HOLD FAST

J. H. GELERNTER

HOLD FAST

· A Novel ·

W. W. NORTON & COMPANY
Independent Publishers Since 1923

Hold Fast is a work of fiction. Names, characters, places, and incidents are the products of the author's imagination or are used fictitiously. Any resemblance to actual events, locales, or persons, living or dead, is entirely coincidental.

Copyright © 2021 by J. H. Gelernter

For information about permission to reproduce selections from this book, write to Permissions, W. W. Norton & Company, Inc., 500 Fifth Avenue, New York, NY 10110

For information about special discounts for bulk purchases, please contact W. W. Norton Special Sales at specialsales@wwnorton.com or 800-233-4830

Manufacturing by Lake Book Manufacturing
Book design by Brooke Koven
Production manager: Anna Oler

Library of Congress Cataloging-in-Publication Data

Names: Gelernter, J. H., author.
Title: Hold fast : a novel / J.H. Gelernter.
Description: First edition. | New York : W.W. Norton & Company, [2021]
Identifiers: LCCN 2020052181 | ISBN 9780393867046 (hardcover) |
    ISBN 9780393867053 (epub)
Subjects: GSAFD: Historical fiction. | Spy stories.
Classification: LCC PS3607.E417 H65 2021 | DDC 813/.6—dc23
LC record available at https://lccn.loc.gov/2020052181

W. W. Norton & Company, Inc., 500 Fifth Avenue, New York, N.Y. 10110
www.wwnorton.com

W. W. Norton & Company Ltd., 15 Carlisle Street, London W1D 3BS

1 2 3 4 5 6 7 8 9 0

Without my parents' advice and encouragement, I might never have written this book, because after school I might have followed my gut and gone to sea, and, because I'm somewhat absentminded, I would probably have fallen overboard by now.

So this book is dedicated, with love, to them.

That said—since one only gets to dedicate his first book once, I would like to append a dedication to Elon "the Musket" Musk, because when you boil it down, space is just a very large, less wavy ocean, and every ocean needs an itinerant writer. Please, someone, tell him I'm available to Darwin his Beagle.

HOLD FAST

I

IN A DARK, oak-paneled room on the second floor of the Admiralty House, Sir Edward Banks tapped his fingers and waited to be asked to speak. He had an unpleasant duty to discharge, and he wanted to get it done with.

It had been judged appropriate, he supposed, that His Majesty's Office of the Admiralty and Marine Affairs be lined with the same oak that built His Majesty's ships. With the war sure to resume—Sir Edward had no doubt that the peace negotiated at Amiens would be brief—he wondered if England might come to regret spending oak on anything besides hulls and planking. He let his gaze wander to the window and out to Whitehall. Such questions were not for his deliberation. He did not sit on the Navy Board; his name was not on the captain's list; he had never been—nor would he ever be—gazetted. He was the chief of naval intelligence, and thus outside the regular hierarchy.

"Sir Edward," said the First Lord, "you had some business concerning Malta?"

"Yes, Lord St. Vincent," said Banks, "but only to report that we've had to recall our man there, and will for a short time have to rely on the conventional channels."

"Wasn't that Captain Thomas Grey?" said a vice-admiral of the blue, speaking for the Mediterranean squadron.

"Yes."

"There is no Thomas Grey on the captain's list, sir," said the lord surveyor.

"Captain Grey was formally a captain of the marines, sir," answered the admiral, "and a very solid man, I'd thought."

"Indeed, Admiral—he has, however, had some difficulties of a personal nature. The gentleman's wife was killed a year ago March."

There was a brief pause, during which Sir Edward hoped—vainly, he knew—that his colleagues would permit him to leave the matter there; he strongly preferred not to add to Captain Grey's troubles by trespassing on his privacy.

However: though (needless to say) it was not uncommon for an English gentleman to be a widower, for his wife to have been killed was most uncommon indeed. As the matter related to work done for His Majesty's secret intelligence, the Admiralty Board would require further detail. The asking was left to the First Lord.

"Killed, Sir Edward?" said John Jervis, Earl of St. Vincent.

"Yes, my lord . . . Sometime in the early winter of the year one, an American ship called the *Agnes* ran aground on the west coast of North Africa. The American crew were taken captive by Sahwari tribesmen, who worked and beat them near to death, before finally bringing the three surviving men—of an original fourteen—to the slave market at Mogador. They were purchased by a local potentate, who believed them to be English, who attempted to ransom them back to us. He sent word to our station at Malta, upon which Admiral Godfrey dispatched Captain Grey to secure the hostages' release.

"Captain Grey had been stationed in Malta for three years, and— as you know—engineered, most successfully, our intelligence network in the Adriatic and on the Dalmatian coast. Because of his experience working in those areas with the Turks and Turkish vassals, Godfrey concluded—rightly, I'm sure—that Grey was the best man for the job of dealing with the Barbary pashas.

"His wife was a keen naturalist—had had a paper read at the Royal Society in '99—and persuaded Grey to allow her to make the trip with him, in hopes of a visit to the Atlas Mountains. In the event, she made her trip, and he secured both the release of the Americans and an invitation for an English embassy to Mogador. The invitation, I make no doubt, you gentlemen will recall."

Several members murmured their agreement.

"During his return to Malta, the fourteen-gun brig which carried Grey and his wife, along with the Americans—*Constance*, I believe, was the vessel's name—was encountered and pursued by the French frigate *Fidèle*, thirty-two . . . this was before Amiens, of course. A stern chase ensued. Before a fresh wind took her aback, the Frenchman was able to close within extreme range of her bow chasers. On a rise, *Constance* was raked at her waterline. Mrs. Grey was then in the cockpit nursing the emaciated and feverish sailors her husband had rescued. The splinters killed her. It was a bad death. She was the brig's only casualty.

"In the subsequent months, Captain Grey attempted to resume his duties, but was judged by Admiral Godfrey to be unable, or at least, not reliably able, owing—"

Sir Edward referred now to a letter on the table in front of him,

"—to 'profound and unshakable melancholia.' Godfrey expressed his hopes that Grey's condition would be attended to in England. I arranged to have him seen on Harley Street, but he wrote yesterday from Portsmouth to say he has returned instead to his house in Kent, at Sheerness. I intend to see him there tomorrow."

Admiral Lord St. Vincent nodded to Sir Edward, who looked around the table to see if anyone else had any questions.

The admiral of the blue cleared his throat.

"How long before we have a replacement in Malta?"

"We will have a new man in place there by the end of the month. I am informed that he passed the Nore yesterday," answered Sir Edward.

But he continued: "The question, though, 'Will we be able to replace Thomas Grey?' remains very much up in the air."

2

THOMAS GREY SAT in the gardens of his estate Marsh Downs, surrounded by an assortment of flowering rhododendrons whose specific names he'd never bothered to learn. Now of course he never would; they'd been planted by his wife. Two or three hundred yards away, the tide was beginning to turn. The waves breaking on the reedy end of his marsh were beginning to push inward, and soon the birds who stalked the mudflats looking for worms and snails would fly inland. He had planned to take one or two for dinner. A shotgun rested across his lap, and his Irish setter Fred rested at his feet. Grey was glad, and frankly somewhat surprised, that the dog remembered him, since Fred had spent the last several years—most of his adult life—as the companion of the Downs' gamekeeper Canfield. Fred seemed sensible of something being wrong. Dogs always are. From time to time, he nuzzled Grey's foot, and Grey reached down to scratch his head and neck.

The fact was, Grey didn't feel much like shooting anything. Fred would be disappointed, but it couldn't be helped. A walk might answer for an acceptable substitute. Anyway, his housekeeper Mrs. Hubble—who Grey believed had now recovered from the shock of his unexpected return—had, no doubt, something in mind for him to eat. It wouldn't do to insult her with a fresh kill.

He stood up, and Fred stood up with him, wearing a keen, gun-ready look.

"Sorry, my boy. Not today. Maybe tomorrow."

Grey took a final deep breath of the flowers and began a slow walk back towards the house, wondering how Canfield had mustered the will to keep the gardens so neat, around an empty house, with no expectation of anyone but himself and Mrs. Hubble seeing them. Before leaving for Malta, thought Grey, he should have opened the gardens to the neighborhood. What a waste were three years of dead blooms that no one had enjoyed.

As he walked south, the house rose up over the gardens. It wasn't especially large, but it was—Grey had always thought—unusually striking; its almost-pink brick exterior topped off by a copper roof tarnished to a beautiful verdigris, set off by creeping, darker yellow-green ivy. He'd bought it with his share of the prize money from a small French fleet captured by his intelligence in '98.

Ninety-eight was the year he'd been married—his marriage being the reason he'd given up his house in town and moved to a country estate. He'd worried that he'd find himself unable to resume living at the Downs, alone. In fact, being back was the one thing that had given him any comfort. He and Paulette had had no children. Thank God there were no children to worry about.

Grey stamped some sand off his feet and stepped into the small, stone-floored mudroom, where he left his coat on a hook and his gun on a table. He opened the door into the larder and paused, hearing three voices in the hall beyond. A woman and two men. He reached back into the mudroom and picked the shotgun up again.

Grey crossed through the larder and into his foyer with the gun dangling from his right hand, adopting as casual an expression as he could. Following at his heels, Fred seemed pleased that perhaps shooting hadn't been stricken from the agenda after all.

Mrs. Hubble was standing in the doorway, speaking to Canfield and another man, who was just beyond Grey's line of sight. The voice was slightly lower than he remembered—too much smoking, no doubt. Equally, though, there was no doubt that it belonged to Edward Banks. Now *Sir* Edward Banks; beknighted since the beginning of Grey's Mediterranean posting. Grey leaned the shotgun against a clock and interrupted the conversation, which was evidently a moot to determine where he might be.

"Sir Edward, please come in," he said, adding, "Thank you, Canfield," and "Mrs. Hubble, would you fix us some coffee—or"—to Banks—"would you prefer tea?"

"Coffee would suit me very well, thank you," said Banks, crossing the threshold. Grey nodded.

"Mrs. Hubble, perhaps you'd bring it to us in my study."

Banks followed Grey down the hall and into a medium-sized room lined on all sides with glass-fronted bookcases. Banks had been in the room several times before. He wondered if the shelves were fronted with glass as a defense against the rich salt air that was filling his lungs and making him—in spite of himself—feel ten years younger.

His mind continued to wander; he wondered if he shouldn't move to the shore as Grey had. Of course Grey was twenty-five years his junior. And had been married, which Banks was not, and had never been. The thought of marriage snapped him suddenly back to the matter at hand. Grey had paused in front of a black oceans globe. He gave it a gentle spin, turned, and gestured to a deep-button leather chair.

"Please to be seated, Sir Edward. I confess, I wasn't expecting you."

"Weren't you?" said Banks. "I should have thought being sent to London and stopping forty miles short would invite both comment and company."

"For my part," said Grey, "I understood that I was being sent home. Haven't you heard? I'm melancholic."

There was a knock on the door. "Come in, Mrs. Hubble," said Grey. The housekeeper stepped into the room, felt the unease in it, set the coffee on Grey's desk, and left again, without a word, closing the door behind her.

The interlude gave Grey just time enough to feel ashamed at his insolence towards a man to whom he owed so much; whom he admired so deeply.

"I apologize, Sir Edward. Please, sit. How will you take your coffee?"

"Black," said Banks, remaining on his feet. He accepted a cup, took a sip, and finally lowered himself into the chair. His face showed no trace of anger; if anything, thought Grey, the unfurled forehead and the slight narrowing of Banks's blue-gray eyes suggested the conversation was proceeding more or less as he'd expected it to.

"I left word at Portsmouth that Dr. Welsh was expecting you at his practice on Harley Street this afternoon. Did you receive the message?"

"I did, sir."

"I won't embarrass you by repeating my sympathies. The service must know what sort of condition you're in, if you're to be of any use to us."

Grey nodded.

"I gathered from Admiral Godfrey that you intend to remain in the service."

This time Grey made no response.

"Do you?"

"I had thought so, sir," said Grey.

"But you don't anymore."

"To tell you the truth, sir," said Grey, "I'm not entirely certain what good I'll be."

"To determine what good you'll be is precisely the reason I've arranged for you to see Welsh." Banks put down his empty cup. "I will expect to hear that he's looked you over by Friday at the latest. Now, I must get on to Chatham and the Yards. My horses are still in the harness."

He stood, and continued.

"As I say, by the end of the week, I'll be back at Admiralty House. If you'll excuse me, I'll show myself out."

Grey waited through two loud ticks of his foyer clock to answer. "Yes, sir."

At the door, Banks paused, turned around, and spoke in a momentarily paternal voice. "Look, Tom——" he said, "it's no good, letting the clouds hang on you forever. Impious stubbornness, Shakespeare called it." The official tone resumed: "There's work yet to be done. War is on the horizon. I will expect you on Friday."

Banks opened the door, and left it open; he retrieved his hat and coat without waiting to be helped, and a moment later Grey heard Banks's man starting the horses.

As Sir Edward's carriage pulled away, Grey poured himself another cup of coffee, and took a seat behind his desk.

3

Early the next morning—Wednesday—Grey presented himself at Dr. Welsh's office, only to discover that the doctor was not yet in; was not in the habit of arriving at his office before nine, and would the gentleman care to wait? Grey declined and said he would return. Perhaps, he thought, after a turn in Regent's Park, which was a hundred yards north. As Grey walked out of Welsh's practice, he wondered that he should be up and about before the esteemed doctor; his picture of a physician—as opposed to the naval surgeons with whom he was much better acquainted—was of an abstemious, scientific gentleman prone to burning the candle at both ends. Of course, to be fair, these days Grey was barely sleeping, which had made it easier to post in from Kent before dawn.

It was the first time Grey had been in London in three years; he'd become used to Maltese weather, and the fresh spring morning felt chilly to him. He watched a farmer's wagon rattle by, leafy heads of vegetables hanging over the tops of wooden crates; a servant on an early-morning errand flagged it down. Other servants passed Grey on the sidewalk, attending to other early-morning errands before their masters woke, mixing with tradesmen and shopkeepers on their ways to work. A cat had decided to lie down on a sun-warmed paving stone by the gutter; Grey picked it up before someone could kick it, and carried it the last few yards to Regent's Park, where it promptly went to sleep, resting against the warm iron of the park's fence.

There was a waist-high granite and brass sundial just inside Regent's Park's southwestern entrance. Grey looked at it, and then narrowed his eyes to look at the sun—unconsciously preferring his own judgment of the sun's progress; a preference not unusual among men who've spent long stretches at sea. It would be at least an hour and a half before the doctor made his appearance. Finding his patience worn unexpectedly thin, Grey retraced his steps from Harley Street, and continued on towards Mayfair, and his man of business. The other man Grey wanted to speak to.

But here was another man not yet at work. Was the whole city asleep? Certainly there was enough bustle about. After the country-side and a few years in the Mediterranean, Grey found London dis-tractingly loud. Perhaps that was the source of the impatience he felt nipping at his heels. At his office, Grey was informed that Mr. Pater was not in—but, said a junior associate, he could probably be found at his club, where Grey knew he often slept.

Pater, that lazy son of a bitch, damn his eyes, thought Grey to himself, offering the associate his polite thanks. Should the gentle-man like a chaise called for him? No, said Grey, he would walk. It wasn't far.

Anyway—he didn't add—there was no sense seeing an old friend whilst in a mood to take his head off. A walk would give him a chance to reflect on Pater's virtues. Such as they were.

Buttle's, halfway down St. James's Street, was just far enough for him to remember what one or two of those virtues were. Though Pater was in fact a lazy son of a bitch whose eyes more than a few acquaintances had damned, he had never stolen any of his clients' money, and through some rather canny investments, had taken the modest sum of prize money Grey had won as a marine captain and turned it into a respectable, if by no means immense, private fortune. In a man of business, he supposed, these were the virtues that mat-tered most.

Pater's sometime residence Buttle's was one of the older gentlemen's clubs, of the several dozen that were now clustered in London's West End. Its brick façade, buttressed by two pairs of Michelange-lesque pilasters, was set slightly back from the street, behind a stone railing and a low hedge. As Grey stepped through the club's front door—into a navy-blue room with cream-colored moldings—he wondered how Buttle's contrived always to smell so clean and invit-ing, so close to the mud and muck of street. Was there a dedicated perfumist crouching behind the desk? Was there a ship's company of youngsters fanning fresh air in from some secret cloister?

"Good morning, Mr. Grey, it's a pleasure to have you back with us," said Mathers, the porter. Grey hid his surprise that Mathers should know his face; it had been years since Grey's last visit to the club, and even when he'd lived in London, he had never been a fre-quent guest. He was not a member.

"Mathers," said Grey, "the pleasure's mine, I'm sure. Is Mr. Pater in?"

"He is, sir," said Mathers, signaling to a page who was waiting in the wings; who now crossed a series of small oriental rugs that led to Mathers's station. "Parslow," said Mathers, "show Mr. Grey into the lounge."

The lounge was a dark, wood-paneled, and candlelit room, where maroon curtains covered windows that had long since been bricked up and paneled over to ensure privacy from the street. Grey had expected to find Pater at breakfast; in fact, he was deep in a game of whist, with coffee at one elbow and a dram of whiskey at the other. The grizzle on his chin suggested this was not an early-morning game, but a hangover from the night before.

Pater noticed nothing until Parslow bent low behind him and spoke a few words into his ear. When he looked up and saw Grey, his mouth fell open; he dropped his cards and stood, to the grunted annoyance of his partner.

"Grey, dear heart, what a damned surprise to see you!" said Pater, with an open, affectionate look on his face. His countenance quickly changed as his memories caught up with his surprise.

"Tom, I was so damned sorry to hear about Paulette. Those f—

French bastards." He offered his hand—which Grey shook—and then took Grey's elbow and pulled him towards the table, pointing to each of the other three men in turn.

"Langley, Slayton, Brummel: Grey." Polite nods from each, and from Grey in return. "Have you had your breakfast?" asked Pater, stroking his unshaved cheek and stifling a yawn. "I say, it's damned early to be out and about. Is the sun up?"

"It is," said Grey, smiling in spite of himself, "and has been for some time already."

"But you haven't eaten?"

"I haven't."

"Marvelous; please to go into the dining room and order something to start—Parslow will take you—and I'll be with you in a few short tricks. In a few shakes of a lamb's tail, ha ha."

In the event, the wait was somewhat longer than that—Grey sipped coffee; wasn't hungry; stared absentmindedly at an etching of a Roman ruin that hung on the dining room's forest-green walls—but the delay did give him time to make his mind up about a notion that had been with him since Kent. Since Malta, in fact. And Pater was the man he needed to discuss it with. Perhaps the doctor's absence was a stroke of fate. Not that Grey believed in such things, he reminded himself.

When the man of business finally sat down, he noticed the absence of any breakfast dish in Grey's vicinity, looked abashed, and waved over the steward. "You haven't begun? I hope you weren't waiting on my account. You'll forgive me, I hope, Tom—I couldn't abandon my post during so warm an action. Ah, here," he said, as the steward took his place at Pater's left hand, "order anything you like. I mean—you remember how it works here, I daresay—tell the steward anything you can think of, and if it's to be had in London, the kitchen'll have it bought and made for you in a trice, before the starters and maybe a tot of rum—ha ha—are disposed of."

"Just a roll and butter and some more coffee, thank you."

"Very well, though I find your lack of imagination worrying.

Oscars, bring me some bacon, scones, some of that currant jam—
and some of those peaches, if they're still on hand. Bring Mr. Grey
one as well, maybe he'll change his mind. But they're very fine fruit,
Tom, you'll see. And Oscars, a pot of the strongest tea that's ever
been brewed this side Tiber."

The steward nodded and backed away, and Pater adopted a more
serious expression.

"Now, Thomas, to what do I owe this meeting? As glad as I would
be for a purely social call, I'm afraid you must have something more
substantial on your mind."

"Yes, I have. I intend to sell Marsh Downs. Or rather, I intend
you to sell it."

Pater nodded. "Lovely place, the Downs—will be sorry to see it
go—but I do understand. It shouldn't take long to sell—you know
I've had several rather brash, unsolicited inquiries about it over the
last few years; such a perfect spot between the sea and London.
Should get a good price for it; yes, a handsome price. I suppose you'll
be looking for a new house in the city? To buy, or to let? Of course I
can put you up here at the club while I have a look around—a mint of
pleasant places have come on the market, now that peace has broken
out and the hangers-on are moving back to the counties. Will you be
bringing Mrs. Hubble with you? I imagine Canfield will go with the
estate—shame, though, I shall miss his advice on shot and powder.
But do tell me what sort of accommodations you have in mind."

"No, not London," said Grey, letting Pater take a breath. "You
may recall: my mother was from Boston."

"In Lincolnshire?"

"No," said Grey, "the other one, in the United States. A rela-
tion in America has considerable interests in lumber. I've long had
a standing offer from him to return there and take a position in his
firm. I've decided to accept."

"Return? Thomas, were you born in America? Forgive me for
being personal."

Grey shook his head once to show Pater no apology was needed.
"That, in fact, was a subject of some debate between my parents. My

mother says I was born in Boston; my father says, having been born aboard a king's ship in Boston harbor, I was on English territory from the first. In any case, it was before the war."

The food arrived, and the two men were silent as the steward laid it out.

"But Tom, damn it, you can't be serious," said Pater. "You intend to go into retirement as, what—I don't know what the term is—a lumberman? A lumbermonger? At your age? Of course," he added quickly, though without conviction, "that's none of my business."

"A lumbermonger," said Grey. "You don't like the ring of that? No, but I'm quite serious. A change is as good as a rest, and, I imagine, the more drastic the change, the better. I'd like a line of credit against the house; I see no reason to wait for the sale. Arrange a stipend for Canfield and Mrs. Hubble, to keep them until they've found new positions, and the rest in a letter I can draw on in Boston."

Pater took a moment to pour himself a cup of tea, and word his response.

"I'll do just as you say, Tom, never fear—but should you be making so great a change so soon after so great a bereavement? Can you possibly be thinking straight? It's awfully goddamned hot in the summers there, I suppose you know, and cold as Lapland in the winter. And business is not at all like a position in the Foreign Office." The Foreign Office being the employment Grey pretended in public. "And after being abroad, mustn't London, and England, be all the change you need? I say again that it's entirely your own affair, but if it were in my power to compel you to wait, I'd say take a week, take some advice, speak to someone in your confidence."

Grey ate his roll and nodded politely. But on Thursday morning, when Sir Edward Banks arrived at his office, sat down at his desk, and began to look through the overnight correspondence, there was a letter from Thomas Grey. He looked it over, then called in his chief of staff.

"Willys, this letter from Grey . . ."

"I haven't looked at it, sir; it was marked personal, for your eyes only."

Banks slid the letter across his desk: "Read it."

"To the Honorable Sir Edward Banks, etc. . . ." read the chief of staff, aloud, "regarding our meeting of Tuesday last . . . I hereby tender, and hope you will accept, my resignation forthwith from His Majesty's Secret Service."

4

Was Fred Canfield's dog or Grey's? Grey had to concede it would be cruel to rip the dog from his home in Sheerness and ship him to the New World—especially having been with him again for just a few days after a three-year absence—but it was with great reluctance that he gave the dog what he assumed would be a final scratch behind the ears. Then there was a firm handshake with Canfield himself, a tearful embrace from Mrs. Hubble, who made Grey promise to write, and then Grey embarked in a four-in-hand coach for Portsmouth—with enough luggage to tide him over; the rest to be shipped by Pater once Grey had a permanent address in Massachusetts.

The carriage ride took most of the morning, southwest through sunken lanes that had been worn into the earth by two thousand years of traffic, and made tunnel-like by canopies of thick, mid-spring leaves. By midafternoon, Grey was on a bumboat being rowed out through Portsmouth harbor; one of dozens ferrying officers, sailors, and passengers among the ranks of merchantmen and men-of-war that stood at anchor waiting on tides and schedules and orders to depart.

He followed his dunnage up the side of the West Indiaman *Ruby*—not as sleek or as graceful as a modern man-of-war, but in its way, a very attractive thing. She was a stout, solid ship displacing perhaps six hundred tons; simple black-and-white paintwork beneath three masts and ten or twelve hundred square feet of still-furled canvas. Most of her cargo appeared already to have been loaded, and most of her crew must have been in the hold ensuring that everything was squared away. The men who remained on deck seemed chiefly preoccupied with questions of the bowsprit and foremast rigging; two others were lashing down a coop of chickens who would be coming along on the voyage west. On the quarterdeck—at the binnacle—a pair of officers were talking with each other, alternately gesturing down at the compass and up at yards; neither was the captain. Grey introduced himself to each, shook hands, and was shown belowdecks.

His cabin was a small but not unpleasant room amidships, directly beneath the waist, with a gunport for a window—a luxury unknown in the service, where all but the forward- and aft-most of the gundeck bulkheads were permanently struck. His chests arrived a moment behind him, and after some cursory unpacking—just some ink he wanted to ensure hadn't spilled, and a book he intended tucking into in short order—Grey stuck his head out the gunport and surveyed the scene.

Despite having formally left the Royal Marines upon his recruitment to the secret intelligence service some years earlier—before Earl St. Vincent had christened them "Royal Marines," in fact; when red-coated, seagoing soldiers were still part of a semiformal detachment from the army, a part of His Majesty's Marine Forces . . . Grey's mind was wandering . . . despite having left uniformed service years earlier, today he had considered wearing his uniform. Because, despite its being peacetime, there was a hot press on—the hottest in years; the country was at peace, but the Admiralty refused to believe it. Men who would normally be exempt from the threat of forced recruitment into the navy—merchant sailors on outward-bound ships, men with no experience in a seagoing profession, even men with formal exemptions from Whitehall—were being seized by the press gangs and read into ships' companies. Ships bound for Java and New Holland were taking to sea with only the minimum, most skeletal crews the press let them keep, hoping they'd make it in one piece to Portugal or Madeira or Gibraltar to restock. Grey knew he'd escaped only by virtue of his booked passage on a West India-man, and because he'd taken the precaution of dressing in his Sunday best—an outfit he'd completed with the unfamiliar process of pow-dering his wig. The clothes and the cabin bespoke him a gentleman, and there was still no press hot enough to risk the navy's vital, and tenuous, support in Parliament by accidentally dragging off to the Cape someone with real interest.

From his gunport, Grey could see the press boat reaching an East Indiaman, on its way in from Ceylon or Sumatra. All the hands who could be spared had doubtless decamped at Scilly, hoping to avoid this. Others would be crammed in endlessly clever hidey-holes. And a few—ah, there was one now, plunging over the side—some of the few men who could swim would chance a breaststroke to shore, and then sanctuary till nightfall in a church or a brothel. Who could blame them? They'd probably been at sea for nearly two years. How could a man in sight of his home stand being dragged off for another two years, under the strict, lash-backed authority of the Admiralty? Grey sighed. The real question was why so few sailors bothered learning how to swim. "If the good Lord had meant us to swim, he'd have given us fins and scales." "Well," he always wanted to ask the foremast jacks in return, "have you got a mainsail growing out of your back?" But it was no good a marine soldier arguing with a sea-man. To a bluecoat, the reds were incurable landsmen.

There was a knock on the cabin door. "Come in," said Grey, pull-ing his head back inside.

"The captain wonders if you'd give him the pleasure of your com-pany at dinner," said a ship's boy.

"Please tell the captain I would be delighted," said Grey, reflect-ing that this sort of invitation was among the dangers of walking around in a powdered wig.

"I will, sir. He dines at eight."

SERVANTS STOOD BEHIND each guest in the captain's dining room, which was the great cabin aft of the quarterdeck. The cabin itself was beautiful—polished to a high sheen, illuminated by the broad row of gently outward-tilted windows on the ship's stern, and by candles in silver candlesticks (their light bouncing off the burnished oak walls and the silver plate on which dinner was to be served). This was very much after the naval style, and its obsession with pristine cleanliness—an obsession of which Grey enthusiastically approved. So were the servants behind the guests' chairs—after the naval style, that is—and so was the cut and color of the captain's coat and the dress of his officers. Grey didn't disapprove of merchantmen imitating the navy, exactly, but he couldn't help but find it a little silly. Most merchant captains were men who, through lack of either performance or family interest, had been unable to secure a position on the captain's list. Why remind everyone of it? There was no shame in successfully running a ship around the globe, with many fewer resources and, at most, a third of the crew that a comparably heavy man-of-war would have at her disposal. And all the while facing the same risks from wind and weather and from enemy ships to which a large commercial vessel was not only fair game, but the most desirable game in the field.

"Captain Grey," said the *Ruby*'s master and commander, one Captain Bavinger, "I don't believe I've seen your name on the list. Were you posted recently?" Booking passage under his former rank had been another precaution against being pressed; Grey generally went by "Mr.," but sometimes one has to play by ear.

"I was a captain of the marines, sir."

"Ah, I see," said Bavinger. Grey didn't expound, and Bavinger turned to the other passengers, a vicar and his young wife, and a botanist wearing a plum-colored jacket.

"Mr. Kefauver, sir," said Bavinger, "have you botanized the New World before?"

"Indeed I haven't, Captain," said the botanist, putting down his wine and shaking his head enthusiastically. "No, so far my study has been an imitation—or, if I flatter myself, a continuation—of Linnaeus, focused on the northern regions of Europe. No, I am most excited to see their brothers in America, sir, in the north of America. Most excited indeed."

"Do you study flowers, Mr. Kefauver?" asked the vicar's wife.

"Yes indeed, ma'am, but also the plants that host them, and in particular, the soil in which they grow. I fear many a botanist has neglected the medium from which his subject derives, the *petrus*, so to speak, on which the church of botany is built! Yes, I'm interested most especially in the variety of soils which may be found from place to place—each of which may be as different from the soil but a hundred yards away as a rose is from a lily."

"And does America have good soil, Mr. Kefauver?"

"I wonder!" said the botanist. "I wonder. The variety of the plants is said to be very great, and yet, the soil is known to suffer from a high inclusion of stones, which must surely steal from the richness of the whole. Agriculture, as you know, has been much more successful in the southern American states—but is the culprit the soil itself? Or merely the interference of stones with plowing? Sure, there is one way only to find out, ma'am. It is my ambition that my work in the New World will allow me to produce a volume on soil as instrumental to the development of our science as *Systema Naturae*."

"Heady stuff," said Captain Bavinger.

"Have you spent much time along the American coast, sir?" asked the botanist.

"Oh yes," said Bavinger. "A great deal. And through the Caribbean, along Brazil; as far south as the River Plate. Though I'm afraid, in the whole hemisphere, the only plant I've had much experience of is the sugarcane."

"Is sugarcane an especially interesting flower, sir?" asked the vicar's wife.

"I meant, ma'am, as the source of rum. It was a poor witticism; forgive me."

"Oh," said the vicar's wife. "Is rum the juice of the sugarcane?"

"It is distilled sugar, ma'am," said the captain.

"Though sugarcane does have a beautiful flower," said the botanist. "A collection of fine tendrils—fine wisps of bloom, very soft, running the gamut of color from brown to white to pink and lavender. I've seen fields of it aflower in southern Spain, in the Andalus country. Most attractive, most attractive indeed."

"How lovely," said the vicar's wife. "I'm glad to know those poor souls who work the cane fields have something pretty to look at."

"Yes, no doubt that makes the task a great deal easier, ma'am," said Bavinger, to be polite.

"May I ask what your business in New England will be, Vicar?" asked the botanist.

"A pulpit awaits me in New Haven, Mr. Kefauver."

He didn't go on. "How nice," said the botanist.

Grey let his mind wander away from the conversation. The captain's mutton was decent. His wine was indifferent. His helmsman was quite good. On a very favorable wind, the ship had already passed Ushant, the small marker island off Brittany's western tip, and was now in the Atlantic proper. The waves had picked up considerably, and the *Ruby* had turned into them without any noticeable loss of speed, which—from the wake—Grey judged to be eight, perhaps nine knots. What a fine sailor she was on a quarter wind, this ship of Bavinger's. Not at all the slab-sided hulk that one always assumes merchantmen to be.

Grey continued to gaze at the wake. The sun had dipped below the horizon now, somewhere beyond the ship's bow, leaving a cloudless pink-and-peach sky behind it. He would be glad for a hot summer in Boston; he'd gotten used to them in Valletta. And no matter how cold the winters would be, the damp would never compare to London. Twice as many sunny days a year, his American relations had claimed. Certainly, the list of all the things Grey wouldn't miss about England was headed by the weather. Good goddamned riddance to it. And, while he was damning things: the same to everything else he was leaving behind. To hell with London, and the service, and the Admiralty, and the mad king. To hell with sealed orders and ciphers and duty. Let the men and the codebooks and the whole stinking Union sink into the North Sea. What had they ever done for him?

Thank God he'd finally let himself say that—if only in his own head. He flushed slightly with the rebellion, draining his glass and enjoying the moment of catharsis.

There was a knock at the door, and Bavinger's second lieutenant— whatever his title in the merchant fleet was—stuck his head into the room.

"Sail, sir, hull down, coming from Brest."

The captain nodded. "Thank you, Mr. Goff," he said, without concern. "Mr.—pardon me, Captain—Grey: the wine stands by you."

Grey passed the decanter to his left and scanned the horizon beyond the great cabin's great windows, wondering if he'd catch a nick of the sail in the smooth sweep of ocean.

"If you'll pardon my ignorance," said the botanist, Mr. Kefauver, "what does 'hull down' mean?"

"It means that only a ship's sails are visible above the horizon— when the rest of her appears, she's 'hull up.' "

"I see," said Kefauver. "Should we be concerned? Mightn't they be pirates?"

"No, sir, if she's coming from Brest, she's certainly a French merchantman—probably on the same run we are. In any case, there are no pirates to be had in these waters, for the time being. We're still too far north for the Berbers, and with the peace, the French and Dutch privateers have had to pull down their colors. So to speak."

The meal dragged on through four courses; chops and cheese and coffee came and went, along with the last of the sunlight. Now it was a waxing gibbous moon overhead, lighting the wake, almost bright enough to read by. Just before the port had begun its trip around the table—just as the sky was turning from deep blue to black—Grey had caught a glimpse of the Brest-outward sail. It was too dark now to see anything, of course, but he kept glancing towards the windows, all the same. It was habit; compulsion. A small prick of intuition at the back of his skull. For the sail to have closed enough for him to see it at deck level, in less than an hour, it must be doing near twelve knots. Not likely a merchant ship, then. Perhaps one of those colors-hauled privateers the captain had referred to; perhaps it was trying to avoid paying off its crew by running mail. It wouldn't be the first. In any case, it was no concern of his. Grey swirled his glass and turned his thoughts towards the book he'd left in his cabin— *A Complete & Scientific History of the Egyptian Kingdoms by the Eminent Geologist Mr. John Folsom.* It beckoned to him.

"Some port, Captain Grey?" said Captain Bavinger, sliding the decanter towards him.

"Thank you, Captain—I'm afraid I must pass it—I'm quite overcome by the breadth of your delicious dinner; I hope you'll excuse me. My eyes are beginning to shut." Grey moved the decanter on to Kefauver and stood.

"Of course, Captain Grey," said Bavinger, standing, along with Kefauver and the vicar, who hit his head quite hard on the ceiling.

"Good evening, gentlemen."

In his cabin, with the gunport open and a heavenly breeze flowing inward, Grey was soon asleep.

"Thomas dear? Where are you?" Paulette Grey was on her husband's arm as they walked onto St. George's Square from the Grandmaster's Palace, which hosted the only Anglican mass on Malta.

"Hmm?" said Grey, turning to her. "Oh, forgive me—my mind wandered off."

"Something troubling you?" asked Paulette, releasing Grey's arm for a moment, tugging at one of her church gloves.

"No, no, just a daydream, Paul, never fear." In point of fact, Grey was thinking about a tear of paper that a strange hand had slipped into his pocket a few moments earlier, during the nebulous well-wishing that tends to follow a religious gathering.

It was less than two months since Grey had assumed his posting as head of the secret service in Malta, but—with Malta the heart of the English presence in the central Mediterranean, and a stopping-off place for so much allied and neutral shipping—it hadn't been long before his identity had leaked out. This, naturally, would make him a target, both of the French and of cranks—but, on balance, Grey felt it was a good thing. It meant people who were willing to do secret business with the British could find him. This, he believed, was more than adequate compensation for the bad. Especially if the mysterious note in his pocket led to something of value.

It was about a forty-minute walk from Valetta, up around the Marsamuscetto, back to the Greys' house on the adjacent Sliema peninsula—during which Paulette gave a disquisition on her first meeting with a genuine African mammal: the North Africa hedge-hog, which had, in late prehistory, made its way from Libya to Malta and Gozo. Paulette had been intrigued to discover that, though separated from its European cousin on Sicily by just a hundred sea miles, *Atelerix algirus* had a number of unique characteristics. It was smaller, but swifter, white rather than brown, it lacked the boldness of *Erinaceus europaeus*—or, indeed, either *Erinaceus roumanicus* or *concolor*, the northern and southern white-breasted hedgehogs—but to her mind, it was markedly friendlier. (Though in fairness, Paulette reminded her husband, an ill-natured hedgehog of any species is hard to find.) She was turning to its rumored immunity to even the most venomous African snakes, and to the difficulty she imagined in procuring a Lataste's viper and a hedgehog willing to meet it on level ground, when she and Grey arrived at their doorstep, and Grey excused himself to his study.

Closing the door behind him, and locking it, he was finally able to retrieve the mysterious paper from his pocket—a tightly coiled cylinder the size and shape of a single dried clove, which Grey unrolled on his desktop.

It read, in a tiny but loopy Italian hand, "*Monday: Eight: Ghajn Tuffieha: Palazzo Parisio.*" The meaning seemed clear enough—someone was requesting a meeting at the Ghajn Tuffieha beach twenty hours hence, at eight on Monday. "Palazzo Parisio" was intended not as a meeting location, but as the writer's credential—it was the villa that had been Napoleon's home and headquarters during his brief stay on Malta, in June of '98, when he conquered the island on his way to Egypt.

After Napoleon's conquest, the French had ruled Malta for two years; to begin with, very successfully. They had abolished slavery and the aristocracy, established freedom of speech, of the press, of religion—for the first time, Maltese Jews were allowed to build a synagogue—abolished the Inquisition and expelled the last inquisitor, devised a semi-democratic system of island government, and announced that France would build a school in every town and village, with teachers paid by France. An additional sixty Maltese students would be given scholarships to study in Paris. And instantly, the French were very popular.

Unfortunately, Napoleon's eyes were bigger than France's wallet. He sailed off to fame in Egypt after just six revolutionary days, and the lieutenants he left in charge could find no way to pay for his reforms other than by looting Malta's churches and despoiling the Catholic military order of the Knights Hospitaller—who, under the leadership of their grandmaster, had ruled Malta for nearly three hundred years, until the French invasion. For the Maltaman on the street, the final straw was when the church loot, used at first to pay the wages of Maltese civil servants created by the new French system, was rededicated to Napoleon's stalled campaign in the Near East. Protests turned to riots, and riots to revolution—a revolution that quickly gained the support of the British, who would ultimately accept the surrender of the French garrison on September 5th, 1800.

The Maltese civil government invited the British to stay, declaring formally in the 1802 "Declaration of Rights of the Inhabitants of the Islands of Malta and Gozo" that Malta would be self-governing under the protection of George III, who they declared was their king. This was perfectly satisfactory to the English, who were quick to make the islands nation an integral part of the empire—but many Maltese, even if firmly in the minority, hankered still & devotedly after the glorious French ideals of Napoleon, and maintained tight personal ties to France and the first consul's government. Along with its central spot in the Mediterranean, this is what made Malta so valuable a cog in the machine of British intelligence. And why Thomas Grey was so willing to accept an anonymous invitation to a secret, seaside, sunrise meeting.

The next morning—Monday morning—Grey awoke, dumped a pair of minuscule filfola lizards out of his boots, and left the house before sunrise. He intended to be the first to arrive at Ghajn Tuff-ieha, to find himself a good vantage point, and make sure no trap had been laid.

It was a three-hour walk to the pastoral side of the island, the northwest coast of Malta, where there was little besides sheepcotes and weavers' huts. As Grey walked, he watched the sky before him turn from inky black to purple, to red and pink, and finally to a perfect crisp blue, without so much as a single cloud in it. By day-light, Grey was crouched among some brush fifty yards back from the beach, and waiting.

At perhaps two minutes before eight, a man wandered, by him-self, onto the sand, leaving a trail of footprints behind him. He stopped a few feet shy of the gently breaking waves and stood there, hands clasped behind his back, looking out at the sea.

For ten minutes Grey watched him. There was no sign of a hid-den third party, and the man never looked back at some hiding spot in which one might have been secreted. No nervous twitching either. Grey stood and walked down the beach towards him.

"Good morning," said Grey, in Italian. The man turned and Grey got a first look at his face—which was perfectly ordinary; clean-shaven, rather suntanned. Cleft chin. Hint of an overbite.

"Good morning," said the man. "You are Thomas Grey. The head of George's spies in Malta."

"No," said Grey, "I'm afraid you must have mistaken me for some-one else; I was most confused by your note. Why have you invited me here?"

"No," said the man, "I'm not confused. I have this for you"—the man reached into his jacket pocket and pulled out a razor, which he flicked open and swung at Grey's face.

Grey had half expected something like this—he bobbed his head backward; the razor missed; Grey grabbed the man's arm as it cut harmlessly through the air, wrenched it a half turn, and threw the man to the ground.

The man landed hard but didn't drop the razor, twisted his body onto all fours and sprang at Grey, tackling him in the midsection.

Both men fell to the ground; Grey beneath his assassin, who was trying to bring the razor to bear, who succeeded in slashing it once across Grey's chest, making a shallow cut, as Grey threw the man off, into the surf.

Grey leapt back to his feet as the attacker got back onto his haunches—Grey kicked the man's hand, sent the razor flying, and now it was Grey's turn to spring his full body weight onto this other man, sending them both into shin-deep water.

The man had turned into a fulminating, wild-eyed animal. He slammed a fist into Grey's stomach; Grey put a fist into the man's face, wrapped his hands around the man's neck, held him under the surface. The man thrashed about wildly. But not wildly enough to shake off Grey's grip.

It took nearly a minute for the man to die. Half a minute for him to run out of air, and another half for the look of fury to be replaced by one of terror. He died with his eyes and mouth wide open. Grey dragged his corpse up the beach, above the high-water line. There was nothing in any of the man's pockets; no identifying mark on the razor itself, which Grey slipped into his own pocket. He would ask the local constables to collect the body and see if they could figure out who he was. Who he'd been.

The cut on Grey's chest smarted, but it had stopped bleeding and didn't seem too serious—only about four inches long, just under his left nipple. It wasn't until more than two hours later, as Grey passed the village of San Gwann on his walk home, that he started to realize something was wrong. His vision was starting to blur. His tongue felt thick. He couldn't draw a full breath. His heart was racing.

His thinking started to become muddled—but not so muddled that he failed to recognize that he'd been poisoned; that there'd been something on that razor.

He collapsed in the doorway of the Chapel of Santa Margarita, after a few weak knocks on the doorjamb. Then he lost consciousness.

He would find out later that the razor blade had been coated in black henbane—stinking nightshade, and enough to kill a horse. Lucky the cut had been shallow. The man had been a schoolmaster who blamed his inability to find work on the canceled French education reforms, whose cancelation he blamed on the English. He'd grown the henbane in his front garden.

This is what the brothers of the hospital told Grey two weeks later, after his convalescence. The only memory he had from the convalescence itself was of Paulette—gripping his hand tightly, never once leaving his side, whispering over and over into his ear:

"I'm here, I'm here with you; so long as I'm here nothing bad can happen, nothing will go wrong, you're going to be fine, you're going to be fine."

As GREY AWOKE from his dream, he thought for a moment he was back on Malta, waking from his delirium, with Paulette there beside him. It was only the sound of seamen holystoning the *Ruby*'s deck that pulled him back to the present, reminded him where he was—it was that *scrape-scrape, scrape-scrape* of men on their knees scouring the ship with sandstone chunks the size and shape of Bibles. Grey couldn't help but notice that the pace of the scraping was considerably slower than it was, invariably, in the navy. On this ship there was no bosun to start the men with a kick in the pants. Nevertheless, the ship was impeccably clean. Perhaps there was a lesson in that.

With that thought, Grey was ready to let himself drift back to sleep—he had nothing in particular to do with his day—but a sudden gust of warm breeze reminded him of the French ship in the *Ruby*'s wake, and after that, sleep was out of the question. He resolved to have a look, have some coffee, and then find a comfortable place to read. Perhaps back here, in bed, where a catnap might eventually be contemplated.

He appeared on deck in breeches and a comfortably worn brown coat; no wig today, and no hat. The captain's steward passed him ascending the companionway and offered to bring Grey coffee on the quarterdeck. Grey thanked him and stepped up into the morning air.

"Captain Grey," said Bavinger, "good day to you."

"Captain Bavinger," said Grey, shaking his host's hand and then looking out over the taffrail. "I see our French friend has gained on us overnight."

"Yes, she's a fine sailor," said Bavinger, with only a hint of concern in his voice. He turned to Grey with a confidential look: "After so many years of war, I'm afraid it isn't easy having a French corvette this close astern without setting topgallants, starting my water, and clearing the decks for action . . ."

More naval pretensions, thought Grey. Or had the captain more fighting experience than met the eye? Bavinger continued:

"But I mustn't give in to baseless worry. Habits may not easily be broken, but by and by, I imagine we will all let ourselves get used to peace again."

Grey nodded and looked at the French ship. She was light and fast; two masts with a short, lateen-rigged bonaventure mizzen hoisted behind them. Twenty guns . . . four-pounders, probably. From the sharp way her sails were trimmed and retrimmed, with the greatest fighting precision and efficiency, she must certainly be an ex-privateer. No run-of-the-mill merchant ship ran the way she did. Or was she not a privateer, but a French regular? Yes . . . yes . . . there, hanging onto the windward rail . . . a man in uniform, Grey was sure of it. Not just a military trim, but a uniform. A rosette on his chest? Perhaps. And the hat worn athwartships, the way the French preferred. But why should *Ruby* be chased by a French man-of-war? Why had this corvette closed to within a quarter mile?

Why had they let her? There was a Greek word Grey was searching for . . . *paranoia*. Was he letting it get the better of him? This was all too familiar.

He wished he hadn't left his guns to be sold with the estate.

Bavinger's officers, on watch or off, had gathered behind their captain. As if reading Grey's thoughts, the sailing master spoke up:

"Could she be trying to post a letter with us? To Montreal, perhaps, or Louisiana?"

The French supplied the answer: there was a flash of light from her bows, a crash of smoke and thunder, and a four-pound ball shot past *Ruby*'s starboard rail, crashing through a wave and disappearing into another.

All at once, the *Ruby*'s naval pretensions ceased to be pretensions; a captain, two lieutenants, and a sailing master—each, Grey was soon sure, having cut his teeth in the Royal Navy—fell decisively back into their martial roles.

Bavinger missed barely a beat as he turned to his first lieutenant and gave the order, "Clear the gundeck for action, Mr. Peters; strike nothing below that you don't have to. And run out the starboard guns." To his second lieutenant, "Mr. Goff, put up the netting, then get every man on the ship not trimming the sails or working a gun gathered at the break of the quarterdeck. Armed for boarding."

"Mr. Kavanaugh"—now he was turned to the sailing master— "keep *Ruby* moving as fast as ever she can with the present spread of sail—we've no time to hoist anymore. As soon as the guns are rolled out, we'll spill our wind, cut sharply across her bows, rake her once, and close for boarding."

The "yes, sirs" trailed behind each officer as he ran to his duty. A second warning shot cracked out of the French ship, split the waves along the starboard rail, and disappeared.

Bavinger turned to the vicar: "Mr. . . . Vicar, please escort your wife belowdecks; find her somewhere to sit in the hold. You may join her if you wish. As may you, Mr. Kefauver."

"No need, sir," said the botanist, who was the only man on deck wearing a smile. "I'm always ready for a good fight."

"Your preparation will be tested in short order, I'm afraid," said Bavinger. "But I thank you."

Finally, the captain turned to Grey.

"Captain Grey, we have four twelve-pounders for each side, and gun crews not entirely out of practice, but of course our only chance is yardarm-to-yardarm. We have double her crew—even if the French have fighting men and we have not—but it goes without saying that we have no marines aboard. I have no right to ask this of you, but if you were to choose to proceed to the tops, there is a chest in my sleeping cabin with a Baker rifle in it."

Bavinger said nothing more to Grey, turning now to the state of his sails, bellowing up to his mast jacks.

Grey hesitated only a moment—only long enough to decide to head not to the captain's cabin, but to his own.

He yanked the larger of his sea chests out from beneath his cot, opened it, tipped its contents onto the floor, and unstrapped from the bottom his sword, in its scabbard, still, he knew, with a fine edge on it. He hadn't let it lose its edge since he'd worn it at Cape St. Vincent.

As he slid the belt into place over his hips, the walls around him—besides the one with the gunport in it—disappeared: the striking of bulkheads had reached his cabin. Quick as he could, he shoved his belongings back into their chest and gave sixpence to one of the ship's boys to drag his things to the hold.

Surrounded by the chaos of a ship preparing for an unexpected fight, Grey pushed his way aft, and then—after a brief tussle with the captain's steward—emerged on deck carrying the captain's Baker rifle, and wearing its accompanying satchel, which had been hastily filled with cartridges, gunpowder, and a spare flint, and slung diagonally over his right shoulder.

More pushing, this time through the men crowded around Goff and the arms chest, drawing swords and pikes and axes, checking their edges, preparing for a close fight. One man, no doubt a former whaler, was screwing the head onto a six-foot-tall harpoon. Grey grabbed a boy by the collar and pulled him out of the path of two men carrying a case of shot for the swivel guns, reminded him to keep his head and avoid being trampled, then grabbed the mainmast shrouds, pulled himself over the larboard rail, and started his nimble climb up the ratlines.

How long had it been since he'd done this? But it felt as natural as walking after a long, restful night in bed—up and up the mast, hand over hand, foot over foot, being blown back and forth by the breeze. Up over the maintop—the platform at the top of the first third of the mainmast—and all the way to the head of the topmast, where, braced against the crosstrees, he could see over the mizzen mast to the corvette, which was now just a few hundred yards away over the *Ruby*'s rear starboard quarter.

Grey pulled back the Baker's flintlock and pulled the trigger, testing for a good spring, and a good spark from a good flint. Finding them, he opened the satchel for a paper ball-and-wad cartridge, which he tore open with his teeth, stuck into the muzzle, and rammed home with the ramrod. A spill of gunpowder into the lock, and he was ready—all told, a fifteen-second procedure that put the end of some Frenchman's life into his hands. Had he ever felt so bloodthirsty in battle before? Suddenly he wanted very much to kill someone at the other end of his barrel. Breaking the peace this way made them pirates. More to the point, any one of them could have been aboard the *Fidèle*—could have given the order or fired the cannon that killed Paulette.

Grey's hawk-sharp eyes picked out two squads of French marines—three of them in the foretop, three in the maintop. They would be focused now on the officers on the *Ruby*'s quarterdeck, waiting to close into the effective range of their muskets. From Grey's position on the masthead, he had a plunging field of fire that would add fifty yards or so to *his* effective range (already lengthened by the rifling in the Baker's barrel). The much greater swing of the mast at this altitude was a small price to pay for the initiative, for the first move. That had always been Grey's position, anyway.

He closed an eye, cocked his rifle, and took aim at a spot in space about three feet over the head of the *républicain* marine with the largest rosette. Gently, Grey squeezed the Baker's trigger. It took more than two seconds for the lead marble to sail two hundred yards from the mainmast of the British ship to the foremast of the French. Grey couldn't hear the man scream, but saw his musket fall towards the deck, followed a moment later by his convulsing body. By the time the French marine had crashed into the corvette's forecastle, Grey was reloaded, and lining up his second shot.

The second marine Grey killed got caught in the rigging as he fell, and dangled there like a grotesque marionette. The third was aiming at Grey when he died, no doubt wondering if he were close enough yet to return fire. It wasn't very sporting, reflected Grey, as he reloaded. But the French had sowed the wind, and he had a clear conscience.

Grey's fourth shot missed—just as he pulled the trigger, the *Ruby* heeled sharply to starboard and fired what would be her one broadside, a four-cannon blast intended to rake the corvette from stem to stern. The merchant gunners' rust and inexperience showed as just one of the four twelve-pound balls struck home. It would, no doubt, do immense damage as it traveled the hundred or so feet down the whole length of the ship. But now it was the corvette's turn.

Grey had been right about the size of its cannon: four-pounder popguns. But now, with the *Ruby* spilling her wind, the distance quickly closed to just twenty yards—at which range the corvette turned sharply, showed her larboard broadside, and began to blast away the *Ruby*'s rigging with grapeshot. Just its rigging—the French didn't want to damage the prize goods belowdecks—but the effect on the men waiting to board was devastating. From his bird's-eye view, Grey could see the ship's waist soaking in blood. A half dozen bodies went over the side. And then—with sails reefed but momentum carrying them onward—the two ships were touching.

Grey was now just forty feet away (and twenty feet above) the French marines in the corvette's mainmast; the second squad of three. He had a shot loaded, and fired at the closest of the three through a forest of torn ropes—quickly swinging his body behind the mast to reload, feeling two balls hit the mast behind him, swinging his body back out, and firing again. Now he was close enough to hear a man scream as he fell onto his crewmates below.

The two ships' yardarms were banging into one another; the wind was driving them closer together and tipping Grey's mast deep into the French rigging—he was now almost directly above the final French marine. Grey fired, and missed; the wood at the Frenchman's feet splintered; the Frenchman fired back at Grey, almost straight upward, and splintered the wood five feet above Grey's head. Grey's perch was too precarious to risk a race to reload. Instead he slung the rifle over his shoulder, drew his sword, and stepped off the edge of the masthead.

He fell onto the Frenchman, who let out a terrified yell as Grey's sword perforated his chest—screaming, still alive, as Grey tried to pull the sword out again, boot on the man's pelvis—a kick and yank, and the man tumbled into the sea, leaving several pints of his blood on Grey's blade and trousers.

Grey looked down. The forecastle of the corvette was now lashed to *Ruby*'s quarterdeck, and that's where the fighting was. The English had the numbers, as expected, but the French had the discipline, and had *Ruby*'s crew back on their heels. The balance of power was shifting in the corvette's direction. To have any hope at all, Grey knew, it had to be shifted back.

With the French marines dead and every French hand now in the boarding party, Grey was alone in the rigging, standing on the French maintop. The main yard was just below him, extending away from him to lar & starboard, the mainsail fully furled beneath it. Grey sheathed his bloody sword, stepped to the edge of the top, and dropped the foot and a half down onto the mainsail yard; then, using the mast to keep his balance, dropped from the yard to the horse line—the footrope—below it.

Now Grey was shuffling along the horse, out towards the yard-arm's starboard tip, wondering how long he had before someone noticed the man in the tops who belonged to the wrong team. At the yard's tip, he wrapped his left arm around the spar itself, and with his right, pulled out his sword and sliced through the clew reef line;

the furthest-out tie keeping the sail reefed under the yard and out of the wind.

Now Grey was shuffling back towards the mast, slicing through reef lines as he went—seeing, hearing the sail unfurl itself in his wake. As he reached the center of the yard, at the mast, he climbed back to the maintop, prepared to duplicate the de-reefing on the opposite arm—but there was no need. The mainsail was starting to take the wind; it was tearing itself the rest of the way free, falling open, yanking at the mast. Even without being sheeted home, the sail caught the sharp breeze, and the corvette started to pull away from *Ruby*, tugging at the lash lines holding the two ships together.

The action on deck changed—the French were split now between their own forecastle and the English quarterdeck. The French still on the corvette started to fire up at Grey; some began a race up the ratlines to take back their mainsail. The French on the *Ruby* tried to keep their lifelines to the corvette in place, while the English focus shifted instantly to cutting them. The two ships continued to separate. It was time for Grey to part company as well.

He pulled a paper cartridge out of his box and stuffed it into the end of his powder horn. Flame was provided by the snap of the flint-lock, and the paper began to burn like a wick towards the explosive powder within. Grey dropped the home-fashioned grenade down towards the French deck and stepped out onto the yardarm in the last moments before the ascending French crewmen reached him. He dove towards the water, and hit it just as the powder horn exploded.

In the fish-eye above him, Grey could see nothing but a pacific blue sky. He kicked towards it—tried to push himself upward—but the dive had knocked some wind out of him, and now the heavy Baker rifle on his back was pulling him downward, down into the sea. The fish-eye view of the world above the water was getting smaller. His lungs were screaming. There was nothing for it. He slipped the rifle and cartridge bag off his shoulder, let them drop into the black depths below, felt himself bob upward, and with a few long pulls of his arms brought his head back above water. He was facing the French corvette—which was burning. Flames licked up the mizzen. All hands were at the pumps.

Grey turned and swam towards *Ruby*: she was twenty yards away, and—thank God—spreading no sail. Someone above the companion ladder threw Grey a line and hoisted him up. The half of the French crew who had been trapped on *Ruby*'s quarterdeck when the ships split were now being held at gunpoint in the waist. They included several officers, one of whom was in deep conversation with Captain Bavinger.

Bavinger broke away from the French officer, saw Grey, and walked quickly towards him. "Napoleon will not remove his troops from Switzerland, and Parliament has abrogated the Amiens treaty. It's war."

5

WITH HALF ITS CREW gone and a fire on deck, the corvette—*Diligente*, her name was—could no longer threaten to take *Ruby*, but she was still capable of mounting an estimable defense. With his own crew diminished, Bavinger embraced the better part of valor and discreetly withdrew, aiming to be over the horizon and running before a fair wind before *Diligente* could consider taking the fight up again. With any luck, the wounded corvette would limp back to Brest, tack on tack, and find herself on the wrong side of the British blockade that was no doubt already being laid.

After the course was set and the sails jury-rigged, Bavinger invited Grey to his cabin for a drink, and to make his thanks for Grey's behavior during the fight. To head off any embarrassment for either of them, Grey changed the subject as quickly as he could to the rifle he'd had to sink—"Please, please, think nothing of it, Captain Grey, nothing at all; should be happy to lose twenty such"—and then to the butcher's bill.

"Only eight men killed," said Bavinger, "and just a dozen more in the sick bay. It was a providential escape, Captain Grey. Perhaps owed to the vicar."

"Oh?" said Grey. "Was he praying especially hard?"

"No," said Bavinger, momentarily confused, then realizing: "Ah, from your place among the masts, you must not have seen him—an absolute devil with a sword, if you'll pardon the expression. Almost single-handedly kept the French boarders from commandeering the swivel guns. I believe he killed half a dozen men. The surgeon pulled a bucketful of shot out of his left leg, but thinks he'll keep it."

"Quite a man," said Grey. "I would never have guessed. He said barely a word at dinner."

"No," said Bavinger, "I'm not sure I would have believed it, excepting I saw it with my own eyes. As I say: providential. Right now the clever money in the gunroom says that he was some sort of an avid duelist at school, always going out. When he sleeps off his laudanum, they propose putting it to him."

"And the botanist, Mr. Kefauver?"

"Oh, he made a very good show of it too, standing on the poop and yelling a blue streak at the French forecastle-men as they closed for boarding, but I'm afraid one of the four-pounders took his right arm at the shoulder. He's one of the men in the sick bay, in the cockpit, but I doubt he'll see tomorrow morning. Though the surgeon says there's still hope."

Grey nodded and waited for Bavinger to continue. When he didn't—instead pouring himself a glass of claret, and offering one to Grey—Grey asked if the French officers hadn't been willing to provide any more information.

"They were quite insistent that only the vaguest news had reached them, and that their orders were no more complex than to make game of British shipping before the escorts were restarted."

"What do you propose doing with them?"

"We'll put in at Oporto for new spars and cord, and then on to Gibraltar to disembark the prisoners."

"Gibraltar?" said Grey. "Not Madeira?"

"No, I'm afraid not—the crossing must be delayed until we can do it in a convoy; *Diligente* won't be the last hungry Frenchman looking for his bread between here and the American coast. I can't risk the company's ship."

Grey nodded. Of course, that was a perfectly reasonable—the only logical—response to the resumption of the war. Every ship with British papers was now a legitimate target, and the *Ruby* having had one lucky escape was no reason to expect a second. Bavinger's plans were changed perforce.

But Grey's were not.

"I understand, Captain. I will disembark at Oporto and complete my journey under a neutral flag."

"I understand, Captain Grey," said Bavinger—with perhaps a trace of surprise that Grey was giving no thought to rejoining the marines . . . what with war breaking out and Grey obviously being fighting-fit . . . but of course, that was none of his business. "And of course," he continued, "the company will make good your fare."

"Thank you, most kind," said Grey, standing, finishing his glass. "Now, I'll leave you to your work."

6

OPORTO: THE CITY in northern Portugal famous for its
tripe and its ships and most of all for its wine—port. It
had been a major center of commerce for northwest Iberia since the Romans had captured it from the Celts two thousand
years earlier. As the *Ruby* shortened sail—leaving just enough canvas
for steerageway—she glided into a harbor packed even more fully
than usual, with English ships who had found suddenly that the seas
weren't safe for them. The sound of old acquaintances greeting each
other, shouting ship to ship, floated over the water as *Ruby* dropped
anchor. The *Ruby*'s gig carried her captain ashore to begin the process of refitting; Grey went with him, and they parted company with
a handshake on the wharf.

As he set off into Oporto, Grey wondered whether the curl-
ing, twisting streets were a remnant of the pre-Roman town, or
if Rome's city planners had simply been thwarted by the steep and
copious hills. Either way, they made for a pleasant place to walk—
among wooden buildings built on Roman foundations, painted in
the cheerful, bright colors that the modern Portuguese seemed to
favor. With two of the oarsmen from the *Ruby*'s gig at his heels—
playing porter, carrying his sea chests—Thomas Grey set his eyes on
the beautiful Torre dos Clérigos, the baroque tower of the Clérigos

Church: as Grey recalled, there was a maritime hotel in its shadow. He figured this as the best place to seek a captain of a ship bound, with a little more determination, across the Atlantic.

The *dono da casa* at the hotel desk greeted Grey warmly. He was always pleased to see a man who could afford not to lug his own luggage. But before the dono d' could launch into his description of the establishment's fine accommodations and many services, Grey cut him off with the question "Have you any sea captains in residence?"— asked in unaccented but grammatically suspect Portuguese.

"We have, senhor; several. I would be happy to make introductions for you. Are you traveling?"

"I am. Please introduce me as Mr. Thomas Grey," said Grey, signing the register, "an Englishman seeking passage to Boston or any American port north of the Chesapeake. I am at any captain's disposal whenever he'd care to meet."

"Very good, sir." The dono d' rang a bell. "Maher will see you to your room. Do you wish to eat?"

"Yes—dobrada, coffee, and a bottle of port. Vintage. Whatever year you'd recommend."

The dono d' smiled gratefully: "Certainly, sir. It will be up shortly."

A young man appeared at Grey's side and picked up his bags. "To number eight," said the dono d'.

7

IN ROOM NUMBER EIGHT, the hotel footman Maher began to unpack Grey's chests into the wardrobe, and Grey began to shave at a small copper mirror beside the bed.

"You're a soldier, sir," said Maher, brushing the red coat of Grey's uniform.

"You're Irish," said Grey, having been caught off guard by the brogue. "I took Maher to be an Iberian name. And no, not a solider. Formerly a marine."

"I am Irish, sir. Lots of Irish in Oporto, you know, and Portugal more general like. It's being the naturalest neutral for us, and not desiring to fight for King George in the last war. Nor this one. I hope that don't offend none, sir."

"It does not. You're not the only one who finds himself in that kettle of fish."

"Indeed, sir? You're not Irish, are you?"

"Are you done there, Maher?" said Grey, who had started to scrape shaving soap off his face.

"I am, sir," said Maher, closing the wardrobe and opening the window. Grey dried a hand on his trousers and removed a shilling from the waistcoat he'd hung on a chair. "Thank you, sir, very much. I'll bring up your dinner soon as it's ready."

"Thank you, Maher. Very kind."

✦

THE NEXT MORNING, after a truly exceptional pot of Brazilian coffee, Grey checked with the dono d' to see if he had turned up any America-bound captains. A vain hope, given so little time for word to circulate. With nothing else pressing, Grey set off for the seamen's hospital, where Mr. Kefauver, the botanist, had been taken on as a patient. Though they had exchanged no more than a few dozen words, Grey felt a certain responsibility to the man, being the only other passenger on the *Ruby* to put ashore in Oporto, and perhaps the only other soul Kefauver knew in Portugal.

That Kefauver was alive to be put ashore in Portugal had surprised everyone, Grey included, once he knew the details of the wound. Of course, the *Ruby*'s surgeon had handled many a lost limb in his career—which had spanned a decade in the navy before he'd begun to dream of a tamer life and obtained a merchant position—but normally, when an arm or leg has to be amputated, either in part or in toto, a flap of skin overlapping the excised portion is preserved and sewn as a cover to the open wound—an essential armor against infection. The unfortunate Mr. Kefauver had had his arm so cleanly severed by a French cannon shot that no bonus skin had been available. In the end, the ship's surgeon had been forced simply to cauterize the wound (before he passed out, Kefauver's screaming could be heard in every corner of the ship) and hope for the best.

When—per those hopes; in spite of expectations—no infection had developed, it was decided that Kefauver's best chance for a full recovery lay in getting him onto solid ground as quickly as possible. While Bavinger had arranged the purchase of replacement cord for his tattered rigging, the surgeon had—at the company's expense—arranged the botanist's admission to the local seamen's hospital. And, with directions from the dono d', that was where Grey headed.

The hospital was halfway up one of the Lordelo do Ouro hillsides, looking down at the mouth of the Douro River. It was a single story tall, with a single long and narrow ward stretching the whole, considerable length of the building. With its shutters wide open and a warm breeze blowing in, it had the feeling of an outdoor bandstand, thought Grey, as he was pointed to Kefauver's bed.

Grey was surprised to find Kefauver wide awake, quite lively—in high spirits, even—and at work: he had a pencil in his left hand and was making notes on a notepad propped against his knees.

Should Grey attempt a handshake? That was the quandary that preempted Grey's greeting the botanist; he was standing silently a few feet from the foot of Kefauver's bed when Kefauver noticed him and waved him forward.

"Why, Captain Grey!" the botanist said, sticking the pencil behind his ear and offering Grey his left hand. "How kind of you to look in on me! Here, here, have a seat." Kefauver pointed Grey to a joint stool sitting at his armless right shoulder. "Would you like something to drink? I was able to secure a bottle of port . . . it's here somewhere . . ."

"No, thank you, nothing for me. And of course, it's my pleasure to look in on a comrade-in-arms. I say, you surprised us all by weathering it so well; I doubt myself I'd have had the mettle to make it through."

"You're entirely too kind, Captain," said Kefauver. "I'm only sorry I couldn't have been on deck at the finale." He was sitting up straighter in bed, trying to tidy himself up.

"Can I offer you any assistance, Mr. Kefauver?" asked Grey.

"No, thank you, but I suppose I might just as well get used to these one-handed operations as soon as possible."

"You seemed to be writing quite adeptly with your left," said Grey. "Are you so quick a study?"

"No, in fact, I'm naturally left-handed. Bit of luck, ey?"

"Indeed . . . though I could have sworn I saw you eating with the right."

"Yes, yes, my governess was quite intent on my learning to use the right for everything, you know—would tie the left behind my back, crack me across the knuckles, and so forth. When I think of all the blood and sweat I put into training the damn thing . . . oh well. It's in a better place now, no doubt." He chuckled. "Feeding the sharks."

"I had proposed to tell you," said Grey, "of all the men I knew in the service who had lost arms and led full and happy lives afterwards, by way of comforting you—but you don't seem to need much comforting."

"Again, you flatter me. Of course, I was in quite a state yesterday, but, oh, we must muddle on. I've concluded that there is little of my professional activity that I can't adapt to a single arm: no, I will only have to draw and record blooms and shoots while they're still attached to their plants, and cut them off after. That way I won't need a second hand in which to hold them."

"I admire your resolve, sir. Now you must tell me, is there anything I can get for you? Oporto has shops aplenty, if there's anything you require."

"Well, I hesitate to ask—do you think you might fill me one of these glasses with soil from the Douro's banks? I should love to see if there is some special mineral in these hinterlands that helps contribute to the richness of port wine."

"Mr. Kefauver," said Grey, chuckling, standing, "it should be my pleasure. I'll return with your sample in no more than half an hour."

AFTER GREY'S RETURN, and another hour or so of botanical talk—and some discussion of Paulette's rhododendrons, which had dampened Grey's mood to the point that Kefauver had tried to buck him up—Grey headed back to his hotel, planning to eat lunch and check in on the westward-bound ship situation. Before Grey had crossed the hotel's threshold, Maher had intercepted him, to pass along compliments and an invitation from a Captain Donald Branson: Branson, upon the chance that Mr. Grey should wish to meet him to discuss passage to the United States, would await the gentleman at Pedrito's coffeehouse until the early evening.

So, turning back into the fresh, warm afternoon, Grey returned down the hill, towards the harbor, following Maher's directions. He found Pedrito's to be a very Portuguese sort of a place, brightly colored but quiet; there was only one customer, a somewhat gray, somewhat grizzled man, immaculately dressed, in velvet, under a cocked hat. Grey approached him.

"Captain Branson?" he asked. The man stood and extended his hand.

"Mr. Grey?" Grey nodded. "Have a seat, won't you? Would you like some coffee? I'll call for a fresh pot. Or would you prefer tea?"

"Coffee would be very welcome, thank you," said Grey. "I gather you have a ship heading west."

Branson called to the waiter for more coffee and a second cup, and then furrowed his brow.

"Not exactly, no. I was anxious to meet you; I hope you'll forgive a false representation."

Grey said nothing. His face was impassive.

"Yes, well . . . You see, I represent an organization in Oporto in which I have been led to believe you might perhaps be interested."

Grey raised one eyebrow, slightly.

"You are familiar with the United Irishmen?"

Grey paused, then answered: "I am."

"The organization responsible for the Irish rising in '98? As you may know, after the rebellion was put down by the English, many of the members fled to the Continent, most of them to France. You will recall that the French Republican government offered assistance, to the rebellion, out of respect for our shared goals. Planning, finances, and the invasion force that Lake defeated at Castlebar.

"Despite our having been removed from our homeland, the work continues, within the aegis of the new Napoleon government. Among our activities is gathering information from . . . travelers, such as yourself, at neutral ports. Information for which we are, of course, willing to pay."

Another pause. Then Grey spoke. "I suppose Maher is one of your men . . . You keep watch at the hotels for disaffected Englishmen?"

"Something like that," said Branson. "And, as I've been given to understand, you were an officer? And not planning to rejoin now that the war has resumed."

Grey kept his face impassive, said nothing, and after a moment stood up. "I'll consider what you've said," he told Branson, who was following Grey to his feet. "Shall I deliver an answer through Maher?"

"Please do," said Branson, reaching his hand out to Grey.

Grey shook it with an assumed air of courtesy and exited to the street.

GREY STOPPED at a tobacconist for a small tin of small Turkish cigars, and began a circuitous walk back to the hotel, smoking and thinking.

Of course, selling information to the French was completely out of the question. But this question had more to it than that.

He paused in a steep alleyway and turned around to face the Douro. A punt barge was being poled along. The men working it were wearing striped shirts, making them look like gondoliers who had wandered away from home.

If he chose, of course, he could do nothing. He could behave as if Branson had never spoken to him. He could be in Boston, and set-tled, in a month.

However, the presence of an Irish-French intelligence network in Portugal—in Oporto, no doubt in Lisbon as well, and probably Madeira—was an important discovery. Naval intelligence and its secret service had done their best to keep track of the Irish rebels who fled after '98, but there was no inkling in Whitehall that they had been organized, and were being used, by the French. And to come on so boldly—to offer, bluntly, to pay him . . . it suggested they'd been emboldened by success. Or perhaps the initial subter-fuge had been called off because of what he'd said to Maher. Either way: though he was free to ignore it, there was no way to deny the enterprise being a serious threat to Britain.

Grey threw away the butt of one cigar and lit another.

Should he pass the information back to London and let them deal with it? It would be a balm to his conscience, and it would not be difficult—no harder than placing a sealed letter in the hands of any honest Englishman on a ship bound for home.

But if such a letter arrived at Sir Edward's office inside a week, it would take at least two weeks more for any action to be taken back here in Oporto. And that was supposing fair winds and decisive action by the Admiralty Board. Realistically it would take a month, maybe two. Maybe more. After all, with war just declared (in the past seventy-two hours, no less), the Admiralty would surely be surrounded by the most intense maelstrom. The letter might not make it through, or not be read if it did.

Grey looked down at the slivers of the Atlantic sparkling up at him from between Oporto's seaside buildings. A two-man fishing boat sculled past, and Grey pinched out another cigar.

Could it conceivably be his responsibility to take action directly? The very point of his departure from London had been to get out of this squalid world. He had done his part; why should it be he assembling the names of Branson's agents? Arranging for them to be secretly knocked on the head. Delivered to the harbor; shipped back to England for interrogation.

. . . Though perhaps the best course of destruction would be to feed the network false information. Distract them from Britain's real plans, point them off in the wrong direction. Like a chess player seeing a game in progress, Grey couldn't help thinking through the possible moves and countermoves . . .

And perhaps . . . Well, there was another possibility too. Vendetta.

Perhaps he could use Branson's offer to induce an invitation to Paris. Perhaps he could discover the name of the man who'd been in command of *Fidèle* when Paulette had been killed. And then kill him.

When Grey arrived back at his hotel, he left instructions at the desk for Maher to be found and sent to his room.

8

BEFORE HE'D BEEN appointed head of the Malta station—that is to say, when Grey had still been based in London—he had had his own small office in the Admiralty building. He had had a secretary he shared with three other intelligence men, and a key to a private entrance, which allowed him to come and go without being observed by the ordinary run of people. Assignments would come in the form of a deputy knocking on his door and delivering the curt message, "Sir Edward would like a word." Nothing more. Intelligence business was not discussed in the halls, nor with anyone not directly concerned. Gossip was taboo even among colleagues. In fact, though Sir Edward's team of spies did fraternize with one another, they did so almost exclusively outside their joint offices. It was an unspoken rule that when they were on the job, it was the job and the job only that occupied their time. Also unspoken was the source of this rule—the men's attempts, whether or not they realized it, to emulate their leader.

None would admit the extent to which each looked up to Sir Edward Banks. Indeed, to admit to such a depth of feeling would run contrary to the Banksian model to which they all adhered. Though he wasn't opposed to dressing well, Sir Edward despised wigs, and never wore one except when performing the official duties for which it was mandatory. Consequently, wigs had been eschewed by every man in the office. Sir Edward may also have hated Whigs—he was widely supposed to be a Tory, but none of his men ever knew for certain, because he never uttered one word of politics outside the narrow confines of budget matters. And neither did they.

Sir Edward was known to have remarked once or twice, in unguarded moments, that a good intelligence man should not only speak but be decently well read in all Europe's major languages. Foreign novels and pamphlets then became common articles in the desks of the secret service. One hearty man had obtained and attempted to read a book of Hungarian poetry. At the same time, Sir Edward found the study of dead languages to be frivolous, and something better saved for retirement. Those men who'd excelled in school at Latin, Greek, and Hebrew kept it to themselves.

Sir Edward was a good rider and a good hunter, but not a fox hunter. ("A damned silly, cruel waste of time.") He was not a naval officer, but he knew his way around a trigonometric table and placed great store in the ability to navigate. He believed every man under the age of fifty should concern himself with fitness, and that no man over fifty should give it a second thought. He was known to play tennis, but purely for recreation, and to have been a champion fencer in his youth. He was rumored to have given up handball after the death of his favorite partner, Major John André.

Of all his foibles, the most strictly accommodated was the obsessive emphasis he placed on promptness. Never be late for a meeting; never dawdle when sent for. So when a deputy knocked on the door and said, "Sir Edward would like a word," every man in the department knew that this meant, "Drop everything and come now— before I give a plum assignment to someone who won't keep me waiting."

That sense of urgency—the just-controlled impulse to run instead of walk to Banks's office—was how Thomas Grey felt now, rolling in a carriage through the Spanish countryside, with a foppishly dressed Mr. (not Captain) Donald Branson sitting beside him.

Getting himself to this point had not been difficult. Grey had sent word, by Maher, to Branson; his story was that, after he left the Royal Marines, his most recent—and final—post in the Admiralty had been in service to the victualing board, and as such, he was familiar with the disposition, condition, crew, and material requirements of near every ship in His Majesty's fleet. He added that his time with the board had ended when he'd been passed over for a promised promotion, a promotion against whose increased salary he'd borrowed money. Knowing then that he'd default on the loan, Grey said, he'd been forced to flee the country to avoid the sponging house and debtors' prison. He explained that his willingness to accept Branson's proposition was not merely a question of money; in fact, he still had funds left from the balance of the fateful loan. He was eager to accept Branson because he wanted revenge for his ruined life. He proved his value, and his story, with detailed intelligence of the Mediterranean squadron—intelligence chosen from the body he had supervised in Malta and knew to be defunct, but rich with detail that he knew could be checked for accuracy in Paris. For the remaining wealth of information he proposed to sell, he set a very high price—a price high enough that he knew Branson would be unable to pay it himself.

As Grey hoped, he had been summoned to Paris by coach, with Branson as handler.

It was a lengthy journey, and a dusty one, that would have been unpleasant under the best conditions, and which was made worse by a badly sprung carriage bumping over the badly rutted roads of northern Spain. Nevertheless, bone-jarring though it might have been, progress was quite quick, and after two uneventful days, they had entered Basque country and were approaching the French frontier.

Here Branson, who (like Grey) had spent most of the first two days' journey silently reading—elbow on the windowsill, pages held up to the bright Spanish sunshine—now seemed to lose some of his sangfroid. Book closed on his lap, he gazed wistfully for a while out at the approaching Pyrenees, occasionally sighing, until Grey had finally to ask what was troubling him.

"I have an apartment in Paris," said Branson. "I've lived there for five years, since after the failed rising, and every time I cross back from Iberia to France, there is a part of my gut that says, We're coming home, and then remembers France isn't my home and never will be."

"Where were you born?" asked Grey.

"Derry," said Branson. Grey resisted the impulse to needle him with a correction to "Londonderry"; any man missing his homeland is a sympathetic character. Even under such rebellious circumstances.

"Beautiful country up there," said Grey instead.

"Yes," said Branson. "Very beautiful. You've been to Eire?"

"Yes," said Grey. "I've been all around Ireland. I was attached to a ship in the Irish squadron, that spent some months in Belfast, before moving to Dublin, Cork, and then to blockade duty in the Channel."

"I see," said Branson, no doubt aware that Grey's squadron had carried not just marines, but regulars, who were a fixture in Irish cities.

For a moment they lapsed back into silence. Not wanting to jeopardize his plans by allowing Branson to develop ill will towards him, Grey struck the conversation up again.

"How do you operate in Paris? Is there some sort of Irish office in the new government?"

"No," said Branson. "I report to an officer of the Committee for State Security, a department of the Maison Militaire"—France's military hierarchy. He didn't go on.

"Are there many Irishmen so employed?" asked Grey.

"Some," said Branson.

Now the coach was starting to rise upward into the Pyrenees' foothills—

"I hope you're comfortable," said Branson. "I'm afraid we won't reach another inn on this road until well after midnight. It's rough country up here. The major crossings run further south, you know, towards Barcelona or Madrid."

"Never fear," said Grey. "I'm a good sailor; quite content to sleep through rough seas."

"Good," said Branson. And those were the last words either spoke for five hours.

The next words they heard were spoken by neither of them; indeed, they were not spoken but shouted, in Spanish, from somewhere in front of the carriage:

"Stop! Stop those horses or you die!" came an angry bellow.

"Damned scoundrels—damned highwaymen!" said Branson.

The carriage bounced lightly on its springs as the driver was dragged off his seat and thrown to the ground; an instant later there were two men standing at the carriage door, each brandishing a pistol, each with a kerchief tied over his nose and mouth.

"Get out," the shorter of the two said. "You first!" He waved his pistol at Branson. "Fast, fast, or you die!"

"Damn them," said Branson quietly to Grey as he stooped towards the door, opened it, and stepped down onto the road. Tucking his pistol into his belt, the shorter man began roughly to frisk Branson, taking his purse and a superb Breguet watch, then pushing him backward and ordering him to remove his jacket and shoes. Branson spit at the ground, uttered an Irish oath, and began to comply.

"Now you!" shouted the man at Grey, pulling the pistol back out of his belt. And now Grey hunched, climbed down onto the road, and walked towards the shorter highwayman, till his pistol was almost touching Grey's chest.

"Keep your hands up!" said the man, lowering his pistol to begin another frisk. With a smooth, practiced motion, Grey grabbed the man's pistol hand and twisted it two hundred and seventy degrees, enough to point the barrel at the chest of the short man's partner. The short man screamed in pain as the bones in his wrist audibly broke; the scream was cut short by Grey pulling the pistol's trigger—there was the concussive *BANG* of the shot going off, and then the *plud* of the taller highwayman falling to the ground dead, not knowing what had hit him.

The first highwayman had resumed screaming in pain, staring

at his perverted wrist; now Grey pulled the empty pistol out of the man's broken grasp, and whipped the butt end across his face, shattering a cheekbone, sending him tumbling backward into a ditch.

Grey walked over to the fallen man and dropped the empty pistol on his chest.

"We'll leave you to see to your deceased friend," said Grey, in tolerable Spanish, reaching into the man's coat pockets and retrieving Branson's things, along with the driver's purse.

Grey turned then to Branson, who had one boot off, and to the driver, who was sitting on the ground where he'd been thrown, beside his horses. "Gentlemen, shall we continue?"

Each in turn nodded his assent as Grey returned their valuables and climbed back into the carriage. He was followed a moment later by Branson, who returned to his seat.

"Thank you," said Branson to Grey, removing a handkerchief from his trousers and wiping at some dark brown stains that the short highwayman had made on his jacket during the frisk.

"You're welcome," said Grey.

Later, when Branson had removed as much of the filth as he was able, he replaced the handkerchief in his pocket and looked over at Grey.

"You're a dangerous man, Captain Grey."

By the next evening, they had crossed over the Pyrenees, and after that, traveling on French roads—perhaps beaten smooth by the goings and comings of the French army—the ride became considerably easier. Aquitaine passed uneventfully, save for a few adventures in ice-cold roadside baths, and the Val de Loire lacked even those, though at one point the driver slowed the coach to allow his passengers and himself to admire a pair of beautiful, remarkably lithe maidens treading on grapes. Each would have been better suited to ballet; Grey remarked to Branson that he found it difficult to believe either was heavy enough to crush a grape, eliciting from the Irishman a good-natured chuckle.

"Do they grow grapes in Ireland, Mr. Branson?" asked Grey as the coach resumed its full speed.

"There have been attempts," said Branson. "So far as I know, each ended in unqualified, undrinkable disaster. I suspect that growing grapes so far north is some kind of an affront to God."

"I agree," said Grey. "I will not say I was disgusted, but let me say that I was surprised when I discovered in Pepys that wine had been made in North London. I think it was Walthamstow."

"Walthamstow?"

"Walthamstow." The men shook their heads disdainfully, in unison.

"Have you traveled much in England, Mr. Branson?" asked Grey.

"I have, from time to time," said the Irishman. "After I left Trinity—Trinity Dublin, that is—I was able to secure a position at Cambridge as an instructor in the Irish language. But that lasted only a year. Then I did some work editing for a publisher in London."

"Did you enjoy London?"

"I did. This was during the period of the American revolution. I attended the Strangers' Gallery in the Commons as often as I could. I found the speeches—from the defenders of the revolution, that is; from Whig members; perhaps you are too young to remember—I found those speeches most inspirational. I took some of those ideas back to Dublin with me."

Many Englishmen had been sympathetic to the American desire for home rule, and now that the independent American states were a fact of life, most Englishmen accepted them. Why, Grey wondered, would it be so much harder to accept an independent Ireland? Was it a simple matter of proximity? Was it because most Americans were Protestant and most Irishmen were not?

Or was the difference that America had won its freedom in battle? Would Ireland have to do the same? Was there truly no other solution?

Grey reminded himself that this was not the moment for indulging sympathies. He guided his thoughts back to Paulette and vendetta.

Now they were closing in on Paris, crossing into the Île-de-France, and Grey was beginning to feel excitement—a lust for action—building up from his feet. He wasn't a man prone to revenge, exactly. But he had killed before, on assignment. During the revolution, he had helped evacuate monarchists from France, and put bullets in the heads of several Jacobins. He didn't regret it. They were savage men. The last one he'd killed—the last time he'd been in France, in the guise of a Swiss anthropologist—he'd assassinated a sans-culotte who'd helped direct the "Republican marriages" at Nantes, where men and women—some of them priests and nuns, but anyone suspected of disliking the new regime—had been stripped naked, tied together, and thrown into the Loire to drown, for the amusement of barbaric revolutionary onlookers. The man in question might still be alive if he hadn't carelessly murdered a British subject, a Scottish magnate who'd retired to an aristocratic vineyard and foolhardily chosen to wait the Terror out. When Grey caught up to the Nantes executioner, he explained why the man had been marked for death, and gave him a moment to say his prayers. The man hadn't begged for his life, and hadn't prayed. He'd told Grey his only religion was the revolution. Grey was not impressed. The man's secretary found him the next morning with a hole in his forehead and the Scotsman's name written on a scrap of paper clenched in his cold hand.

That was the last time Grey had seen Paris. And he had to admit, it looked much better now. Gone was the crazy profusion of revolutionary banners and slogans and egalitarian unswept streets. Bonaparte was a tyrant, but at least he wasn't an unhygienic tyrant as Robespierre had been. Grey could forgive many things, but wanton filth was not one of them.

The carriage rattled over a wooden bridge, over one of the Seine's tributaries, signaling that their arrival was near and waking up Branson. Feeling perhaps that the grape discussion had marked the establishment of a friendship, Branson had relaxed noticeably, and for the last twenty miles, had been snoring in the most irritating way. He wiped his chin and straightened his clothes before addressing Grey.

"I'm afraid I drifted off," said Branson, turning to look out the window. "It won't be long now. Have you ever been to Paris before?"

"No," said Grey, as they passed through a bottleneck of traffic that had formed at one of the gates through the toll wall surrounding the city, "though of course I've long hoped to."

"Well, I don't expect she'll disappoint. The first consul has things running very well—yes, very well. The city is more alive than it has been in years."

"That's good to hear," said Grey. "Of course I followed with great interest the excesses of the revolution."

"Who didn't?" said Branson. "But the old regime is dead, and since the Thermidor Reaction France has been much more civilized. And now Napoleon has made it every bit as cosmopolitan as London."

"I'm told the cathedral has been reopened."

"Yes, mass in Notre Dame has resumed, and churches are allowed to ring their bells again, and priests to wear their vestments." Grey briefly wondered how so-Catholic Ireland could have sustained an alliance with so brutally anti-Catholic a regime as the Jacobins', but of course war makes strange bedfellows. Branson continued:

"The first consul has likewise commenced a building project— many building projects—to turn the city into what he feels it ought to be. Slums are being razed, the sewers are being repaired and a new aqueduct built—an iron bridge is being constructed across the Seine! I will show it to you, you must see it—it's quite remarkable; quite beautiful."

Again they lapsed into silence, each looking out at the city rising up around them, admiring the beautiful homogeneity of the pale golden sand-colored stone façades that gave Paris its charmingly consistent style, even with modern and baroque buildings mixed with the medieval.

"I look forward," said Grey, after a while, "to meeting some of the new regime."

"I'm sure they're looking forward to meeting you as well," said Branson.

9

A ROOM HAD BEEN arranged for Grey on the newly refurbished Place Vendôme, in one of the several luxurious hotels revived by the Bonaparte government: clearly Napoleon had made it a priority to see Paris return to her place as the Continent's center of art, culture, and fashion. Indeed, the velvet & tricorn that had made Branson look like a fop in Oporto seemed ordinary, perhaps even a touch conservative, amidst the ladies and gentlemen moving in and out of the lobby of the Hôtel d'Orsigny, where Grey was to be lodged.

The lobby itself was splendid: orange walls in baroque molding surrounded a trio of three-layer brass chandeliers, which hung in a line from the front door to the hotel's desk. At the desk, Branson negotiated terms with the maître d'hôtel, producing the official papers calling him, with Grey, to Paris. As they debated, a soft tinkle of porcelain drew Grey's attention away . . . It was the sound of chips in a gaming room, which—despite its continental appointment; everything in excess—more brass—brass fixtures—brass everywhere—shot silk drapes on the walls—reminded Grey, pleasantly, of Buttle's. The patrons were playing Basset, that fortune-breaking game which the French aristocracy had loved so well that the Sun King had been forced to ban it outright, for fear of destroying the credit of the ancien régime.

Now, the nouveau régime was back at it, and with his unusually sharp eyes, Grey could see the banker's stake was something on the order of five hundred francs, an astonishing amount in a country wracked, as France had been, by so much political turmoil. And a new war, to boot. Someone had made a *quinze-et-le-va*.

"I'm sure a line of credit can be arranged, if you like," said Branson, who had come up behind Grey. He didn't have to add, "With what you're demanding in payment, I'm sure the government is anxious for you to lose as much of it as possible here in Paris." Perhaps that's why this particular hotel had been chosen. And Grey was glad for an easy chance to play up a mercenary façade.

"Thank you, I would appreciate that," he said, turning away from the green baize tables.

Branson nodded. "Your cases are already on their way up. I will leave you here to rest and recuperate, as you will. I will call for you tomorrow."

"Very well—till tomorrow, then. Bid you good day." Grey turned and, catching the eye of a footman, was led up to his room.

After the long trip—and glad to be in a room that was stationary—Grey had fully intended to bathe and go straight to sleep. However, during his bath, which was hot as anything and wonderfully restorative, a note was slipped under the door, signed by the management, informing Grey that the surprisingly immense line of a thousand francs' credit had been established for him. He had only to present himself to the cashier.

Of course, the first step in obtaining information is to be sociable. And, if he were to be quite honest with himself, the tables called to him. Though Grey had no love for endless trick-taking games like whist, he had a soft spot for Basset. Yes, it was a game of luck. And true, the odds favored the banker—though they could be controlled somewhat by familiarity with their predictable variance, and by keeping track of the cards that had been played. Still, what mattered most in Basset was courage. It was the one game that measured not just a man's luck, but his fortitude.

Freshly dressed, feeling clean and relaxed for the first time since Oporto, Grey collected from the cashier eighty francs of markers, in chips and plaques. The law, in place since the Sun King's son had relegalized the game, said that initial stakes of Basset could not exceed sixpence; half a shilling—one fortieth of a franc. The fact that the smallest chip denomination here was a sou, a full shilling, spoke to the tone of the d'Orsigny's game. But the rich always play by their own rules.

A hand ended at a central table, with a young swain winning his bet against the banker, declining his *paroli*, collecting his winnings, and making his exit. Grey took his chair and spoke to the croupier:

"A book of spades." That is, a full suit of thirteen cards, ace through king. The suits play no role in the game, they are simply a personal preference; most women played hearts, or some of the wealthier and more gregarious ones, diamonds. Frenchmen tended to play clubs—it was something about those silly cockades.

The croupier handed Grey his cards, and Grey lit a cigar, watching the movement of the shoe. Basset is not too complex a game; it is a series of individual duels between the banker—a private player who has volunteered to deal and stakes all bets—and the players who bet against him, one by one. The first to play is the man at the banker's right, who lays out between one and thirteen of the cards in his book; as many and whatever denominations he chooses. On each card he chooses to play, he places a bet—say, a sou (which was evidently the minimum bet of this table). The banker then deals two cards; the first is the winner, the second, the loser. If the player had laid a bet on a card matching (in rank, not suit) the first card dealt, he doubles his bet. But any bet laid on a card matching the loser, the second-dealt card, is forfeit to the banker.

What makes the game interesting is what happens on a winning bet: the player is given the option of *paroli*—to forfeit his winnings back to the banker, in exchange for the right to play the same card again, with the same bet. But this time, if he wins, instead of paying off at two-to-one, the bet will pay off at seven-to-one. This is the *sept-et-le-va*. If the player wins his bet on the *sept-et-le-va*, he may *parol* again, at fifteen-to-one: the *quinze-et-le-va*; and then again, for the *trente-et-le-va*: thirty-to-one. On those rare occasions when a *trente-et-le-va* is played, and won, the player may *parol* one final time—the *soixante-et-le-va*. These sixty-to-one bets were the ones that brought men to their knees; wealthy aristocrats banking against table stakes of one hundred francs, suddenly owing six thousand— more, certainly, than their annual incomes. More possibly than the value of their estates. And if they had accepted side bets, as was common, the total could be more, far more, than that. Enough to ruin families.

For his part, Grey had no intention of winning any money. Only of ruffling a few feathers. To that end, after a few hands—the banker addressing himself slowly around the table—Grey spoke for the first time, when the player to his left won a *sept-et-le-va* off a seven-franc wager, on an ace, and chose not to *parol*.

"Perhaps," said Grey, "the gentleman will pass his *paroli* to me, if the bank has no objection."

"I have none," said the banker. "I would be glad of the chance to win that money back, Mr. . . . ?"

"Grey. Thomas Grey."

"You are an Englishman."

"I am."

"Are you lost?" There was laughter around the table, and a smile from Grey.

"Let us say I am a pilgrim, Mr. . . . ?"

"Polignac. Jacques Polignac." Grey looked him over—late twenties, handsome, vaguely ruthless-looking, with a hint of smallpox scarring on his cheeks.

"Did your parents give all their children rhyming names, Mr.

Polignac?" More laughter from the table, and a strained smile from the banker.

"Indeed not, Mr. Grey. But some of us are just fortunate. As we shall see. Play your ace."

Grey slid the top card off his book of spades, the ace, and played it on the table in front of him, laying atop it a stack of two twenty-franc plaques, a five, and four single chips. On his side of the table, Polignac placed a five-franc plaque on top of a hundred, and slid them towards the croupier.

"*Quinze-et-le-va*," said Grey, as a matter of form. Polignac drew two cards from the shoe, sliding the first towards Grey, into the middle of the table, and the second back towards himself. After a brief pause—the French and their drama, thought Grey—Polignac turned up the first. It was an ace. A murmur went up around a table. Polignac turned up the second card. It was an eight.

"The player wins," said the croupier, who readied a tapered ivory baton to slide the winnings to Grey. Grey shook his head.

"*Trente-et-le-va*," said Grey. Polignac nodded, smiled, and dealt two more cards from the shoe. His smile vanished when he flipped the first—another ace. Another, somewhat louder murmur moved around the table. The murmur turned to a gasp when Polignac flipped the second card. Also an ace. No hand; no winner. Relief read on Polignac's face. Nothing at all read on Grey's.

"*Suivi*," said Grey, calling for another two cards at the same stake. Approving nods, excited chatter from the crowd that had formed to watch. Polignac dealt. He flipped the first up:

An ace. Gasps and laughter from the onlookers. Polignac flipped up the second card. A six. Grey won again. There was a single shout of *Bravo*. Grey smiled.

"How many decks do you play here?" he asked the croupier.

"Twenty, sir."

"Very well," said Grey. By his count, eighteen aces had been played, and there were around forty cards remaining in the shoe. Whether an ace came up for or against him, they would know soon enough.

"*Soixante-et-le-va*," he said. Polignac nodded, now on the hook for four hundred and twenty francs—enough to buy a house. He slid the ponderous stake of plaques towards the croupier, and dealt two cards.

They were a four and a nine. No winner.

"*Suivi*," said Grey. Polignac dealt two more cards.

Both kings.

"*Suivi*," said Grey. Polignac dealt two more.

He flipped the first. The onlookers gasped. There was the ace! That rarest of coups, of the *soixante-et-le-va*, would pay off . . . if the final ace was not now turned up.

Polignac hesitated, then flipped the second card.

A knave. Several more shouts of bravo, and some excited jostling as people leaned forward to see the fatal cards for themselves.

The croupier slid the porcelain pile of winnings to Grey, who thanked him, and thanked Polignac:

"A most spirited hand, sir," he said, with the traditional grace of a good winner.

"Yes, Mr. Grey," said Polignac, in an affable tone. "I admire your dumb luck."

The murmuring stopped, replaced by an uncomfortable silence at Polignac's rudeness.

"Well," said Grey, "perhaps you would like to test it a final time. A cut for high card, at double or nothing? If you can afford it."

A stunning riposte. Polignac's rude smile turned into a sneer.

"I believe I can, Monsieur Grey," said Polignac.

"*Capitaine* Grey, Monsieur Polignac," said Grey. "A fresh deck, if you please?" he asked the croupier. The croupier retrieved one from a small cupboard beneath the table, slid off its paper cuff, and handed it to Grey. Grey shuffled, then offered the deck to Polignac.

"Would you like your own shuffle, sir?"

Polignac shook his head. "I am satisfied."

Grey placed the deck halfway between them.

"Make your cut." In the large game room, one could have heard the drop of a pin. Polignac made his cut and held it up for Grey to see.

"Queen," he said. Grey reached forward and made his own cut.

He looked at the card, and held it for Polignac to see.

"Ace," said Grey. "Quite a lucky card for me tonight."

Polignac nodded, and stood.

"I will have to visit the cashier," he said, looking, perhaps, a little pale. "Excuse me; I must pass the shoe."

Polignac walked away, and Grey slid a ten-franc plaque to the croupier before himself standing.

"Good evening, gentlemen. Ladies." The glow of victory followed Grey away from the table. One of the onlookers leaned down to the player who had watched the whole affair from the front row, so to speak—seated to Grey's right, to whom the bet now passed.

"*De l'audace*," he said, quoting the recently rehabilitated revolutionary Georges Danton. "*Toujours de l'audace.*"

10

"I UNDERSTAND YOU CAUSED quite a stir at the tables last night," said Branson, as he and Grey walked, the next evening, from the Place Vendôme towards the Tuileries.

"Did I?" said Grey. "I had a run of luck. I shouldn't have thought it was anything remarkable."

"On the contrary, it was the talk of the clubs this morning—some Englishman at the d'Orsigny room who had doubled a *soixante-et-le-va*. I presume that was you?" said Branson.

"Social clubs, or political?" asked Grey.

"Social. I do not belong to the political clubs—such as they are, and, of course, they are diminished under Napoleon. But I am no citizen, just a confederate. My Société des Jacobins is in Dublin."

"Yes of course."

"But let us say, around the coffeehouses, you were wondered about. Particularly by my contact in the Maison Militaire, who wished me to tell him, first, if you were the anonymous Englishman, and second, if you might not be persuaded to adopt a slightly more . . . discreet posture."

"Were I he," said Grey, "I should have been more concerned that my winnings would alleviate my desire to sell to him."

"The thought occurred," said Branson. "However, it was hoped that your private grievance with the Admiralty House would exceed in importance your financial considerations." A timbre of concern had entered Branson's voice. Grey supposed the man had staked quite a lot on the value of what his new recruit could provide.

"Just so," said Grey. "I trust my report on the Mediterranean situation proved reliable?"

"It did," said Branson, with constrained relief. "I was specifically desired to mention to you the satisfaction with which its certification was met. It was proved true from start to finish."

"I am gratified to hear it, Branson."

For a moment they walked in silence.

"Some—possibly all—of the men who certified it will be at the debut tonight," said Branson. "I had preferred to introduce you to the relevant parties in a somewhat less frivolous atmosphere, but I'm afraid it can't be helped. The size of the payment you've asked for—"

"Which is not at all out of step with the wealth of information you stand to receive, Branson—"

"I don't dispute that, Captain Grey. No one has. But the fact is, under the first consul's new system of checks and approval, there is a passel of men whose imprimaturs must be sought in order to move forward. Most have expressed a desire to look you over first. To arrange to meet them one by one might take so long as to render your intelligence passé. Our hands are tied—tonight you shall be the belle of the ball."

"The young lady coming out, I fear, will be disappointed to hear that."

Branson shrugged. "Perhaps, but you will never know; she's from one of the old families, with the requisite manners, I'm sure."

"I didn't realize any of the old families had survived," said Grey. "Not with houses for parties, anyway."

"They've been returning quite rapidly since Napoleon's accession, in fact. And he has made it quite simple for those who support him to reclaim their homes and property. The estates are thriving again."

"And feudalism too?"

"No, that at least was successfully defeated. Wages must be paid, and those smallholders who were able to make a go of it—so many of them collapsed, you know, unable to make small plots profitable amidst the Jacobin price controls—yes, the smallholders I believe are allowed to keep their land, so long as they continue to work it. This is it—"

Branson gestured to a large town house near the west end of the Tuileries Garden. Its steps to the street were carpeted, and its carpet flanked by footmen, who—along with the house, and everyone entering it—were lit in gentle gold by braziers suspended over the doorway.

"Very imperial," said Grey.

"Old money," said Branson.

"I should have worn my sword," said Grey.

"I don't think that would have been a good idea," said Branson.

Branson presented an invitation to one of the footmen, and he and Grey proceeded inside, into a crowded foyer that smelt strongly of perfume. Knots of men and separate knots of women provided obstacles for the servants marching back and forth with flutes of champagne and canapés. Grey wondered how long it would take to get all the wig powder out of the carpets.

One well-powdered man in late middle age spotted Branson and walked over to introduce himself, pulling in his hilt as he came, to avoid tripping any of the champagne men. He wore the uniform of a general in Napoleon's Grande Armée.

"Monsieur Branson, good evening," he said.

"Good evening, Général de Chambrun; may I present Capitaine Grey."

"Captain Grey," said de Chambrun, in English, "it is a pleasure to meet you, I've heard a great deal about you over the last few days."

"You may perhaps have heard of the *général*'s endeavors in the battle of Rivoli," said Branson, to Grey.

"But of course," said Grey. "The general's reputation has preceded him across the Channel."

"Has it, has it indeed?" said the general with a wide smile. "How nice. I understand you have come to us from His Majesty's chandlers."

"From the victualing board, yes," said Grey.

"I was told the story of your maltreatment at the hands of your government," said de Chambrun, shaking his head, clicking his tongue. Branson blushed slightly at de Chambrun's lapse in manners. "Contemptible," he continued, "most contemptible, their behavior. But I do like a man who gets his own back! And I've read your report on the Mediterranean—it was most illuminating. Most illuminating! I look forward to your reports of the other six seas." De Chambrun smiled at what he considered an elegant turn of phrase.

"I look forward to preparing them, General," said Grey. "And in the meantime, if the Mediterranean portion left anything to be desired, I should be happy to answer any questions."

"That is most accommodating of you, Captain. I have none at the moment, it not being my field, but I am sure you will find others to take you up on the offer. If you will excuse me." With a shallow bow, the general moved off to his next glad-hand.

"Come," said Branson. "I know much of the staff of the *amiral de France* is in attendance; we should start with them."

Branson climbed a step into a drawing room and cast his eyes about for the blue-coated officers.

"There," he said, leading the way towards three men who seemed to be examining a bottle of cider.

"What do you think it's doing here?" asked one, to the others.

"There must be a Norman around." They all chuckled, and Branson cut in.

"Officers, I am Branson of the staff of the Irish chargé d'affaires; this is Captain Thomas Grey, late of the British Admiralty Board and the Royal Marines."

The man with the bottle placed it back onto a drinks table and extended his hand. His expression said that, like de Chambrun, he'd heard Grey's story.

"Captain Grey," he said, "it is a pleasure to meet you. I am Captain Roquebert; this is Captain Peley de Pléville, and Captain de Vance."

"It is an equal pleasure, gentlemen," answered Grey, shaking their hands in turn. "I'm afraid I don't know many French officers by name, but I may know you by your ships."

"*Sans Pareil*, sixty-four," said Roquebert, pointing to de Vance; "*Sévère*, sixty-four," pointing to Peley de Pléville. "My most recent command was *Impérieuse*, forty. And this dashing gentleman"—he pointed to a fourth French officer, now joining the conversation—"is Captain d'Aumont. Of *Fidèle*, thirty-two."

Grey felt a hot flush run through his veins. The muscles in his neck tightened and his vision narrowed. His heart pounded in his ears. Captain d'Aumont was an average-looking man, slightly taller than Grey—an inch or two over six feet. Thin but muscular. Solid looking. A tanned face and light brown hair. Pale blue eyes, slightly close-set. A sharp pointed nose; thin lips on a wide mouth. A narrow chin.

Grey was face-to-face with the man who'd given the order to kill his wife.

D'Aumont was extending his hand. Grey shook it, and tried to sound normal. "Captain d'Aumont—yes, I remember news of *Fidèle*. A very fine ship; I'm sure our admiralty would have liked to lay down His Majesty's frigates along her lines."

"You flatter me, sir—but by my word, you're quite right; she is the most weatherly ship it was ever my pleasure to sail on. I'm afraid, though, that Roquebert does me an injury—I've had to leave her to join the staff."

"A tragedy, sure," said Grey, fighting an urge to shatter a wineglass and slit d'Aumont's throat with it. "But it was you on her quarterdeck as she went tearing through our Gibraltar trade?"

"Indeed, sir. Are you a navy man?"

"A marine, sir. Captain Thomas Grey."

"Of that Mediterranean report—yes, I had hoped to make your acquaintance."

"*Kismat*," said Grey.

"You speak the Turkish, sir?" asked d'Aumont.

"One picks it up, serving in their orbit," said Grey.

"Indeed one does," said d'Aumont, smiling congenially. "We must trade anecdotes when the opportunity presents itself."

We'll trade a great deal more than that, thought Grey as he nodded agreeably. A life for a life.

"Let us drink to new acquaintance," said Roquebert, flagging down a footman and handing a glass of champagne to each of the five men before lifting his own. "Branson and Grey": Branson was plucked up to have been included. They all drank, and before the footman had put much distance between himself and the toasters, Roquebert called him back and deposited the bottle of cider on his tray.

"My good man, take this outside and have it shot."

They all laughed; d'Aumont unaware of the hole being bored into the side of his head by Grey's eyes.

GREY SPENT the next few hours shaking hands, being looked over, and occasionally probed about the circumstances that had driven him to Paris—though without much severity: Napoleon's army was filled with foreigners, both mercenaries and believers in the revolutionary French cause, so Grey's presence struck no one as especially remarkable.

Eventually the young lady made her debut, descending a grand staircase and floating into the ballroom in a beautiful gown of mousseline, cut conservatively in a style Grey gathered was reminiscent of the couture of Joséphine: long sleeves, absent décolletage, and touches of Egypt in tribute to Napoleon's triumphs there. Touches of Rome, too, or perhaps Greece: the lady looked statuesque, and white as marble save for a touch of peach in her cheeks. None of it was to Grey's taste, but at least she wasn't wearing a turban, as so many of the ladies were . . . another remnant of the Egypt campaign. They would have looked less silly with pyramids on their heads.

"Lovely, isn't she?" said d'Aumont, who had appeared at Grey's elbow, swirling a glass of red wine as if it were brandy. Grey found it hard to deny—she may have been pale as death and dressed in fashion beyond his ken, but she did have a certain Venus-on-a-half-shell bearing to her, something intrinsically regal that men find hard to ignore.

"Older than I'd expected," said Grey, hearing himself fail at his act of congeniality; feeling the hatred well up in him again.

"No doubt she was put off by the revolution. Can I offer you a cigar?" As d'Aumont reached into his jacket, a French naval officer—a senior captain—approached, with Branson and two of the French officers Grey had already met in tow. The two Frenchmen, Roque-bert and de Vance, looked ambivalent. Branson looked mad.

"Pardon, Captain Grey," said the new officer, "I am Captain Aubert; we have not met, but I have just been learning of you."

Grey nodded politely. "Captain, a pleasure." Aubert did not nod back.

"My colleagues and your countryman—"

"I'll trouble you to remember that I'm Irish, Aubert," said Branson, still looking mad. Aubert shrugged.

"My colleagues, and yours"—he gestured with a tilt of his head towards Branson—"have been telling me about your magnificent report, which has raised you far in their esteem. They say it proved true, and that it proves you as well. But I've said to them, at sea we haven't only a single stay to support a sail; we don't have only one sail for each yard. Redundancy, Captain Grey, keeps a ship safe—I'm sure you know that. I have only today returned from Le Havre, where my own ship *Marengo* is kept at bay by your blockading fleet—"

"My former fleet, Captain Aubert?"

"So perhaps these procedures of prudence are fresher in my mind than in the minds of men who have spent more time ashore."

Roquebert's jaw tightened slightly at this insult.

"Not to cast aspersions," he said, intending the contrary. "In any case, if Christ could be doubted, why not you, Captain Grey?"

Grey spread his hands in a gesture of agreement. "Doubt away, my captain."

Aubert had spoken in English; Grey had answered in French.

"Good," said Aubert, continuing in English. "Then perhaps you will indulge me: You were a chandler, yes? For your admiralty's central board of victualers."

"I was," said Grey.

"Until only a matter of weeks ago?"

Grey nodded.

"In which case you would have had a hand in outfitting the blockade fleet that is now off Le Havre and Calais—indeed, I am told it is knowledge of the disposition of ships in this theater that henceforward will make you so valuable to us."

"Indeed," said Grey.

"In which further case—and I'm sure you will forgive my asking—please to identify for me the first-rate ship of the line which I observed off our coast only yesterday evening."

Over Aubert's shoulder, a dance line was beginning to form; a chamber orchestra had appeared, and appeared ready to begin a waltz.

As Grey's eyes wandered over the men and women awaiting the music, his mind was racing.

Since the catastrophic accident in which His Majesty's ship *Queen Charlotte* had burned and exploded—673 men lost—there were only four British first-rates—only four British ships that carried more than a hundred cannon. *Queen Charlotte*'s sister ship *Royal George* was in the Mediterranean; Grey had seen her heading east from Gibraltar during his journey home from Malta. He'd seen *Victory* as well, at Chatham, just a few miles from Marsh Downs, undergoing repairs. Which left only *Royal Sovereign* and the confusingly named HMS *Ville de Paris*.

Grey had seen both ships anchored at Portsmouth when he'd joined *Ruby*; either of them could now be patrolling the north coast of France, while the other was likely headed west around Ushant. Aubert was right; if Grey had been what he claimed to be, he would know which had been fitted out for which duty. It was a coin toss. Grey hoped he hadn't wasted all his luck at the Basset tables.

"*Ville de Paris*, I believe, is blockading the Channel; she was loading close stores when I left."

Aubert raised his eyebrows and shook his head.

"I'm afraid not, Captain Grey." He looked smugly at Branson and the other French officers. A woman in her middle twenties approached Aubert; a brunette with a small mouth, freckles, and large green eyes that matched her gown.

She curtsied to the men and said, placing her hand on Aubert's forearm, "Captain Aubert, you asked me——"

"Not now, my dear," said Aubert, waving her away. "Grey: Have you some explanation?" The woman took a step or two back, looking embarrassed and annoyed.

"There is only one possible, Captain—a vote in Parliament. No doubt you know that many of our naval officers have seats in the House, and are recalled for crucial votes on naval funds. I am not privy to the men assigned to command; only to the supplies with which they're provided. But I would wager *Ville de Paris* has a new pennant, and her former master is a member of the House of Commons. And that HMS *Royal Sovereign* took her place."

Part of this was true: There were indeed several dozen rich or landed naval officers who sat in the House, for various rotten boroughs. And they did indeed take leave of their posts, temporarily, when they were asked or inclined to attend votes. It was also true that Grey had no idea who was commanding *Ville de Paris*; it was a stab in the dark.

"Yes," said Aubert, "it is *Royal Sovereign* now on patrol. As for the master of *Ville de Paris*? I don't know his name either—but I imagine we have a dossier on him."

"Well," said Grey, "how happy that you can check my theory." Aubert smiled acidly and waved to an *aspirant*—a midshipman—to come over.

"We can," said Aubert.

"And while you do," said Grey, turning to the woman Aubert had brushed aside, "perhaps, mademoiselle, you would give me the honor of this dance."

She smiled, slightly, as Grey extended his hand.

"Go," said Aubert, maybe worrying she wouldn't seek his

approval. "I have more important matters to attend to." The woman took Grey's hand; he pulled her in towards his body, and—with the music having already begun—waltzed her into the whirl of dancers.

Her face lit up with surprise at how quickly he swept her into the fray—the waltz was upbeat, and the new style of dancing disdained the order of the cotillion, leaving partners instead to find their own way across the floor, with structure confined to the steps of each individual pair, rather than to all the dancers as one group.

Rather than organized, a waltz was intimate; a celebration of uninterrupted contact between two people of opposite sex. It was considered too risqué for parties in England; Grey had picked it up in Malta . . .

But it appeared to be too risqué for this party as well, as the hostess was calling the music to a halt and ushering the dancers into squares for a quadrille, while the orchestra leader was left, red-faced, to remake his program.

Grey smiled at his partner. "Shall we continue, Mademoiselle . . . ?"

"Montcada. And yes, if you will, Monsieur . . ."

"Grey," said Grey. "Montcada: a Catalan name?"

Mademoiselle Montcada nodded. "And Grey is Irish?" she asked.

"English," said Grey. They were placed together on one of the four sides of a square of eight dancers.

"How interesting," said Mademoiselle Montcada as the music began, and with it, the quadrille's complex interlacing choreography.

Grey and Mademoiselle Montcada bowed to each other, then to the dancers to their left and right, then to the dancers on the opposite side of the square. And then everyone began to change places and partners, and Grey—doing his best to follow along with this particular French variation—made a quick estimate that this would be one of the numbingly long routines; maybe a quarter of an hour. Maybe more.

Grey hoped so, anyway: he needed time to think.

At that moment, presumably, one of Aubert's lackeys was running a message over to the Maison Militaire, or whoever kept files on English officers. There were approximately five hundred full captains in the Royal Navy. Grey guessed that twenty, or at best, twenty-five, had seats in the Commons. Which gave him one-in-twenty odds. Not too good.

But of course, the senior officer of a first-rate would not be a captain, but an admiral, with a flag captain serving under him. And that improved the odds considerably. There were only a hundred admirals, and probably a good . . . thirty of them? maybe more? had seats in Parliament. In the Commons and the Lords.

So a one-in-three chance, then?

Grey briefly swung about the center of the dance square with a debutante-aged, black-eyed blonde.

One-in-three was still not enough to count on. There was a two-in-three chance he would be exposed. And that was what he had to plan for.

Grey changed places with the gentleman to his right, and then with the gentleman on the opposite side of the square.

He was unarmed. What was worse, about fifty men at the party *were* armed; carrying their best ceremonial swords, which, in wartime, would be sharp, and would kill just as well as their workaday counterparts.

He could pull the sword from another man's scabbard.

Of course if the cloud of suspicion had already fallen, the man might be on his guard.

Grey could break a bottle, hold it to a man's throat, and then take his sword.

And then what? Fight the other fifty-odd, one at a time?

He could forget the sword and make a dash for the front door. Once he was on the street, he could lose himself in the evening crowd.

But there were too many men between him and the street; he would be taken before he made it outside.

As Mademoiselle Montcada was briefly again on his arm, as they mirrored one another's steps at the square's center, he looked out the window. There was a small courtyard and garden; at its end, a wall of about Grey's height, and beyond that, another street.

That would be his way out: straight through a window, through the garden, over the wall.

Now Grey and the Mademoiselle Montcada were dancing a quick turn around the square, and returning to their original places.

An arm fell on Grey's shoulder.

It was Aubert, holding a folded slip of paper in his hand. Branson was beside him, as were d'Aumont, de Vance, and Roquebert.

"A word, Captain Grey?" And to the other dancers in the quadrille: "Forgive me the interruption."

That was fast, thought Grey—we must be very near the security offices; an interesting detail. He nodded to Aubert, and looked at Branson . . . who now wore a sneer on his face. But at whom was it directed?

"I owe you an apology, Captain Grey," said Aubert. "I am informed that the most recent commander of *Ville de Paris*, of whom we are aware"—he looked down at the folded paper in his hand—"is in fact a member of your parliament, from Yorkshire."

He said this with the minimum possible noblesse oblige. Grey returned the courtesy with the shallowest of bows.

"Think nothing of it, Captain Aubert. I'm only sorry that the confusion cost you a very pleasant dance."

As they'd spoken, the music had finished and the dance squares begun to break up; Mademoiselle Montcada now stood at Grey's left elbow and Aubert's right, halfway between them.

"But perhaps a drink will compensate," said Grey, signaling to a passing, champagne-bearing waiter.

"No," said Aubert. "I am in Paris only briefly before I return to my ship, and I must get on. If you will forgive me."

A shallow bow, and another from Grey.

"Gentlemen," said Aubert to the others, who nodded in return.

"Mademoiselle, a word?" he said to Mademoiselle Montcada, who followed him away—flashing a slight, conspiratorial smile at Grey as she did.

D'Aumont noticed and laughed. Branson excused himself—perhaps to splash some cold water in his face. Roquebert and de Vance made their own excuses and moved towards the dancers, who were beginning to re-form for a second round.

"When we were interrupted," said Grey to d'Aumont, "I was about to accept your offer of a cigar."

D'Aumont smiled and shook his head. "But of course," he said, reaching into his jacket and removing a cedar case the size of a pocket Bible.

"Thank you," said Grey, accepting first a cigar, then a paring knife to trim it with—the knife slid beautifully out of its flush hiding place in the case's back—and finally a long cedar match.

"Beautiful," said Grey, nodding to the case as d'Aumont slid the knife back into it and returned it to a jacket pocket.

"Thank you—I had it made at the Palais-Royal, at a shop in the colonnade. Have you seen it yet? It really is the true heart of Paris— anything in the world your heart desires can be found there . . . I hope it survives a new English blockade."

Grey nodded and began to draw on his cigar, and d'Aumont gestured for him to take a seat in a wingback by a window. D'Aumont took the seat next to him.

"So," he said, placing his empty glass on the floor between them and knocking some ash into it, "what's next for your reporting? We on the admiral's staff are most anxious for the next tranche of information."

"As soon as Branson receives approval from—whomever—"

"I expect he will tomorrow, based on the general discussion tonight," said d'Aumont, looking at his cigar.

"Then I will set about a detailed evaluation of the British naval situation in the home ports, in the docks, in the Channel, on station off France, and in the Baltic. I can add my estimation of the African stations and the Indies, but they will be mostly conjecture, as they were beyond my remit." Of course, Grey reflected, it was all beyond his remit, but the eager glow of d'Aumont's eyes told him any misinformation he turned over would be eagerly accepted. He knocked some ash into d'Aumont's glass and took a long drag. It was a very good cigar.

"Well, *well*, what have we here. The lost pilgrim." Grey looked up—at his erstwhile Basset partner, an obviously drunk Jacques Polignac.

"Good evening," said Grey, coolly, not standing.

"Do you know this man?" asked d'Aumont, falling easily into the role of Grey's host.

"We met at the tables at the d'Orsigny," said Grey.

"Yes," said Polignac, "We met a-gaming. The *capitaine* pulled off a remarkable coup. Most remarkable. Too remarkable."

"I beg your pardon?" said Grey, narrowing his eyes. Beside him he could see d'Aumont tense slightly, in embarrassment.

"Come, sir, come"—Polignac was almost spitting out the words—"that final cut, where you alone had the shuffle? You planted your ace, and I'm sure we can all recognize a cheater when he stands before us like the nose on one's face."

Before the last word had left his mouth, Grey was standing bolt upright, and d'Aumont beside him.

"You will withdraw that remark," said Grey, "or give me satisfaction of it."

"You may be satisfied *anytime you wish*," said Polignac, stepping closer. Grey could smell his breath.

"I would advise you to step back, sir, before I lose control of my manners and embarrass us both. You in particular."

"Come, Captain Grey," said d'Aumont, "let us withdraw; the next words should be between your seconds."

D'Aumont led Grey back towards the foyer, where a footman was sent to fetch Branson.

"I'm sorry about that," said d'Aumont. "Too much wine in the man, I'm sure."

"You needn't be sorry, Captain, it's nothing to do with you," said Grey. "Though I appreciate your intervening . . . Perhaps you would second me?"

This caught d'Aumont off guard. For a moment it seemed he would suggest Branson as the more natural candidate, but then he regained himself and said, "Yes of course, I would be happy to. I will meet with his man, whoever he is, and inform you of the arrangements. Ah, here's Branson. I will send word to you. At the d'Orsigny?"

Grey nodded and d'Aumont withdrew, just as Branson stepped forward and asked, in a restrained panic, "What in God's name is going on?"

II

O VER THE NEXT two days, considerable pressure was brought to bear on Polignac, by the government author-ities, to persuade him to issue an apology. He refused, and Grey would accept nothing less—rejecting, for instance, a letter expressing that "Mr. Polignac regretted their difference of opinion." When it became clear that nothing could be done to head off the actual crossing of swords—short of arresting one or both parties, and this was impossible, because of Polignac's family connections—Branson and the men to whom he was responsible resigned themselves to hoping for the best. Grey, they knew, had been a royal marine—and the marines were a martial force well respected on the Continent. On the other hand, Polignac—foppish though he might be—was prone to giving insult, and had been out many times in the past. And the evidence suggested he had never, hitherto, been killed.

The duel was set for the late afternoon two days after the chal-lenge had been made, in a remote corner of the Bois de Boulogne, where such matters were often attended to. The meadow that was to serve as the field of honor—flat and level; surrounded by mulberry trees; dotted with red and lavender wildflowers—was filled with the sounds of springtime birds and insects. Grey wondered how many his beloved Paulette could have recognized by their calls. He glanced at d'Aumont, then turned his focus to the matter at hand.

D'Aumont and Polignac's second, a man named Caron, made a final motion for reconciliation. It failed. The lengths of two *épées de cour* were measured, found to be equal, and the two principals were told to stand sword tip to sword tip.

Caron asked Polignac if he was ready.

"Ready," said Polignac. Caron turned to Grey.

"Are you ready, Captain Grey?"

"I am."

"Very well. On my word, then, gentlemen."

There was a momentary delay as Caron retreated a dozen paces and took his place next to d'Aumont. Grey and Polignac waited. Neither looked nervous.

"Gentlemen—*En garde.*"

Polignac lunged forward; Grey slid Polignac's jab out to his right and took a step back. Polignac lunged again. Grey batted this jab away and closed ground, thrusting at Polignac's chest. Polignac parried the blow to his left, and Grey swung the tip back towards Polignac's face, slicing through Polignac's lower lip and chin. Polignac grimaced and spit blood. He lunged a third time towards Grey, and Grey gave ground. Their swords clattered off one another, and on the rebound, Polignac lanced his *épée* through Grey's right forearm, taking a tear of shirt and some blood with it.

But now Polignac's weight was on the wrong foot, and Grey stepped to his left and swung his sword in a tight arc around Polignac's outstretched arm, towards his throat. Polignac's only defense was to buckle his knees; he ducked the blow and tried an aggressive slash across Grey's midsection, which missed; Grey jumped out of the way and thrust again at Polignac's chest. Polignac's knees were still buckled, and as he rotated his shoulders to avoid the tip of Grey's blade, he lost his balance and toppled. Grey's edge was at Polignac's throat before he hit the ground.

Suddenly everyone was still:

Grey holding his *épée* against Polignac's neck. Polignac holding himself up on one elbow, looking at Grey with the wide eyes of a lamb on the altar. D'Aumont and Caron holding their breaths, waiting to see what would happen. Would Polignac ask for quarter—beg for mercy—or be killed?

Grey waited. Polignac said nothing. He was ready for the coup de grâce.

Grey took a step back and lowered his sword:

"I am satisfied." The seconds exhaled, and so did Polignac, who laid his sword on the grass. Grey offered Polignac a hand; pulled him to his feet.

"In that case," said Polignac, though a bloody mouth, "I will now offer my apologies. It is clear to me that I was mistaken, and I will freely say so in any company you choose to name."

"That won't be necessary," said Grey. "You acquitted yourself honorably, and I consider the matter closed."

He turned and walked towards d'Aumont, while Caron stepped forward to examine Polignac's split lip.

"That was a most damned gentlemanlike thing," said d'Aumont as they withdrew towards a waiting fiacre. "Let me see your arm."

IN FACT, the cut on Grey's arm was quite deep—deeper than he'd realized—and when the bleeding could not be staunched, d'Aumont directed their driver to the office of a retired naval surgeon of his acquaintance, for whom he had the greatest respect in matters of open wounds. The surgeon's practice was in the colonnade of the Palais-Royal; as they approached it, walking down a row of sand-colored stone columns, d'Aumont pointed out a closed shopfront nearby.

"Do you know who works there?" asked d'Aumont. Grey shrugged.

"Who?"

"That is the studio of Jacques-Louis David."

"Well, well. Somehow not what I would have expected." Though

Grey was no great student of contemporary art, even he had heard of the brilliant, guillotine-happy painter.

"After Robespierre fell, how did he avoid the chopping block himself?" asked Grey.

"Ha ha——" answered d'Aumont, smiling, "but it was quite amusing. You may know how close Robespierre and David were—not only was David himself a member of the Committee of General Security, but he designed the—hmm—the art, the style, of those great festivals of atheism, with the idols of the revolution, where he and Robespierre planned to retrain the people in the new faith. So they were joined, you might say, at the hip, until the very end. David was beside Robespierre when he was arrested—he shouted to him, 'Maximilien! If you drink hemlock, I shall drink with you!' But when it came time for his friend to be sentenced, Jacques-Louis sent word that he had a 'stomachache,' and could not attend that session of the National Convention. Otherwise he would have been——"

D'Aumont mimed a guillotine blade descending.

"—as well. But in the end, they took pity on him—partly because of his fame and reputation, I imagine. So he was merely imprisoned. Lucky for him, his fame and reputation extended to the notice of our first consul Bonaparte, who is a great admirer of David's Roman epics. I believe it was Napoleon who had him released. In any case, he keeps himself to himself now, in there, painting and teaching. He won't talk to you about politics."

D'Aumont laughed again; Grey shook his head.

"How much would a portrait cost?"

"With what we will pay you, and what you won at the tables— you might have enough."

"Well," said Grey, "you truly can get anything at the Palais-Royal."

"Jean-Anne!" came a voice from inside the surgery, whose door was hanging open. Now a man appeared: "If it isn't our honored lieutenant, Jean-Anne d'Aumont! I haven't seen you for, oh, it must be nearly a year."

"Sébastien—how nice it is to be back, and not for a wound of my own," said d'Aumont, shaking hands with a red-haired man in his late forties. "Captain Grey, allow me to introduce Dr. Berger, Sébastien Berger. Our doctor aboard *Guerrier*."

"What a fine ship she was . . . a seventy-four, burned at the Nile. A goddamned tragedy, sir."

"A pleasure to make your acquaintance, Dr. Berger," said Grey, now shaking the surgeon's hand. "Captain d'Aumont speaks most highly of your skills with open wounds—says when he served with you, he couldn't recall the smell of gangrene."

"He flatters me, Captain Grey. But enough of this talk, let me look to your arm—we can become better acquainted once I'm certain you aren't infected. For if you are, what's the point?" He waved Grey and d'Aumont inside.

Berger's surgery was about ten feet wide and thirty deep, and quite dark; there was an oil lamp on a desk, but the only natural light came through the door onto the colonnade and a single window beside it.

"Take a seat there, and stick out your arm," Berger said to Grey, pointing to a stool beside a heavy wooden table (which bore an unfortunate resemblance to a butcher's block). "Roll up your sleeve," he added as he lit a second lamp and adjusted a thick lens to focus the light on Grey's wound.

The surgeon now sponged away the blood on Grey's forearm, leaned in towards it, squinted at the sliced flesh, sucked his teeth, and walked away to a tool bench nearby.

"A good clean cut, sir," said Berger to Grey as he retrieved a needle and thread. "I applaud whoever gave it to you, he keeps his blade impeccably sharpened. He nicked a vein, but not an important one—not an artery. You shall knit up nicely." As Berger threaded his stitching needle, he said to d'Aumont, "Jean-Anne, there's a bottle of Dunkirk gin on that shelf behind you. Pour Captain Grey a double. You can have one too if you like."

D'Aumont poured three drinks—"The third is for you, Sébastien, for when you've finished"—and clinked glasses with Grey. The surgeon took a seat on a stool opposite Grey and began, with the total lack of ceremony that is a custom of naval medicine, to stitch the wound.

The procedure took less than a minute. When it was through, Berger again sponged away some blood, and spilled a little of his gin over the closed cut.

"It's good luck," he said, as Grey winced. "Cheers."

Grey couldn't help but admit that it was the finest, tightest stitch he'd ever received—and Grey had been stitched up more times than he could count.

"With this needle talent of yours, Doctor, you should close your surgery and open a dress shop," said Grey, accepting another pour of gin from d'Aumont.

"Nonsense," said Berger, accepting another as well. "If I ever close this practice, it will be to make lingerie." Grey and d'Aumont chuckled, and all three downed their drinks.

"Now," said Berger, standing, retrieving a cloth sling from a drawer, "wear this, and don't use that arm or wrist for anything unnecessary for at least a week, until the skin's holding together on its own. Then you can cut the stitches and pull them out yourself, or if you're a coward, you can come back here and I'll do it for you."

Grey put the sling on, stood, and shook hands again with the doctor. This time, left-handed.

"Thank you very much, Dr. Berger," said Grey. "I'll do as you say."

"Good," said Berger. "It was my pleasure."

"What do I owe you?"

"A franc," said the surgeon. "But if it festers and you die, I will return half the fee to your next of kin."

ON THEIR WAY BACK through the colonnade to the waiting fiacre, Grey was able to place an order with a deluxe carpentry shop for a duplicate of d'Aumont's cigar holder.

D'Aumont took this as an outstanding compliment. As for his arm, Grey took that quite in his stride, as did d'Aumont, who had seen so many limbs taken off after sea fights that he was quite inured to the dangers of infection.

But it nearly overwhelmed Branson, who said—in so many words—that Grey's wound and the affair as a whole were jeopardizing his position and, in consequence, the position of Irish revolution in the plans of Napoleon. He was most insistent that Grey should desist from any more *provocative* behavior, though he gave himself the worst of it for having established the near-mortal line of credit in the first place. He could be mollified only by an assurance, at last, from d'Aumont that the French captain would deem it part of his responsibility as Grey's second to see the arm healed and none of his vital work delayed. To this end, he said to a fawningly grateful Branson, he would invite Grey to his estate in Champagne—where he was in any case headed, still in the process of reconstituting his family's holdings under the new regime. It would be nothing but fresh country air and clean living, and a chance for Grey to begin his naval report amidst general tranquillity. Provided Grey wished to accept his offer.

Grey did; he accepted most eagerly—this was good fortune in its very essence. The vastness of opportunity provided by a country retreat—opportunity for him to settle his score with d'Aumont, that is—excited him. The welcome taste of revenge was back in Grey's mouth.

It was early the next morning when a Hôtel d'Orsigny footman informed Grey that Captain d'Aumont's chaise (and, indeed, Captain d'Aumont himself) awaited him on the Place Vendôme. With two footmen along to carry his things, Grey made his way outside. There he found d'Aumont standing beside his carriage, lighting a cigar and offering one to Branson, whom he seemed to be trying to calm. Branson waved the cigar away and started in again on whatever point he'd been trying to make—but d'Aumont cut him off as Grey drew near.

"There you are, Captain Grey," he said. "I was just explaining to Mr. Branson that it wouldn't be necessary for him to join us——"

Indeed not: Grey had no desire to find himself in the position of having to kill Branson too.

"—and that I am happy to take responsibility for you, and for your completing your work," finished d'Aumont.

"Quite so," said Grey, turning to Branson: "I had hoped, Mr. Branson, that you would take up my part in securing my fee, without which, of course, we cannot proceed. I had expected everything to be settled by now."

"Yes, Captain Grey, so had I," said Branson, with a dismal look. "But I'm afraid there's nothing else I can do, besides wait for the approval to make its way through the necessary channels."

"Yes, but there's nothing you will be able to do in the country either," said d'Aumont. "Do you not believe I can keep our man on the march?"

"No of course I do, Captain, it is only that—"

"Then it is settled," said d'Aumont, gesturing for the hotel footman to hand Grey's luggage up to the driver, who tied it in with the rest of the movables on the chaise's roof. Branson was defeated. He stuck his hand out to Grey, who shook it awkwardly—his arm being still in a sling.

"I look forward, then," said Branson, "to reading your report . . . on your return?" He spoke uneasily. Hopefully.

"I have no doubt," answered Grey, "that it will be well in hand by that time. Let not your heart be troubled." Another dismal nod from the Irishman.

"I'll have him back in a week," said d'Aumont. "His arm will be recovered but his feet will have been kept to the fire. Now—we mustn't spend the whole day here in conversation, spilling the wind from our sails. *Entrez*."

On d'Aumont's gesture, the footman held open the door of the carriage, and Grey pulled himself up—left-handed, minding the sling, which seemed destined to catch on every hinge and screw. D'Aumont climbed up behind him, rapping the ceiling as he did. The carriage began to move.

"I hope the argument with Branson didn't embarrass you," said d'Aumont, settling himself into the seat beside Grey, so that they were both facing the direction of travel. "I know that in this new enlightened age we are supposed to be egalitarian, to love the proles—but I have no time for functionaries."

"No, I wasn't embarrassed," said Grey, instantly liking Branson more than he had at any point since they met.

"And I am well prepared for some fresh country air," continued d'Aumont. "Not as fresh as sea air perhaps, but it shall be a pronounced improvement over the riot of horse manure that fills our beloved capital."

It took a half hour for the smell of excrement fully to recede, and as the gentle Champagne breezes began to waft in, Grey let himself drift to the beach at Malta, where he walked beside Paulette.

It would be early evening on the Sliema peninsula, across the harbor from Valetta. Grey and Paulette walked the beach in the evening whenever they could—Grey to make sure no day passed without some exercise, and Paulette to make her daily search for the fossils that frequently were exposed in the limestone cliffs. If the rising night was clear, they might linger afterwards for a swim, or whatever else they felt in the mood for. Then Grey would fill his hands and pockets with Paulette's findings, and lead her inland towards their house while she mused on geology. There were no words to describe the pure, unadulterated contentment he felt. Rather, the contentment he had felt. Now there were no words to describe his sorrow, nor the upwelling of hatred for the man sitting next to him. He might have killed d'Aumont right then, wrapped his hands around the man's throat and squeezed out the life. But here was a man on the French admiralty staff. He could prove as valuable a source of intelligence for England as d'Aumont took Grey to be for France. For the time being, killing him was out of the question.

"This is Château-Thierry." D'Aumont was gesturing out the window on Grey's side of the carriage. A small village had appeared on the slope of a modest hill.

"My estate is not far on the other side. But we'll stop in town to change horses . . . Is something wrong?" D'Aumont was looking at

Grey's hands, which were so tightly clenched that the knuckles were beginning to turn white.

"No," said Grey, "just a bit of nausea. I can never get used to traveling by land."

"Ah, I'm so sorry, my friend. We will be there soon."

12

WHEN HE HAD spoken to Grey of his family's estate, Captain Jean-Anne d'Aumont had been deceitfully modest. The estate was exceptional. A superb, late Renaissance, large but not vulgar house sat on a rise at the end of a long entry drive; the drive was flanked not by the traditional gardens, but by several acres of vineyard. And as pleasing to the eye as vineyards tend to be, these were especially lovely. They had been treated as gardens—hedge gardens—with immaculate grass paths leading in and out of them, and billowing fountains visible in their interior.

"Do you approve?" asked d'Aumont, relishing Grey's admiration.

"I should say so," said Grey, earnestly. "What do you grow?"

"Only pinot blanc," said d'Aumont. "For an uncommon Champagne blanc de blancs."

Grey chuckled. "I had no idea."

"No, I don't make too much of it in the ministries—I'm not sure there is any cachet in a naval officer producing his own vintage."

"I'm not sure you'd prove right in that," said Grey, admiring the perfect rows of vines, "but I follow your reasoning."

"But you understand why I have to check in, periodically."

"Of course. Who runs the place in your absence?"

"There is a vigneron who is chief gardener, winemaker, and man-

ager, when I am at sea. Or now, when I am in Paris. I have him report
to my mother, who runs the house. She keeps me informed. And my
sisters help. I am the only son of my father's house, but I have four
sisters, of whom three are unmarried."

Those three, as well as the matron Madame d'Aumont, awaited
the carriage in a circular gravel patch, thirty yards across, which
stood before the house. Beside them, at a decorous remove, was a
line of servants—indoor and out, some apparently having emerged
direct from the vineyards. Everyone seemed pleased at the master's arrival.

D'Aumont climbed out first, with the assistance of a footman,
then lent a hand to Grey, whom he walked over to his mother—a
handsome lady of about sixty, with pale gray hair and a dark purple
dress. D'Aumont made the introductions in French:

"Captain Grey, may I present my mother, Madame d'Aumont."

"Captain Grey, welcome to Val de Thierry."

"Madame, thank you, you are very kind to have me."

"My sister, Miss d'Aumont," a beauty in her late twenties and a
navy blue dress; tall, with dark hair wound tightly around her head,
and golden amber eyes.

"Captain Grey, a pleasure."

"Miss d'Aumont, the pleasure is entirely mine."

"Miss Yvette," the same height as her sister; middle twenties with
a paler complexion and darker eyes, in light purple.

The middle sister curtsied.

"Miss Yvette, your servant," answered Grey.

"And Miss Christine," shorter than her sisters and with a wide,
welcoming smile on her face; perhaps fifteen or sixteen years old,
in pink.

"Good afternoon, Captain Grey,"

"A lovely afternoon, Miss Christine."

"Brodeur," said d'Aumont to the butler at the head of the servants' line, "put the captain in the Red Room, won't you?"

"Of course, sir." Brodeur bowed.

"Come," said d'Aumont to Grey. "Let me show you about."

+

BEHIND THE HOUSE was a large pond, or a small lake—of about an acre, Grey guessed—bounded by a ring of flat, manicured lawn. The lawn was bounded by limestone hills covered with further rows of vines, and beyond them, thick forest, which gave the estate an enclosed, private feel.

"More pinot blanc?"

"Yes," said d'Aumont. "Nothing but. My father experimented with Petit Meslier further out, but ultimately he decided that to grow two varieties satisfactorily was no more difficult than to grow one, superbly."

"Sounds a thoughtful man," said Grey. "I had assumed he was a naval officer like yourself, and you a part of a seaman's legacy."

"Indeed he was, and I am—he didn't plant these until later in life, tearing out our gardens and replacing them with the vines. And lucky he did, this place might otherwise have been burned to the ground like so many of its peers. But as a working vineyard, it fell under the protection of the peasants. Added to that is the agreeable fact that there is no Frenchman alive—no, not the most inveterate Robespierrist; not Marat himself—who would wantonly destroy a vine. We were very lucky."

Grey nodded as they proceeded around the lake. A pair of swans alighted on the surface, their dangling legs drawing V's behind them.

"Do you hunt?" asked d'Aumont.

"I do," said Grey, "though not in the English style, on horseback."

"You mean you prefer retrievers to hounds?"

"Just so."

For a moment d'Aumont was silent. Then, "Come, let me show you a new toy—I think you may enjoy it."

D'Aumont turned on his heel and led Grey back towards the house, through a greenhouse, to a gun room.

The object that d'Aumont removed from a felt case was like no gun Grey had ever seen. He stared.

"Is that . . . ?" He tried to work out the mechanism as d'Aumont smiled like a child with a secret. "Hmm. What is this for?" Grey was referring to a metal cone, with a domed end plate, where the rifle's butt should have been.

"Air!" said d'Aumont.

"Air?"

"Yes, air, compressed! It is a Girandoni air rifle. From Austria. I was able to procure one during the peace. And: it's a repeater."

"Really? I've never fired a repeater."

"This rifle can fire twenty-two shots—in twenty-two seconds."

"You must be joking."

D'Aumont was still smiling excitedly. "Come along, I'll show you!"

Back out on the lawn, d'Aumont pointed to a line of trees to the east. "Pick out any tree you like, at one hundred yards."

There was a single white birch in the midst of several yews, at approximately the correct distance. "The birch," said Grey, brimmed with curiosity.

"Very good," said d'Aumont. "Now, see this?" he said, gesturing to a metal tube running down the rifle's barrel. "This is a magazine—it holds twenty-two balls of .46 caliber. Now see this?" He pointed to a slide where the gas canister met the rifle's breech. "This is a spring-loader. When I slide it to the right"—which he did—"a single ball falls into a depression. And when I release it"—which he did—"it slides the ball back into the air channel. Now I cock it so"—he pulled back the hammer—"which primes it for a single gout of compressed air, for one shot. With practice, the process takes less than a second."

"Please to proceed," said Grey.

D'Aumont raised the rifle to his shoulder and fired. There was a quiet *pffft*—a sound like a very short sigh—and nothing else. No bang, no smoke, no powder smell. Just the escape of air, and the plug of a ball hitting a tree a long way off.

Pffft

Pffft

Pffft

Pffft

D'Aumont fired four more shots in quick succession. "Let us inspect my target."

As they walked to the birch, Grey could not contain his genuine awe at this demonstration.

"How many shots can you get out of a cylinder?" asked Grey.

"On a single charge of air, two magazines' worth, before muzzle velocity begins to drop. But at close range—perhaps a hundred lethal shots."

"You stagger me. A gun like that will change warfare forever. How do you load the air?"

"Ah, there's the rub. You use a device that is something like a hand pump for raising water out of a well—but it takes fifteen hundred strokes to load it fully, along with considerable patience and stamina. The cylinder is iron, yet when fully charged, somewhat fragile. And once pierced, of course, the gun is useless. Worst of all, though, is the difficulty of manufacture. For the price of giving an infantryman one of these guns, you could issue him his own personal cannon. So, for the moment, warfare may remain the same."

Grey shook his head. "Shame. Think how beautifully quiet they would make a battlefield." D'Aumont chuckled as they arrived at the birch.

There was a constellation of holes—"You're not the first to suggest the birch," said d'Aumont, with a grin. Grey stuck his finger into several. Some of the holes were an inch deep. Some were deeper.

"Someday I'll have to cut this tree down and recover my shot," said d'Aumont. "Would you like a try? Can you manage it with that arm?"

"I would, most certainly," said Grey. "And the arm is fine—in fact, I don't think I'll humor your doctor friend with this sling any longer, the damn thing is just in my way." He stuffed the cloth into his pocket and rotated his shoulder in a circle, working some of the stiffness out.

"Yes, that's much better. I'll just be careful not to crash into anything." He reached out for the gun. "Have you any particular tree in mind?"

"That oak over there, shall we say?" said d'Aumont. "It's closer to a hundred and a half away. But let's see what my toy can do."

Grey raised the gun to his shoulder—with only slight objection from his stitched forearm—and gave the slide a test push. He took his aim, exhaled, and—

Pffft

Pffft

Pffft

Pffft

Pffft

"Wonderful, is it not, Captain Grey?"

"Brilliant," said Grey, holding the Girandoni out at arm's length. "Exceptional."

At the oak in question, d'Aumont was surprised to see not five holes, but a single large one beaten through the bark, about the size of a Spanish silver dollar.

He looked curiously at Grey. "You must be quite a hunter."

Grey handed the gun to d'Aumont.

"I am."

AS THEY WALKED BACK towards the house, Grey and his host were intercepted by Brodeur carrying a passel of correspondence that had arrived by the afternoon post. Grey could see from the impressive seals and franks that this was official business from the French admiralty. D'Aumont knit his brow, begged Grey's pardon, and excused himself to his study.

Brodeur assumed d'Aumont's place as guide, offering to show Grey to his room, which was now adequately prepared. The name Red Room was no misnomer: it proved to be a curious chamber in which warm shades of red covered every surface and created the impression of being inside a raw beefsteak. A series of golden-fringed vermilion rugs covered most of the floor, exposing between them strips of an ochre-stained wood. The walls were a pure blood-red, with a satin finish. The ceiling, trim, and curtains were scarlet; the ceiling with a motif of stars in cobalt blue.

"Most impressive, Brodeur," said Grey as the butler led him inside. Grey's luggage had been unpacked and laid out—searched perhaps? But who would have searched it—d'Aumont had been with Grey, and it strained credulity to think d'Aumont's household staff doubled as intelligence men.

"Please ring if you would care for hot water, sir," said Brodeur, bowing shallowly. "Dinner is served at nine."

"Thank you, Brodeur. Have that water sent up now, would you?"

"Certainly, sir," said the butler, backing into the hall, closing the Red Room's door as he went.

Turning to his unpacked things, Grey checked his shaving kit. He always buttoned it out of alignment, putting the second-to-top button into the topmost loop. When, in the past, his things had been secretly searched, his shaving kit tended to end up rebuttoned correctly. It was still out of alignment, and Grey told himself not to be paranoid: through Branson, the French had sought him out. Had it been the other way around, he would have had cause for concern.

There was a knock on the door, and a footman appeared with a kettle of hot water. Grey deposited the shaving kit on a stool by the bath and began to clean up for dinner.

After changing into something formal—his best waistcoat and high-collared jacket, and his wig—Grey descended to the drawing room. He found d'Aumont's mother and sisters already there, sitting amongst a quartet of bright oil lamps in the high-ceilinged, chartreuse-walled room—but d'Aumont himself was still at work on his correspondence. Grey accepted a glass of the family blanc de blancs from Brodeur. It was, in fact, very good; of the first rate. Perhaps just a little heavier in taste than Grey liked, but still—

"Madame d'Aumont," said Grey, "allow me to compliment you on your exceptional wine. I have rarely encountered its equal."

"You are very kind, Captain Grey," answered Jean-Anne d'Aumont's mother. "I am pleased to hear you say so. And, indeed, I am always curious to learn how our small house appeals to foreign palates."

"To mine, madame, its appeal is considerable," said Grey.

"Tell me, Captain Grey," said Yvette d'Aumont, the middle daughter, "how do you find France compares with England?"

"Favorably, Miss Yvette," said Grey.

"Of course, I was in England once," said Madame d'Aumont. "With my husband, in the late seventies. To visit the Royal Academy's summer exhibition. You know, they had just started then—'69 was the first year, I believe."

"Indeed, Madame d'Aumont? That must have been most interesting."

"Do you enjoy art, Captain?" asked the youngest daughter, Christine.

"I do, Miss Christine, when given the opportunity."

"I have always been a particular connoisseur of the theater, Captain Grey," said Madame d'Aumont. "I had the chance to see Garrick play Shakespeare, during his final season, as Lear—'77, I believe it was, while the exhibition was on."

Grey smiled. "Madame d'Aumont, I was lucky enough to attend a performance in that very same run. Perhaps we were there on the same night. In fact, it was my first time in a theater; my father felt it was an occasion I would remember for the rest of my life. And indeed it was."

"What a small world it is, Captain," said the eldest Miss d'Aumont, whose Christian name Grey had not yet discovered.

"Did you really?" said Madame d'Aumont. "Well, well, well! Did you really! Why, it's as if we are old acquaintances! You know, I saw Mozart play once, as well—in Prague. I don't suppose you were at my arm there, were you?"

Grey bowed his head slightly. "I regret not, Madame d'Aumont. Would that I had been." There was general smiling, and Jean-Anne d'Aumont finally made his appearance.

"Forgive me for being late, Mother; the admiralty has me quite overwhelmed; I shall go mad. Shall we go in?"

"Jean-Anne, I will shock you now," said d'Aumont's mother. "Captain Grey and I have crossed paths before!"

"Have you?" asked Captain d'Aumont, earnest surprise spreading over his face.

"Yes! We both attended a performance of Shakespeare, Garrick's last. During my trip to London with your father."

"You astonish me, Mother," said d'Aumont. "What a small world, Captain Grey."

"Funny," said Grey, "that's just what your sister said."

DINNER ITSELF was a pedestrian affair; a continuation of their pleasant small talk, which revealed little of substance. Twice during dinner Grey tried to steer the conversation in the direction of Jean-Anne d'Aumont's evening work, the admiralty correspondence that had made him late for dinner, but d'Aumont parried both attempts, turning the conversation instead to Grey's own admiralty work. Grey wouldn't risk a third foray, which might imply that his professional curiosity was covering a second motive. Consequently, by the end of the meal, Grey had made only a single discovery—that d'Aumont's eldest unmarried sister did indeed have a first name, and that it was Julia.

A little after ten, Madame d'Aumont suggested the ladies retire. Grey and Jean-Anne stood, and Grey, being the closer to the door, held it open for the ladies to pass through—the servants had served dessert and then, evidently following the same tradition in France they did in England, withdrawn.

Three or four minutes later, after serving the ladies their digestifs, Brodeur returned to the dining room with a decanter of port. Grey and d'Aumont were already deep in conversation and smoking a pair of cigars d'Aumont had produced from his pocket case.

"Aha!" d'Aumont was saying, producing a large billow of blue smoke as he waved his cigar in imitation of an easterly wind. "But it was a trick of fate, my dear Captain Grey—for the Spanish fleet would have made port safely at Cadiz had it not been for that damn levanter blowing all through the day and night, pushing them back out to sea!"

"Perhaps," said Grey, nodding in agreement. "Perhaps, but of course we will never know for certain."

"So you were on *Victory* herself?": the flagship of then-Admiral Sir John Jervis, commander-in-chief of the British Mediterranean fleet, as he lay off Cape St. Vincent.

"No, I was a supernumerary aboard HMS *Captain*, under Commodore Nelson—Horatio Nelson; I joined him when he touched briefly at Gibraltar to collect a prize crew he had displaced to the frigate *Santa Sabina*. We knew the Spanish fleet was between us and the balance of the British fleet"—Grey excluded the fact that he had been the source of this intelligence—"but the fog was so thick that we were able to pass through their lines unobserved—and then to pass word onto Old Oak—that is, Admiral Jervis—himself, of the Spanish fleet's disposition—but not its numbers; no, the fog was too thick to get any count; all we had seen were a few shapes coming in and out of the gloom.

"And though I was not aboard *Victory* herself, I have the account from the lips of at least three men who were: Old Jervy got our signal, our intelligence of the Spanish fleet, before nightfall and sailed to intercept. We and the whole fleet along with him."

"Fifteen ships of the line? And five frigates," said d'Aumont.

"Yes, exactly! Along with a small sloop and a cutter. Jervis formed us into two lines of battle, then turned to his quarterdeck and said, 'A victory to England is very essential at this moment.' A very serious-minded fellow, John Jervis."

"And at this time, he had no idea of the size of the Spanish fleet?" asked d'Aumont.

"None!" said Grey. "None of us did. How could we? We knew only that a Spanish fleet was bound for Cadiz as an escort for their merchantmen, to try to break our blockade. But then, it was the fog that started to break.

"On the quarterdeck of *Victory*, a supernumerary named Captain Hallowell is counting out sails for Old Oak as the Spanish fleet appears. 'There are eight sail of the line, Sir John,' says Hallowell. 'Very well,' says Jervy. Not a moment later, Hallowell corrects himself: 'There are twenty sail of the line, Sir John.' 'Very well,' says Jervis. Hallowell still has the glass to his eye: 'There are twenty-five sail of the line, Sir John,' he says. 'Very well,' says Jervis. 'There are twenty-seven sail of the line,' says Hallowell.

" 'Enough sir, no more of that,' says Jervis, perfectly calm. 'The die is cast, and if there are fifty sail, I will go through them.' "

"What a man!" said Jean-Anne d'Aumont, admiration lighting up his face.

"Well," said Grey, "you're not the only one who thought so: hearing this, Captain Hallowell clapped Admiral of the Fleet Jervis on the back and shouted, 'That's right, Sir John—and by God we'll give them a damn good licking!' "

D'Aumont roared with laughter, almost spilling his port, banging the table three or four times to emphasize his approval.

"Good man! But hold: please correct me if I'm wrong, but did not the English fight at St. Vincent in a single line of battle, not in two?"

"No, no, you're quite correct, Captain. Well, three of those sail of the line turn out to be armed merchantmen, with a fourth besides, so the numbers end up at twenty-four Spanish ship of the line, four armed merchantmen, seven frigates, and a brig. Against our fifteen of the line, five frigates, a sloop, and a cutter."

"Astonishing," said d'Aumont. "Astonishing."

"Now, the Spanish fleet is in two lines—or I should say, two groups, since they were all ahoo and hadn't formed up yet—so Jervis gives the order for the English fleet to re-form as a single line of battle, and says, 'We're going to fight both sides!' We see his signals from *Victory*, on *Captain*, 'Engage the enemy; admiral intends to pass though the enemy lines.' And so we do, fighting the cannon on both sides, laying into them.

"But on *Captain*, we're near the back of the procession, and Commodore Nelson is anxious not to miss the fighting—a great fury in battle, you understand, is Nelson, and now he fears by the time we reach the Spanish lines closing on us, the battle will already be won or lost. So with the Spanish lines breaking, Nelson wears from our own line of battle and heads straight for the Spanish van—three ship of the line, *San Nicolas*, eighty guns, *San Josef*, a hundred and twelve, and *Santísima Trinidad*, a hundred and thirty. And this aboard *Captain*—a seventy-four!"

"My God," breathed d'Aumont, transfixed.

"And may God strike me down if Nelson didn't begin to fight all three—all three!—at the same goddamned time! First firing a broadside into one, then cutting across the bows of another and raking her! It was beautiful chaos.

"Now, *Culloden*, another third-rate, another seventy-four, sees us fighting and comes to help, which gives Nelson the chance to close with *San Nicolas*—he lashes *Captain* to her, raises his sword in the air, and bellows to his men—to me too; I was there on *Captain*'s deck— 'GLORIOUS VICTORY OR WESTMINSTER ABBEY!'—Westminster Abbey, I should say, sir, is where we bury our dead heroes."

"Remarkable! Remarkable!"

"So with all of us at his heels, Nelson runs and takes a flying leap—I swear to God in heaven, sir, a flying leap—and crashes through the windows of the *San Nicolas*'s great cabin! Right through her quarter gallery! He charges up the companion ladder, swashbuckling as he goes, coming out on her quarterdeck, giving her officers the shock of their whoreson lives."

Again, Jean-Anne d'Aumont banged the table to express his deep excitement.

"Now, damn it, we're winning, we're taking her, and the *San Josef* sees this: she comes over to reinforce *San Nicolas*, and you know what Nelson does? What he says? He shouts that we're going to take *San Josef* too, boys, and leaps from the quarterdeck of *Nicolas* into the waist of *San Josef*, fighting like a devil as he goes—and bringing all of us with him, in sheer astonishment. It felt like hours—I felt I saw the Spaniards fighting in a slowed motion—but they say it was just a few minutes before both had hauled their colors down. And Nelson collects the swords of an infernal lot of officers right there on the quarterdeck of a Spanish first-rate. His bargemen had a job getting them all back to *Captain* again!"

D'Aumont roared with laughter—couldn't stop roaring—and shouted to Brodeur:

"Bring another bottle—this calls for a toast. To the English fighting man!" He added, in English: "Especially those who have crossed the floor."

"Thank you," said Grey.

When d'Aumont had drunk and replaced his glass on the table, his faced turned somewhat serious.

He took a moment choosing his words.

"It must be—I don't mean to discourage you, of course—but it must be hard for you to be here with us now. After all you went through for your country. You must have felt the injury it did you very deeply. Very deeply."

"Yes," said Grey. "You heard the story, I trust. In an instant, my life was ruined."

"And all that was left was revenge, yes?"

"Yes," said Grey. "And seeking revenge makes all things possible."

13

THE NEXT BOTTLE had been extinguished, and one after that, and now Grey hoped d'Aumont was sleeping soundly. Night was the pure black of the unilluminated countryside, and Val de Thierry was not one of those self-important houses that fill their hallways with torch sconces. After the last glass of port had been drained, Grey had said good night and taken a candle with him to bed. Now, by its light, he dressed in black trousers and a black jacket, closed at the collar to hide his pale skin. He pulled on black socks cut low, which, by habit, he kept wrapped around his lock picks and buried in the pocket of a pair of trousers. He slipped the picks, along with a box of matches, into the pocket of the trousers he was wearing, snuffed out his candle, and slipped himself out the door, into the pitch-black hallway.

He was on the second floor, in a bachelors' corridor. D'Aumont's room was opposite his, and both were opposite the ladies' rooms, which fell on the other side of the main stair. No light shone from under d'Aumont's door. Good.

It was thirty silent paces to the top of the stairs, with no light at all for Grey to navigate by. Anticipating this, he had counted off the route on his way to bed. After those thirty steps, Grey stuck his arm out to his left, found the cool surface of the thick limestone bannister, and turned onto the stair downward.

It was a squared spiral, descending about thirty feet. At the bottom, Grey turned towards the rear of the house, and the corridor he'd seen d'Aumont take towards his study. Which, evidently, was somewhere in the house's northeast corner.

Suddenly: light.

Someone with a candle was coming in the other direction. Grey stepped lightly up into a statuary nook cut in the wall—a remnant of a more religious age—and crouched behind some sort of large oriental vase. The someone with the candle was a hallboy doing his rounds, wearing an overcoat that was too big for him, humming softly to himself. He walked by Grey's hiding place without an instant's hesitation.

Once the boy was well past, Grey climbed out of the nook and continued down the corridor, which terminated in a small library. There were openings to hallways on two adjacent sides, and a closed door opposite the opening Grey had entered through. This would be d'Aumont's study. Grey approached the door—

And it swung open.

Grey dove for cover, into the lee of a daybed—bumping, in the process, the leg of a small decorative table, on which teetered a small decorative vase. Why did this goddamned house have so many goddamned vases? Instead of settling back in place, the vase fell carelessly off its perch and into Grey's hands; he caught it inches from the polished floor. Grey felt a stitch tear out, bit his tongue, and held his breath.

It was d'Aumont who had opened the door, closed it again, and was now locking it with a jangle of keys—a jangle that had happily concealed the sound of Grey's emergency evasion. So d'Aumont worked late, the bastard. He returned the keys to his pocket and, carrying a candle, crossed the library into the hall from which Grey had entered, then disappeared, the light of his candle receding behind him.

Grey counted off five minutes before he moved, to give d'Aumont a chance to return for anything he might have forgotten. When he didn't, Grey climbed to his feet, replaced the precarious vase (with a silent curse), and closed the remaining distance to d'Aumont's office door.

Grey slid the lock picks and the matches out of his pocket, striking a match to get a look at what he was dealing with, quickly blowing it out, lowering himself to one knee, and beginning to work by feel. Grey had picked he-knew-not-how-many locks in his professional career . . .

And this one was no particular challenge. He felt the mechanism give way to his prodding, release, and twist left. Grey pushed the door open, still on one knee, edged around the door into d'Aumont's study, and shut it again.

Grey struck another match. The room was square, fifteen feet to a side, high ceiling, with two walls of windows that opened onto the rear lawn. At the center was a large desk, covered with d'Aumont's papers and correspondence. Grey lit one candle on a candelabra sitting among them, hoping that any sort of night watchman who might see the light from outside would ascribe it to d'Aumont's late-night work habit.

The letters d'Aumont had been reading—each of them written in a wonderfully clear hand—was Bonaparte a stickler for penmanship?—were from the admiralty; the first from a senior officer directing d'Aumont to lose no time in extracting a full British naval report from Grey, the others from d'Aumont's secretary, transmitting developments in discussions to which d'Aumont was evidently a party. The references to secret projects were not specific, referring instead to documents that seemed to be already in d'Aumont's possession . . . But they appeared to touch principally on two things. First, plans for movement of the French Mediterranean fleet past the British blockades, past Gibraltar, to Brest and Normandy, where they were needed for unspecified reasons. Second, plans for the mass construction of flat-bottomed troop ships in the yards of Normandy and Brittany. And indeed, in every Channel harbor, however small, which could accommodate them . . .

The document alluded to had, therefore, to be a précis of a plan to invade England—of Napoleon's designs for landing an army and conquering the island of Great Britain. There could be no other reason for building an armada in the Channel, much less for building landing craft there. There was no other explanation.

Grey felt his chest tighten.

Carefully, Grey searched through the rest of d'Aumont's desktop papers—careful to keep them in the order d'Aumont had left them. Grey needed details: where Napoleon's forces would land; in what numbers; with what artillery, and what offshore support; what their short- and long-term objectives would be. But there was no sign of the master document. Grey looked through the desk drawers. Nothing there but records of the vineyard and cellar. He looked around the room. There had to be a safe somewhere.

There were several portraits on the walls, and a large tapestry. Grey checked behind them, one by one, running his fingers along the walls' paneling to feel for a hidden release catch. There was nothing. Nothing he could feel. Nothing at all. He swore. Besides the desk and the wall hangings, the room was bare. Wherever d'Aumont was secreting the secrets he guarded most closely, it wasn't here. His bedroom perhaps. Grey knew that would mean a daytime operation. Damned inconvenient.

After a final rearranging of the desk to match precisely the state of disarray d'Aumont had left it in, Grey snuffed out the candle, and left the way he'd come.

14

"GOOD DAY, BRODEUR," said Grey the next morning, entering the dining room, finding its cheerful, lemon-colored walls suitable to the sunny weather, and finding it empty save for the butler.

"Good day, sir," said Brodeur. "You will find breakfast in the silver service on the table to your right. If there's anything you'd like that is absent, please inform me and I will locate it for you."

"Thank you, Brodeur, most kind—I'm sure I will find everything I need without difficulty—though perhaps you could tell me where I should expect to find the d'Aumonts?" As he spoke, Grey poured himself a cup of coffee from a large silver pot.

"It is the practice of the family to dine early, sir, and thus begin their day. Madame d'Aumont has taken Miss Christine and Miss Yvette to pay a call on neighbors; Miss d'Aumont is attending to some matter with the vigneron. Captain d'Aumont is at work in his study—I will carry a note to him, if you wish."

"Never in life, Brodeur—I shouldn't think of disturbing him at his work. I'm sure he will find me when he's ready for me."

Brodeur bowed shallowly; Grey continued, "In the meantime, I wonder if you would object to my taking this"—he held up his coffee cup—"out into the gardens, or I should say, the vineyards. I find myself in the mood for some fresh air."

"Please feel at liberty, sir, to take your coffee wherever you like," said Brodeur, with only a slight frown. "And please to leave the cup wherever you find yourself when it is empty—a footman will retrieve it."

"Thank you, Brodeur."

"Shall I have the rest of the breakfast cleared away, sir?"

"By all means, if it stands on my account. Coffee is all I want."

"Very well, sir," said Brodeur, bowing again.

Cup in hand, Grey stepped out onto the back lawn and imbibed some of the light and deeply refreshing breeze. Not that he particularly needed refreshing. He had slept excellently. This was his peculiar tendency in difficult circumstances; the more serious the occasion, the better he slept. He'd often wondered why this was. As a young man, he would wake on the morning of a sea action to discover his marine colleagues had slept barely or not at all, and he'd count his lucky stars. Paulette had always said that hot action made him coldhearted.

It was lovely out, and Grey began a slow circumnavigation of the pond—sipping his coffee and pondering the best way to work out d'Aumont's schedule for the rest of the day without drawing too much attention to himself. This Brodeur fellow was no pushover. Perhaps he would try to make the acquaintance of the vigneron— surely he and d'Aumont would have a meeting planned, something lengthy enough for Grey to search d'Aumont's bedroom.

"Good morning, Captain Grey."

Grey turned. It was Julia d'Aumont, the elder sister—the one with the amber eyes.

"Good morning, Miss d'Aumont. A beautiful day, isn't it?"

"It is, Captain. I was just passing up to the front of the house—I walk portions of the vineyard every morning to check for vermin, to shoo away birds." She smiled slightly. "I am the family's human scarecrow."

Grey chuckled. "An admirable occupation. May I join you?"

"If you like."

Grey downed the rest of his coffee and placed the cup on a stone bench—"Excuse me"—and off they walked, around the house and into the rows of pinot blanc.

"Are you very involved in the winemaking?"

"Not much more than this, I'm afraid. Occasionally I'll get into the vat at pressing time and stomp a few rounds to show the men I'm a good sport. But aside from that, I confine myself to scaring crow and sampling the final products."

"Essential functions, no doubt."

"You're too kind, Captain. Have you ever done any farming?"

"My father had a small orchard that I sometimes ventured into—occasionally we even made cider and perry. But certainly nothing on this scale."

"What is 'perry'?"

"Ah, perry is cider from pears—yes, I don't imagine it has made many inroads in France; it's popular mostly in the North of England and Scotland. But it is quite delicious, if you have a taste for it."

"I must tell my brother—Jean-Anne is always anxious to try new things. He has shown you his new toy gun, no doubt?"

"The air rifle? He has. I confess I was quite as excited about it as he is."

"Oh, you men. That thing is but the toe of the elephant—it's lucky the Bonapartists are drinking champagne by the shipload to celebrate themselves, otherwise my brother's proclivity for tinkers might spend us out of hearth and home."

This she said mostly in jest, but Grey took it as an opening into d'Aumont's private affairs.

"Of course you must have his naval income too—forgive me for being personal, but during my service in the British admiralty, his ship *Fidèle* was known to have taken many rich prizes."

"Oh yes, there was that. But most of that was spent recovering the outlying portions of the estate nationalized in the revolution. And there won't be any more, now that he's on the staff. Though of course it's well worth it to have him home and out of danger."

"Yes, yes. I'm sure."

"You must forgive me for speaking so freely—I hope I am not embarrassing you. He and I crossed swords this morning, and it has left me in a cloudy mood."

"On the contrary: you flatter me with your confidence."

"Because you are an Englishman, you mean?" She shook her head. "Jean-Anne explained to us something of your circumstance. You must understand: many of the families in this area, many of our friends, were ruined at the hands of their government. More than a few fought their government, during the last war, and will during this one. Some now serve the English Crown."

"The Chasseurs Britanniques, you mean?" asked Grey. "From the men of the Condé's army."

"Indeed," said Julia. "So you see, your being here evokes no shock. Only sympathy. If I may say so."

"Again, you flatter me," said Grey. "And please feel free to speak of anything you wish."

"I thank you, though I won't tax your manners any further. It's only that Jean-Anne is seeking to leave the staff and return to active duty, and he refuses to listen to any sense about it. Stubborn, pig-headed fool."

"You mean he wishes to be assigned to the Channel squadron."

"He's spoken about it to you? And there he was, making so much of its being a secret. Yes, he wishes to go north. As if we both had not had enough of death and war."

"Has the estate been touched?"

"I have been touched, Captain Grey. I don't know if Jean-Anne spoke at all of his family before he introduced us to you—my older sister and I were both engaged in the year '99. Her fiancé survived Winterthur and returned to marry her. Mine did not."

"I am so terribly sorry to hear it."

Julia had a deep frown on her face. "I must be mad to speak so openly of this to you, when we've known each other only a few hours. Jean-Anne was so worked up this morning, and it has me worked up as well. And I gather it has something to do with you—though he instructed me not to inquire into your business here, so I won't. Even so—if I may continue this unseemly boldness—if there's anything to be done to keep him from returning to active duty, I should be most grateful if you would do it."

She blushed and looked away from him, and began to walk more briskly.

"I shall, Miss d'Aumont."

"Forgive my melodrama. Do you enjoy champagne particularly? Or do you choose to stick to your perry and cider?"

"Oh, I enjoy a crisp blanc de blancs; I never turn up my nose at anything dry. The vintage from dinner last night was most agreeable. Or was it a blend?"

"A blend—there was never a strong enough harvest during the nineties to produce a drinkable vintage. But for my sins, I prefer the blends. You know more what to expect from one drink to the next."

"A contretemps, Miss d'Aumont, I'm afraid. I prefer each bottle should be its own adventure. Even if that means a false step once in a while."

Julia picked a stone off the ground and flung it into a small congregation of starlings hopping their way down the row.

"I should have brought a shotgun," said Grey. "I could be more use to you."

"No, I don't require the little pests dead, just away."

"They're quite smart, though, starlings. Kill a few and the word might spread that these were fruit to be avoided."

"I'm certain you're right. But I haven't the stomach for it."

Grey and Julia arrived at the end of their row, and into a small clearing with a fountain in the middle.

"This really is remarkably lovely," said Grey. "What did it look like as a garden? Were these hedges?"

"Some of them were—but low hedges, only up to your waist, or a little lower. And a great assortment of flowers. Though of course I never saw them myself, they were changed to vines a few years before I was born. But there's a painting of the house somewhere that shows how it looked in the old days."

They crossed past the fountain and back into the vines. A rabbit was nibbling some fallen grapes, and Julia stooped again for something to throw at it.

"Allow me," said Grey, picking up a stone.

"Very well. Don't kill it."

"I wouldn't think of it," said Grey, sailing the stone into the gravel at the coney's lucky feet, giving it a start it could tell its innumerable grandchildren about. The throw made the torn stitch in his forearm wince; what a damned nuisance it was.

"Though I was under the impression the French were most partial to rabbits, in roasts and stews and so forth."

"Not to rabbits we've been acquainted with," said Julia.

Another few steps in silence. They reached the end of the row of vines and began up another.

"Your brother surprises me somewhat. I had expected him to be nipping at my heels all day about this work he's brought me here to do."

"I'm sure he will be later on. There was another great haul of papers in the post this morning—all of which he has, no doubt, to put his initials to, losing not a moment, as these naval men say. I imagine he'll be along to nip at your heels before the sun climbs too much higher."

"I hope not; I confess I'm rather enjoying this tour. We don't have vineyards like this in England—we certainly don't grow champagne. From the moment your brother revealed the nature of his estate, I've been hoping for some insight into its secrets."

"If you like," said Julia. "What do you wish to know?"

"Well—for instance, where do the bubbles come from?"

Julia sighed and shook her head at Grey's naïveté. "Oh, but Captain Grey, champagne is so much more than its bubbles. Forget I asked you what you wished to know, I will start instead from the beginning. How closely did you look at the rock you hurled at my rabbit?"

"How closely should I have looked? It seemed normal enough—white; limestone. Chalk? Like the cliffs of Dover."

"Quite so, Captain. You must understand that all of our province of Champagne was once beneath a sea, which has made all of our soil very much like your white cliffs—it is composed of the shells of ancient things. And the shells have little holes in them, you see, so water drains from the roots in a constant, slow, steady way—not drowning them one minute and parching them the next, as in normal vineyards. Besides that, Champagne has a unique climate—cooler than all the surrounds in summer, but milder in the winter. This means a slow, steady, and lengthy growing period for our grapes. These together give them their special flavor."

"Fascinating. Why do you grow white grapes instead of red? Isn't most champagne made from pinots noirs?"

"Yes—that's why most champagnes you see are golden; a golden wheat color—"

"Like your eyes, you mean; a most unusual shade," said Grey, casually, catching Julia off guard. She blushed slightly but continued as if he'd said nothing.

"That's the color of the juice of red grapes—without the skin being permitted to contribute color of its own. Blancs de noirs. By using white grapes, we can leave the juice to soak with the skin, giving the final wine a deeper taste. As you would get from a rosé champagne, but without the sweetness, and without the fairground color."

Grey smiled. "You don't approve of pink champagne?"

"I can't say I approve of its being called champagne at all, Captain. It is a drink for children."

Grey laughed. "Lucky children. I suppose milk became passé during the revolution."

"Milk is white and champagne is golden. Or perhaps now the wet nurses of the new bourgeoisie produce rosé milk as well. But no matter what madness seizes the world, our champagne, the blanc de blancs, is of the finest shade of gold—white gold, clear and pure. Like bottled golden sunshine . . . but am I carrying on?"

"Only to my great enjoyment," said Grey, "though you continue to neglect the bubbles."

"Ah yes, our little friends, the bubbles," said Julia. "Well, come, I will show you the caves."

"The caves?" asked Grey.

Julia waved him to follow, and walked off towards the nearest hillside, out of the vineyard, onto a well-trodden path.

After a few twists and turns, taking them up the hill and back in the direction of the house, the path led through a wide semicircular mouth directly into the hillside, into a man-made limestone cavern. It was lit by a few dim torches, but so much light reflected off the stark white walls and ceilings that Grey had the impression of being outside at twilight.

"These are the caves," said Julia as they walked further inward— the temperature dropping as they did. This remarkably cool, remarkably silent, chiseled-out burrow was filled with several thousand bottles of fermenting champagne. The bottles rested in peculiar, angled wine racks—shelves that leaned backward against one another, forming triangles.

"The racks are made this way to collect sediment in the bottles' necks—our men rotate the bottles a few degrees, twice a day, and over a year and a half, for non-vintage years, the sediment is all shaken, gracefully, to just under the cap. There it can be frozen, and the sediment-ice plugs shot out by the bottles' pressure, when the metal caps are replaced by corks. This is called 'riddling,' the technique of sediment capture. It is very new . . . invented by our friends at the house of the Veuve Clicquot. Jean-Anne was able to— shall we say—liberate it with a few pieces of silver placed into the right palms."

"Thirty pieces at a time, no doubt," said Grey.

Julia cocked an eyebrow and grinned.

"So, your brother brings his work home with him."

"I don't follow you, Captain."

"He is concerned with espionage for the admiralty, is he not?"

"Oh. I'm sure I don't know. Are you? . . . No, but we mustn't discuss it. What do you think of our caves?"

"They're delightful," said Grey. "How long did they take to excavate?"

"Near a decade. Before that we had to ferment our wine in the cellars. Much less space; much less consistent temperature. No good."

"No doubt. What do you use the cellars for now?"

"Oh, wine, still—but now finished bottles, not works in progress."

Grey nodded politely, filing away the fact that he would have to discover the cellars' entrance, give them a look-over when night fell. But for the time being, he was coming dangerously close to the point where Julia might find his probing for private information suspicious. "But I'm afraid you lost me with the riddling, Miss d'Aumont," said Grey. "What sediment is it that has to be removed? Though it occurs to me now I've never seen a bottle of champagne that had to be decanted."

"Yes, exactly—and this brings us to your bubbles: to produce them, the wine is fermented twice—once for alcohol, and then, after, a second batch of yeast and sugar is sealed in. Sugar for the yeast to eat, and to give off bubbles in return. But double the yeast means double the sediment—and with so crisp and clear a wine, how unappealing it would be to leave it behind in the bottle."

"I see."

"Did you know that it was your own countrymen who popularized our sparkling champagne? Most of France saw the bubbles as a grievous fault, but the English loved it, and from the Court of St. James's it spread back to Versailles, and all over Europe."

"I did not know that. I'm afraid I have grossly neglected my grape studies; you must think me terribly ignorant."

"I do," said Julia. "But no more than the other Englishmen I've met."

"Well, perhaps you'll take pity on me," said Grey. "You're a most excellent teacher; you've captivated me. And there are all sorts of things I'd like to learn about."

The cave was verging on cold, and Grey saw Julia's cheeks turn rosy with another slight blush.

"Such as what, Captain? I suspect that in other subjects you would prove much more knowledgeable than I."

"Perhaps I would," said Grey. "But prudence demands I make certain."

Grey took Julia by her chin, tilted her head up, planted a kiss on her lips. She let the kiss linger for just a moment, before pulling away.

"Really, Captain Grey . . ."

The voice of Julia's brother rang out from somewhere beyond the caves' entrance:

"Julia my dear, are you in there somewhere?"

"I am, Jean-Anne," she called back. "Shall I light a flare?"

In a moment he was by their side. "Julia dear, I'd been hoping you could tell me where Captain Grey had got off to, and here it turns out it was you who carried him away. Will you mind terribly if I steal him back from you?"

Who was this treacly man? wondered Grey, silently. Not at all seamanlike. But perhaps he was teasing her—it's never easy to guess at the games of siblings. And Julia had intimated that they were at odds over something.

"You may have him, brother. But don't work him too hard, I believe that arm of his is still a bother. Captain Grey: you're bleeding."

Grey looked down at his arm. That son-of-a-whore stitch, he didn't say.

"It appears I am. Oh well. I have blood to spare. Though that may be the end of this shirt."

"Nonsense, I can get a little blood out," said Julia. "God knows I've beaten it out of enough of Jean-Anne's shirts. And jackets, and trousers."

"I would be most obliged to you, Miss d'Aumont."

"Some other time for that, though," said Jean-Anne, cutting in. "For the time being I need him. Shall we?"

"Yes of course," said Grey. "Miss d'Aumont: a pleasure."

Julia nodded but said nothing as Grey followed d'Aumont back out into the light.

"Did you have an interesting chat?" asked d'Aumont.

"We did," said Grey.

"What did you talk about?"

"Wine," said Grey. "And rabbits."

15

GREY FOLLOWED D'AUMONT through the library, on the route he'd taken the night before. "Pleasant little room," he said, entering d'Aumont's study as if for the first time. "You must get a lovely breeze through here."

"Yes," said d'Aumont. "I've cornered the market in paperweights. Now let us turn to this."

He gestured to his desktop, which was covered by a large, detailed map of the British Isles.

"Please indicate," said d'Aumont, handing Grey a pen and gesturing to an inkwell, "which shipyards are active, what is the capacity of each—in ship type and volume, which are favored by the present government, and what is the quality of their work. We've heard, for instance, of the Forty Thieves."

Yes, thought Grey. Forty *Vengeur*-class line-of-battle ships, Seventy-fours, whose outstandingly shoddy construction had caused enormous scandal in Whitehall. Grey had sailed in one once. You could feel the dry rot all around you. He shook his head, dipped his pen, and ruminated.

The trick to misinformation is telling the truth about what's known, and lying, plausibly, about what's unknown. That the French knew about the Forty Thieves was not entirely surprising, given the ships' infamy—there was nothing stopping the French reading English newspapers, after all—and that meant too that they would have noted the yards where they'd been laid down, at several southern ports. He could safely mark each of these as out of favor. It was unlikely the French could know of First Lord St. Vincent's ongoing campaign to root out the men responsible; it had been kept reasonably quiet, because several remained politically well connected. It was likely too that the French would know, in general terms, the state of production in the northeast, where so many of the laborers were Irish. He would keep their details vague but accurate. No, the best opportunity for misleading the French would be the North Sea yards—at the Wash and the Humber, the Tees, the Tyne, and the firths. British naval power was totally unchecked in the North Sea; no French spy ship would have dared venture in for a look, and any French spy attempting to survey them by land would stand out like a smashed thumb. No doubt these were the holes that Napoleon's admirals in the Maison Militaire were so desperate for Grey to fill.

The principal question—as he dipped his pen; shook away the excess—was how far he could inflate the true numbers without making the French suspicious.

"I'm sorry," said Grey, after a few long moments. "You know, I can't simply spit this out. There's a considerable demand for detail that requires plumbing the memory. But if you'll leave me alone for an hour with the map and some notepaper, I believe I can give you what you want."

D'Aumont hesitated.

"Yes, very well, if that will assist your recollection. Perhaps you will take the map to your room and return again when you're ready."

So, thought Grey. He doesn't want me alone in his study . . . Could I have missed something?

"Yes, certainly," said Grey. "I'll find you here?"

"Yes," said d'Aumont. "With bated breath."

UPSTAIRS, GREY made short work of the map, noting the construction of a dozen phantom first- and second-rates, two dozen thirds, and two dozen frigates—these he would explain as a consequence both of the war and of the Whig governments' efforts to increase employment in the northeast, where much of their political support lay.

He made a final note of a new squadron of gunboats being built at Boston—the one in Lincolnshire—then rolled up the map and exited to the hall: this was his chance to investigate d'Aumont's room.

No one was coming. He tried d'Aumont's door and found it unlocked. A poor sign that there were secrets within, but not a conclusive one. He walked inside as casually as he could, leaving the door open behind him.

There was no desk; instead there was a table fit for a dining room, extensively laid out with papers in neatly squared stacks. Grey quickly circled the table looking from pile to pile—household accounts, almanac reports, vintage reports, notes on bottles, notes from vintners, statements from bankers (d'Aumont was even wealthier than Grey had realized . . .), but nothing whatever relating to his official duties.

There was a bureau and a wardrobe; Grey rifled through each, discovering nothing of interest. There was a humidor on a bedside table, with nothing in it but cigars. On the walls was a single painting, which Grey now looked at for the first time. It was a widely smiling d'Aumont standing beside his mother, behind a couch with five women on it: the three sisters Julia, Yvette, and Christine, and two others. One presumably was the married, absent fourth sister. There was no indication as to the identity of the fifth.

"What are you doing in here, Captain Grey?"

It was Brodeur, in the doorway, with a polite tone but narrowed, accusing eyes. Grey held up the rolled map.

"Delivering this to your master. This is his room, isn't it?"

"It is, sir. But Captain d'Aumont is in his study. Waiting for you, I believe."

"Is he, indeed? Well, I mustn't keep him waiting any longer. It's a lovely painting, isn't it, Brodeur."

"Yes, sir."

Grey walked towards Brodeur, who was still in the doorway, still with a dissatisfied look on his face.

"Move," said Grey, with the stern but casual authority one uses to cow a misbehaving horse. Brodeur moved, and Grey strode past with enough guiltless confidence to put the butler back on his heels. Maybe this was an innocent mistake after all.

Downstairs, Grey presented d'Aumont with the map and watched him scan it first with excitement, then with growing concern. That concern was exacerbated (intentionally) by Grey's broaching an uncomfortable subject.

"Captain d'Aumont, of course I'm happy to cooperate with you as far as I can—however, there is a matter of my payment."

"Yes of course," said d'Aumont, without meeting Grey's eyes. "Your fee has been approved by everyone from whom it was necessary to obtain approval . . . with the proviso that you provide your intelligence first and receive your remuneration afterwards."

Grey put on a look of insult. "That was not the agreement I reached with your representative. How long have you been aware of this intention to renege?"

D'Aumont blushed. "I received word only today, in the morning post, I assure you."

"Just before you asked me to fill in this map, then?" said Grey, nodding towards his handiwork.

"Yes." D'Aumont placed the map on the table and drew himself to his full height. "I must ask you to accept my apologies—I was not forthright with you on this matter. The fact is everyone accepts the value of the information you can provide, *except* those in the orbit of the first consul himself. I'm afraid, you see, Monsieur Bonaparte thinks very little of naval matters; he sees ships as satellites of the land, and believes all sea battles must be won on land, through capture of ports and supply lines and so forth. He has therefore conditioned payment to naval intelligence sources on the quality of the complete information provided. He is unshakable."

"And you intended to keep this from me . . . until when?"

D'Aumont cleared his throat. "I had hoped to keep it from you altogether . . . After you asked me to serve as your second, this unfortunate responsibility was transferred to me from Branson. You may read my orders if you like."

D'Aumont retrieved a folded document from a billfold and handed it over. Grey read it quickly.

"You are directed to obtain the information from me in a timely manner, or place me under arrest."

"I am afraid so."

"Is this how the government of France treats its friends?"

"I wish that were for me to say, Captain. However, I restate my apologies for my hand in deceiving you. And there should ultimately be no difficulty in paying you—"

"You will understand my doubt on that point—"

"Of course, but surely you have bureaucracy—surely you have accountants—in England."

"Have I a deadline?"

"Three days. I was disappointed in efforts to obtain a delay because of your arm. If you like, I will get you a secretary and you can dictate."

"That won't be necessary," said Grey. "I believe I can meet your date. Though under the circumstances I'm not sure what choice I have."

"I appreciate that, Captain Grey."

Brodeur knocked on the study's door and entered. "Captain d'Aumont, your mother, Miss Yvette, and Miss Christine have returned, and await you in the drawing room."

"Thank you, Brodeur. Would you please have writing paper and ink delivered to Captain Grey's room?"

"Yes, sir."

"And tell my mother I will join her shortly."

Grey moved towards the door. "If you will excuse me, I have some thoughts to get in order."

"Yes, certainly, Captain Grey. Thank you."

Grey walked past Brodeur—who moved out of the way unprompted—crossed through the library, and navigated himself towards the front of the house. Considering he had never had any expectation of collecting his traitor's bounty, and that this French subterfuge had no bearing at all on his own sub-rosa plans, Grey should not have been put out. But he was. He was damned irritated. Who wouldn't be, being welshed on and threatened with arrest?

Grey wore a little of this on his face as he ascended the stairs; Julia d'Aumont, coming in the other direction, noticed.

"Is something the matter, Captain Grey?"

"Hmm? Oh, Miss d'Aumont, forgive me. No, there's nothing the matter, my mind was wandering."

"I thought perhaps your arm was getting the better of you," said Julia.

"Oh no. In fact, everyone, myself included—myself in particular—has made far too much of it. It's really nothing. Though I believe," he said, looking up at her, "you were going to do something with this shirt?"

. . . Had he been too forward? Did he detect a moment of iciness in her expression?

"Come along, then," she said, turning back up the stairs.

"If you'd prefer, I can give it to a servant," said Grey, following her.

"Why?" said Julia d'Aumont. "Don't you think I've ever scrubbed anything before?"

Julia's room was at the far end of the north wing, whose corridor was lit by a skylight; it illuminated Miss d'Aumont as she walked, swaying back and forth. A little more than she had been in the vineyard? Grey would have had to know her better. It's hard to judge a French girl on that score.

She opened her door and strode into her room: "Come in."

Grey did, and closed the door behind him. She didn't seem to notice, walking over to a washbowl and pouring some water into it from a pitcher beside her bed. Grey looked around the room. It was bright and cheerful; the color scheme was sky blue, gilt-and-white trim, with a lacquered cherry coffee table before a sofa. On the table was tea service.

"Do you entertain here frequently?"

"Let's have that shirt."

Grey removed his jacket and draped it over a chair, then slipped his shirt up over his head.

"My, you have seen a lot of action, haven't you?"

Grey's chest and stomach were badly scarred from his years of service at sea. Sword wounds, healed over bullet holes, splinter wounds; a large burn over his left shoulder, where he'd been hit by shrapnel from an overheated cannon that exploded as its powder charge was put in.

"Here and there," said Grey. "You'd be astonished at how many shirts I've gone through."

"I don't doubt it," said Julia, rubbing soap onto the bloodstain and dipping it into the water. "You must really try to take better care of yourself."

"I could say the same to you," said Grey. "Of course it's not my place to notice, but you seem—well . . . unhappy."

"Do I?" said Julia, beginning to scrub. "I'm not sure I can tell anymore. I was unhappy after Mathieu died, and I suppose I have gradually returned to normal. I try not to think too much about it. It has been four years now."

"Do you spend all your time out here in the country?"

"Yes. Though I don't particularly mind being alone. Of course I have my family—though I see surprisingly little of them; I don't expect you've seen much of them either; they're always out paying calls or arranging some charitable garden party, as if we were in the neighborhood of Versailles. But I've never been one for calls. I came out the year of the revolution, so my exposure to society was cut short, until my engagement. When Mathieu was stationed in Paris—and he was for several years; he was lucky, his father was very political—I stayed in Paris with my sister, at Jean-Anne's apartment. But once Mathieu was killed . . . I couldn't bear the pitying looks. I seemed to drive every other emotion out of a person, till they could manage only to see me as a wounded puppy. It was intolerable; it made everything so much worse. So I retreated to the country, and have stayed here ever since."

"Well, if it makes you feel any better, I have no pity for you."

"Don't you?"

"No. We all have our problems. And yours are common ones."

"That's very forthright of you," said Julia, rubbing the stain with the edge of her fingernail.

"In war, people die. I'm afraid there's only one thing for it."

"To put it behind you, you mean?"

Grey was pouring himself a drink from a decanter sitting on a bedside table. "No. To revenge. You're French, you should understand that."

"We're a Norman family originally, the blood is cooler . . . On whom do you suggest I seek my revenge? Shall I fight the Habsburgs myself? Shall I play Charlotte Corday?"

Grey laughed.

"And who is the target of your revenge?" asked Julia.

"No one, my dear. I was just putting myself in your shoes."

"Oh. I thought you were trying to put yourself in my bed."

She was still working on the stain. Grey put down his drink.

16

AFTERWARDS, JULIA BROUGHT Grey a fresh drink, and began to dress herself.

"Shouldn't you have a maid for that?" asked Grey as he leaned onto one elbow, sank slightly into Julia's mattress, and sipped his brandy.

"Very funny," she said. "I think it's best in these circumstances to be able to handle your own repairs. Speaking of which, you had better repair to your own room. Be careful, though—peek out before you go—there are often hallboys and footmen and things about."

"It's a shame we couldn't find someplace more discreet than your boudoir. The cellars, perhaps."

"The cellars are hardly discreet; they are also the servants' quarters. And the kitchen. It's like a county fair down there."

God damn it to hell, thought Grey, having started to pin his hopes on those cellars being d'Aumont's secret hideaway.

"But really, Captain, you must go."

"Call me Thomas, and I'm not sure I can yet—is my shirt done?" Julia glanced over at the washbowl, most of whose contents had been wicked up into Grey's sleeve.

"It's a little damp, I'm afraid. But I'm sure you have another somewhere."

"I do. I suppose this will take me down the hall at least."

"You had better hope it does," said Julia. "If he finds you here, my brother will throw you into the oubliette."

"Into the what, my dear? What is 'oubliette' in English?"

"I don't speak any English . . . it is a hole, you know, a dungeon."

"Oh," said Grey, swinging his legs off the bed and looking for his pants. "You mean one of those awful things they had at the Bastille? A prison pit where the only way out is a hole in the ceiling? I'd wondered if those really existed."

"They do—many estates have one, from the old days of feudal privilege." Julia was starting to touch up her makeup.

"Well, I suppose that demystifies the revolution somewhat . . . And you still have one, you say?"

"Well, not exactly, it hasn't been used in fifty years . . . My father converted it into a special cellar for his most precious vintages, when he added the greenhouse. He converted the room over it into his study at the same time. It's Jean-Anne's study now."

"How nice," said Grey, emptying his glass.

THAT NIGHT, Grey crouched at his keyhole until he saw d'Aumont retire for the night: tonight's trip to the man's study would not risk an encounter with the man himself. In the same black outfit he'd worn the night before, Grey made his way down the stairs, down the hall, through the library, past the lock, and into d'Aumont's private office. Tonight, he wouldn't leave without the papers he was looking for. He was certain now that they were somewhere beneath him.

Once again Grey lit a candle on the desktop candelabra, and shined the light over the floor. There was no obvious trapdoor . . . but there was a small carpet directly behind d'Aumont's desk. Grey set the lamp on the floor and began to roll the carpet back.

And there it was. A heavy oak door, perfectly flush with the rest of the floor—with a large, recessed brass ring with which to haul the thing open. Grey slid the rolled rug clear and pulled upward. The door swung open easily; it was heavy, but well greased: clearly it got a lot of use. It opened onto wooden steps that descended into a cold, damp blackness below. Grey picked up the candelabra and followed them.

After an initial straight descent, the stairs began to wind around the outside of a cylindrical room, about eight feet across and (Grey squinted downward) perhaps fifteen or twenty feet deep.

In the center of the room was a freestanding, cylindrical wine rack, seven or eight feet tall. Grey held the light towards it. These presumably were the special vintages to which Julia referred. Now Grey moved the light out towards the exterior wall. Its continuous curve gave the distinct impression of being in the hold of a ship. Or at the bottom of a well. Which, Grey supposed, he was.

Along the exterior wall were cases of this and that . . . wine from other estates, it looked like. Some beer too. Was it too déclassé for the main cellars, or too good for them? Grey followed the boxes around the room's circumference . . . Case upon case . . . and then the gold strike:

A safe.

A large one, almost Grey's height, with a door like the vault of a great London bank.

Grey held the light down towards the door's locking mechanism. In the center was a spoked wheel, something like the wheel of a ship, in brass, to draw open the bolts that held the thing shut. Beside it should have been a keyhole, for the mechanism's release. Instead there was a dial, made of ivory, with numbers carved around its edge. No . . . he looked closer . . . three concentric dials.

A permutation lock? Grey had heard of them, but never seen one . . . He searched his memory. . . . weren't they an Italian novelty, one of those things invented during the Renaissance that hadn't managed to spread across the Alps? D'Aumont and his whoreson toys. Grey held the light closer.

The innermost dial had the numbers one through ten carved into it; the second, one through twenty; and the outermost, one through thirty. The math was not complicated. Assuming the principle was to line up an arbitrary set of three numbers in order to create a channel for an arresting bolt to pass through . . . there were exactly six thousand possibilities.

Six thousand. How many could Grey try a minute? He twisted the dial in his hand. Perhaps one every twenty seconds? Three a minute? Two thousand minutes. Thirty-three and a third hours. He cursed under his breath. If he started now, he could try . . . eight or nine hundred variations before the sun came up. If he could keep it up. That would give him a one-in-seven chance of guessing right. (*Sept-et-le-va*, he said to himself.) But how long before dawn did the servants begin their duties? No, the odds were too long; it was a bad risk.

Could he blow the safe open? What with? Powder from d'Aumont's gun room. But the explosion would bring everyone in the house running, trapping him in the oubliette. Just as it was intended.

. . . What about one of those gas canisters? For the Girandoni? No doubt puncturing one would cause an explosion—the pressure inside them was plainly immense. But would it be enough? He had no point of comparison to guess against. And that would, at very least, make a sound like the crack of a rifle. Amplified by these circular walls.

It was no good. There was only one way this safe would be opened: at the point of a sword. Here was a happy convergence of his two missions—tomorrow night, as soon as the ladies went up, Grey would make some excuse to accompany d'Aumont to his study, and then make him open the safe.

Grey would then escape with the secrets, and leave behind the corpse of one Captain Jean-Anne d'Aumont. Stabbed in his oubliette.

Grey turned to climb back up the stairs . . .

He turned back to the safe. Was d'Aumont a lazy man? No. But just in case . . .

Grey turned the dial to read 1-1-1, and pulled.

Nothing. 1-2-3, and pull. Nothing.

Oh well. Never hurts to try. He spun the dials back to where he had found them, gave that a pull as well, just to be sure, and then returned to the study above.

17

W HEN GREY CAME down for breakfast the next morning, he passed the two younger daughters, Christine and Yvette, standing in the foyer, waiting and chatting. He bowed politely to them, and would have deployed some courteous small talk if he hadn't been cut off by a severe look from d'Aumont, who waved him to follow, into the empty dining room, closing the door behind them.

"Captain Grey, I have something . . . delicate to discuss with you."

Instantly Grey's mind spun through the events of the previous day and night. Had he been seen leaving Julia's room? Had he left something out of place in d'Aumont's study or his cellar? Did something on the map ring false?

"You will forgive me, I hope," said d'Aumont, "for being personal. Are you Catholic? I know it is not very common in England, but perhaps with your evident sympathy with the Irish? Or perhaps I presume too far. It's Sunday morning, of course"—Grey had forgotten—"and I wondered if you wouldn't like to accompany my family and myself to hear the mass. Of course you need feel no compunction at saying no."

Grey had to keep himself from sighing his relief.

"It would be a pleasure to accompany you, Captain. I've made strong progress in my work, I feel I can take the morning."

"Good," said d'Aumont. "I'm very glad to hear it. Normally of a Sunday we walk down to the church in the village. We will leave in ten minutes."

"Very good," said Grey. "Just enough time for a cup of coffee, and then I am your man."

Grey had imagined the walk might permit him a chance to speak to Julia, who had gone up quickly after dinner the night before, but she was locked in conversation with her mother. Instead he found himself paired with the youngest daughter, Christine—she was very sweet and very chatty, not terribly bright, and hadn't yet grown fully out of an adolescent plumpness.

She wanted to know everything about England. Did they really still have a king there? She was almost too young to remember Louis Seize. Did it rain all the time, the way it did in Normandy? She understood the cheese was very hard. In Champagne they mostly ate brie, from Brie, which was in Champagne—it was where they were right now! How did he learn to speak French so well? Did everyone in England speak French? She should love to learn English, but her governess said it was more important to learn German, though she disagreed, but of course her governess probably knew best, though her governess was German, so that might suggest a certain bias, and anyway, her governess didn't speak English, so it was a moot point. What religion was Grey? she wondered. They had discussed it before he'd come down. Mama says England is a country with a thousand religions but only one sauce. She did hope it was a pleasant sauce. And how could there be a thousand religions? She only knew five: Catholic, not Catholic, Jew, Mohammedan, and pagan. She had met Jews in Paris—people said Mr. Napoleon admired them for being the lawgivers, so they were quite fashionable at the moment, and that Jean-Anne had met many Mohammedans when he was at sea, though some were quite unfriendly, and took Christian slaves when they could, rowing north from Africa, which seemed a terribly long way away, but others he said were quite friendly, and had helped Mr. Napoleon when he was in Egypt. But she had never seen or heard of someone seeing a pagan. Did Grey know any? Did he think they looked like other men? She had heard they had narrow eyes, but she found this difficult to believe. She wondered why they shouldn't just become Christians—it was such a pleasant way to be—though perhaps there was some obstacle, they living so far away. She should love to see the Orient. Perhaps Jean-Anne would take her someday. Or perhaps her husband would. She giggled. Grey and the family rounded a corner, and finally there was the church. He marveled at the girl's, Christine's, stamina. When did she inhale?

Grey had attended several Catholic masses before; when he was younger, out of curiosity (he had in fact been somewhat disappointed, at the time, to discover that there was far less "folderol" than he had been told), and then later on assignment in Catholic countries, when good manners required it. He wasn't especially religious, but even for a laissez-faire Anglican like himself, it was impossible to kneel before a crucifix on the day you intended to kill someone without contemplating questions of sin and hell and redemption and life everlasting versus everlasting torment. Christ had advised men to turn the other cheek. Grey saw himself as more of an Old Testament Christian. "Thou shalt not hate thy brother in thine heart; thou shalt in any wise rebuke thy neighbor, and not suffer sin upon him." Grey had been, at times, a professional rebuker. It had been his job to see that eyes were repaid with eyes, or sometimes, to take a foreign eye preemptively, to prevent the loss of one in Britain. Perhaps Christ wouldn't see things his way, but Grey felt confident that Christ's father did. If he troubled himself with this sort of thing.

After several ups and downs, a sermon (quite a good one, Grey thought), and communion (which he didn't take; neither did Julia), the service concluded. Christine was ready to resume her conversation with Grey—was preparing her opening salvo—when Julia told her family that she wished to remain behind and make confession.

Jean-Anne d'Aumont tut-tutted, said he couldn't take the time to wait for her, and that he didn't wish her to walk back to the house alone. Julia tut-tutted at that, and was considering a riposte when Grey interjected.

"Might I be permitted to see Miss d'Aumont home?"

Jean-Anne seemed ambivalent about the suggestion. So in fact did Julia. But after a moment's thought, d'Aumont said:

"Yes, I would appreciate that, thank you," and then to his mother and sisters, "Come, let us go." They filed out of the church with the rest of the parishioners, and once the priest had shaken the last departing hand, Julia approached him, and they two disappeared into a booth.

Grey stepped outside to give them their privacy. He lit a cheroot from a box he'd purchased in Paris, which had become regrettably stale. It was a warm, gusty day. A breeze carried away Grey's ash and made the end of his cigar glow. Grey followed the smoke's circuitous path through the air, twisting here and there, and was wondering at the vagaries of wind at a small scale—how wind was so much studied and harnessed, but still imperfectly understood—when Julia emerged.

"I hope I wasn't too long," she said, brushing the knees of her dress.

"Not at all," said Grey. "Shall we?" He gestured up the oak-lined road back towards her house.

Julia didn't say anything until they were a respectable distance from the church. "I suppose you know what I was confessing for."

"You won't tell me that that was your first encounter. I'm not certain I could believe you."

"What a terribly ungallant thing to say," said Julia d'Aumont.

"I meant it in jest, my dear."

She refused the offer of his arm. "If you don't mind, I would prefer not to discuss it further."

For a few moments, neither said anything, until finally Julia spoke again:

"You have some conflict with my brother? I don't know what it is, but you and he are both wearing it out on your sleeves this morning."

"No, not a conflict, just a transaction. Of mutual interest."

"You mustn't lie to me," said Julia. "When he said he had to speak with you this morning, there was murder in your eyes. As on the staircase last night. And perhaps you made love to me in order for me to intercede with him."

"No, of course not."

"My brother had told me you were a man of honor——that you had so impressed him in your conduct on the field of honor. What nonsense."

"And so I should have refused your advances? Or warned you against mine?"

"Please leave me be." Grey grabbed her by the arm; turned her towards him. She slapped him across the face, repeated, "Leave me be!" and added, after a moment, "We've had our sin. That will be enough."

They walked the rest of the way in silence.

18

UNFORTUNATELY, GREY WOULD have to leave the bulk of his possessions behind—everything that didn't fit conveniently into his jacket and trousers. He had a long walk ahead. Would he have a chance to return to his room after dispatching d'Aumont, for a trousseau to take with him? Possibly, but he decided not to count on it.

There was a sound from behind him. Grey turned. It was a note, slipped under the door. He picked it up. It was his note; an apology he had sent to Miss d'Aumont an hour earlier. Unopened; still sealed. Returned to sender. Oh well. He no longer needed anything from her—but he was sorry it had ended badly. He hadn't intended to hurt her, and he regretted it—he always regretted hurting innocents, and she was a civilian in all of this. He couldn't help the feeling that Paulette would have approved of her, in some roundabout way. But it was something he had no time to think about right now. Julia was hurt; he had hurt her; she was a casualty of war. Regrettable, but there it was.

As Paulette had been? he asked himself. No, of course not, you damned fool. None of that moral equivalence nonsense. Leave that to the French philosophers.

· · ·

When the dressing gong rang, Grey had already filled his pockets—as much as he could without drawing attention to them—with the few small items he couldn't bear to leave behind. Most of them remembrances of his wife, along with his warmest socks. He considered wearing his sword. It might draw some attention, but he might say that he expected to depart shortly with d'Aumont, at the completion of his work, and wished first to honor the house with his full fig at dinner. He could even say it was a Shetland tradition, and that he was of a Shetlandic family. He'd used that in the past. It proved hard to dispute; who had ever been to the Shetlands? However, the plan he'd developed went like this: At dinner he would say that the report was nearly done; imply that he'd been working on it right along and being discreet about the progress, for the sake of his financial arrangements. D'Aumont would ask to look at it. Grey would offer to bring it to his study after dinner. When Grey went up to get it, he would actually be getting his sword, which he would roll up in a large map he had earlier procured from his host.

Dinner itself proved uneventful. Grey was asked several times what he thought of the church and the service, et cetera, how his arm was recuperating ("I had almost forgotten it, ma'am"), how his work for Jean-Anne was coming. They said they were sorry when he told them it was virtually done, and that he would be prepared to return to Paris the following day, with Captain d'Aumont's approval. The announcement caught Captain d'Aumont himself off guard, but he was pleased to hear it, and expressed his desire to see the in-progress draft.

"Certainly," said Grey. "Why don't I bring it to your study after the ladies have gone up?"

"I would appreciate that," said d'Aumont. And the dinner conversation swung to other topics. Champagne and vineyard-related topics. Anticipating a return to Paris the following day, d'Aumont had a few things he wanted to set in order before he left. However, per Grey's plan, there would be no notifying Paris to expect him: the final post had already gone.

. . .

WHEN DINNER concluded, Madame d'Aumont adjourned her daughters to the drawing room, suggesting the gentlemen proceed directly to their business. Grey and d'Aumont stood as the ladies left; again Grey held the door for them. As Julia passed Grey by, she slipped him a note.

With d'Aumont's mother and sisters gone, Jean-Anne stared for a moment at Grey, then turned and walked in the direction of his study.

"Come with me, please, Captain Grey," he said.

"Shall I get my papers?" asked Grey, following d'Aumont out of the room.

"Not yet," said d'Aumont. "One thing at a time."

Neither said anything else until they were through the library, and the office door closed behind them.

Now d'Aumont stood behind his desk, wearing a solemn expression, his hands clasped behind his back. His brow was furrowed; a countenance more in anger than in sorrow.

"My sister handed you a note?" said d'Aumont to his guest. "I must ask you to show it to me."

Grey had not yet looked at it himself, having slid it as subtly as possible into an inner pocket of his jacket. Now he removed it, unfolded it, examined it:

Captain Grey,

Perhaps you think me too capricious, too like a girl. I am sorry I have been so cold to you. I do not blame you for what passed between us. I gave in to an improper impulse. Do not tempt me to do so a second time.

With my regrets,
Julia d'

Grey looked from the letter to d'Aumont. His frown had deepened.

"My dear Captain d'Aumont," said Grey, stepping towards d'Aumont's desk, "this note concerns a most private matter between your sister and myself. I'm sure you understand"—Grey stuck the letter into the flames of the desktop candelabra—". . . being French." Grey smiled his most distasteful smile. It gave him no pleasure to bandy Julia's name about. He took solace in the fact that the only one hearing him do so would soon be dead.

D'Aumont's color changed to a dark red. *"Swine!"* He was gripping the back of his desk chair, digging his nails into the leather. "You will not spend another night in this house!"

"I will gladly leave, *mon capitaine*. But I'll take Julia with me." Grey dropped the smoldering remains of the note into d'Aumont's ashtray, where it lay glowing amidst the butts of d'Aumont's smoked-out cigars. "And of course . . . Julia will take whoever she might be carrying with her."

D'Aumont let out a roar of fury that shook the walls:

"DAMN you!"

He stormed around the desk—Grey half expected the man to pounce on him like a wounded bear. Instead he threw open the door to the library and crossed the room to a pair of crossed sabers, hung beneath a portrait of a naval officer.

Brodeur and a footman were coming quickly up the hall in response to d'Aumont's shout.

"GET OUT," he bellowed at them. "This is a personal affair. I'll see the next lackey who interrupts me STRUNG UP BY HIS THUMBS." The footman was already retreating. Brodeur hesitated. D'Aumont turned an even darker shade of red. "OUT, I SAY—GOD DAMN YOU!"

As Brodeur backed away, d'Aumont wrenched the sabers from the wall:

"These belonged to my father; they are a matched pair." He threw one to Grey. "You will give me satisfaction or by God I'll kill you where you stand. On your guard."

Grey felt the blade's tip—sharp—felt its balance—good—and its grip—adequate. He swung it back and forth, listening to it cut the air. Then he swung it wide to his right, listening for the *crash* and *tinkle* as the vase he'd knocked over two nights earlier exploded into a pile of porcelain debris. Grey smiled.

"Ready."

D'Aumont began to circle with his sword held out in front of him, parallel to the ground. Grey let his own saber dangle from the parallel, pointed somewhat towards the floor, and waited for d'Aumont to make the first move.

The Frenchman took a quick step forward and sliced at Grey's chest. Grey banged the blow away and sliced back at d'Aumont, who let Grey's blade run up to his hilt before shoving it away and laying a quick riposte back at Grey's face.

Grey leaned back and the riposte sailed wide of his head; he leaned forward again as d'Aumont swayed, looking for balance, and swung at d'Aumont's stomach. A chunk of jacket and shirt came along with the blade, and the two men circled apart.

Now it was Grey's turn to lunge forward—but not at any vital organ. He needed that safe opened. He nicked d'Aumont's sword arm; d'Aumont exhaled sharply through gritted teeth and took two steps backward. Duty. Damned duty. He hated the word, as he hated hell, all Montagues, and Capitaine Jean-Anne.

Grey parried a weak blow as d'Aumont tried to keep Grey at bay and simultaneously tear off a bloody strip of cloth that had wound itself around his hand. Grey took a step back and lifted his sword. A courtesy. D'Aumont ripped the cuff of his shirt away and shouted again—

"*En garde.*"

Slice, parry, slice, parry, lunge, parry. Grey's focus was sharp; d'Aumont was no slouch with a saber. They fenced back and forth; Grey waiting for his chance at a disabling cut, d'Aumont still with bloodlust in his eyes. Grey twisted away from a deep lunge and sliced at d'Aumont's hip. D'Aumont took three quick paces backward, passing back through the door into his study, stumbling just slightly on the threshold. Off his balance again, he fell back towards his desk, reaching out behind him for support as he was forced to lean away from Grey's slices about his head.

D'Aumont fell against the desk—his concentration snapped, and in a snap, Grey struck at d'Aumont's sword hand and the saber flew across the room.

There was now nothing between the tip of Grey's blade and the bits of fabric covering d'Aumont's heart except a foot of empty, heavy air.

"WELL?" said Grey, charged with passion from the fight, waiting for d'Aumont to beg for his life. Instead d'Aumont reached behind him, grabbed the flaming candelabra on his desk, and lunged with it at Grey's face.

Grey stabbed between its prongs and, with the torque of his sword, wrenched the candelabra out of d'Aumont's hand. Grey's motion was smooth and contemptuous. The candelabra clanged loudly onto the ground.

"Pick it up, before you burn your damned house down. NOW." With Grey's sword still pointed at his heart, d'Aumont knelt to retrieve the still-burning lamp. He was in a heavy blush of shame and anger. He placed the candelabra back on his desk, which he once again leaned on, trying to catch his breath.

Grey stuck the tip of his sword into the hilt of the sword d'Aumont had dropped, and flung it out of the room, back into the library. The two men listened to the sound of metal skittering across the wooden floor with their eyes locked together.

"Well?" Grey repeated.

"Well, what. You expect me to beg for my life?" answered d'Aumont, wiping some blood from the corner of his mouth.

"I did, rather; yes. You want to keep it, don't you?"

The two men stared at each other still, neither blinking, neither flinching. D'Aumont broke the line of sight first, turning his head to the left, exhaling loudly with a mix of hate for Grey and for himself.

"Very well," he said. "I ask for my life."

"And I will grant it to you, if you do as I ask."

D'Aumont's mouth curled into an even deeper scowl than the one he'd worn till now.

"And what's that?"

"There's a strongbox directly beneath us. You will oblige me by turning its dials to the correct combination of numbers required to open it. And I will oblige you by letting you live."

GOD DAMN IT, thought Grey—what did I just do? I promised the man his life. What have I done; I'm here to kill him. But Grey knew—hated that he knew—that the contents of the safe were more important than his revenge. Damn it all to hell, but they were. If it meant he had to make this deal with the devil—so be it.

Slowly d'Aumont's frown was replaced by a look of confusion; then one of understanding, of revelation.

"So," he said, "that's what all this has been about. You're not an informer, you're a spy. This entire affair . . . all our confidences . . . everything by design."

"Not exactly," said Grey. "I'm afraid I can't take that much credit. But the heart of what you say is correct. You have information in that safe that I need."

"You will have to kill me, then."

"Don't tempt me," said Grey. "You have no idea how thin is the ice upon which you stand."

"That safe will never be opened for you while I'm alive," answered d'Aumont, regaining some of his manhood. "Nor when I'm dead, I daresay."

"How many fingers can you afford to lose before you change your mind?" asked Grey, menacing his sword around d'Aumont's nether parts.

"And let us suppose you do extract the documents in my safe. What would you do with them? Walk them to the Sleeve"—he used the French name for the English Channel—"and swim across? Will you swim across the Rhine? Will you walk to the Pyrenees? Evading every Frenchman, every troop movement, every patrol between here and there? Come. You are being absurd. The information you seek will prove useless."

"Then there's no reason not to give it to me."

For a moment d'Aumont's eyes seemed to wander.

"Very well," he said. "First I must catch my breath."

D'Aumont said this in the same contemptuous snarl he'd used since Grey had burned the note . . . but now there was just the hint of a twinkle in his eye.

Grey twisted around just in time to see the stocking-footed form of Brodeur, behind him, with d'Aumont's saber raised over his head.

Grey drove his own saber deep into Brodeur's gut. Brodeur gurgled blood, dropped the sword, then dropped to the ground beside it, dead.

Now it was Grey's turn to snarl, turning back around to face d'Aumont. "Shall we begin cutting off those fingers, then? Or would it be more persuasive to begin cutting off sisters?"

D'Aumont was staring at the lifeless body of his butler.

"I bring you into my house, and this is how you repay me."

He shook his head—and Grey couldn't help but feel pangs of shame. Despite his hatred for the man, Grey knew that d'Aumont had done his best to act honorably towards him. Even with the threatened arrest. Grey had wanted to flee to Boston to avoid any more of the ugliness that went with this kind of life.

But there was nothing to be done about that now.

"If you please," he said to d'Aumont.

Wordlessly, the French captain walked around his desk, kicked away the carpet, and opened the trap.

"Would you like to go first?" he asked Grey.

"Take the light," said Grey, nodding to the candelabra, "and move."

D'Aumont wound his way down into the oubliette, with Grey, and Grey's saber, at his back. At the bottom of the stairs, d'Aumont handed Grey the lamp, turned the dials to 9-12-29, and took a step back.

"Someone's birth date?" asked Grey. D'Aumont looked at him but said nothing.

"Open it," said Grey.

D'Aumont rotated the safe's locking wheel, pulling back the

bolts, which made a groaning sound as they were drawn. Then, with a slightly grand gesture, he threw the door open.

Inside were four shelves; the top two stacked with neatly divided piles of gold currency: an assortment of pre-revolution French coins—louis d'ors; francs *à cheval* and *à pied*—Spanish doubloons in several denominations, along with some smaller escudos. Some Swiss duplones and Prussian friedrichsdors. Exactly one pund Scottis. All told, several hundred pounds English.

Beneath the gold was jewelry; evidently valuable family pieces; a piece all in rubies, and various smaller diamond and semiprecious trinkets.

"I suppose I could not interest you in taking the money and leaving the documents. I would be happy to aid your escape with the gold; I will send my own carriage to see you unmolested back to Spain."

"Very generous of you, d'Aumont, but I'm afraid you suppose correctly." Grey was looking at the bottom shelf, the one on which stood one careful pile of notes and letters, and beside it, several scrolled maps.

"It's a very great deal of money. Allow me to add to it the contents of my wallet." D'Aumont reached into his jacket.

"Keep your hands where I can see them, Captain."

D'Aumont withdrew the hand from his inner pocket . . . something in it flashed . . . then it was buried in Grey's gut, tearing, tearing . . .

The knife . . . thought Grey, collapsing to the ground, feeling himself slowly soaked in his own blood.

The knife . . . from his cigar case . . . the damned cigar case . . . the damned cigar case . . .

Grey lost consciousness.

19

THE NEXT TIME Grey drifted up towards consciousness, he was on the floor of a carriage, being rocked back and forth. There was a sharp pain somewhere in his belly. He tried to reach for it but couldn't. His hands were tied down, on either side of him. Was he on a litter?

Above him sat d'Aumont, looking out the window, deep in thought. The Girandoni was balanced across his knees.

Grey drifted back into darkness . . .

. . . Two men, men in uniforms, two French soldiers, were standing over him now, pulling him out of the carriage, on a litter, banging his shoulder into the doorsill.

"Careful!" snapped d'Aumont. The soldier at Grey's feet murmured something in apology. Grey couldn't make out what.

Now the tops of towers loomed into his field of vision . . . some great gray edifice, dark, uninviting. Hostile. Hateful. The Conciergerie? He couldn't quite bring his eyes into focus. All his blood seemed to be in his feet. He closed his eyes again . . .

• • •

. . . Now he was in a white plaster room. Vaulted ceiling. He was staring up at it. Someone was probing about his waist. A sharp, burning pain. He wanted to shout out his agony, but he didn't seem to have any air inside him, nothing in his lungs, no tongue in his head.

"I will replace these stitches, but not a bad job for a country man," said someone standing by his hip. "I don't see any infection . . . he's quite lucky, really. The question now is: has he lost too much blood."

I'LL HAVE A PINT OR TWO OF YOURS, VILLAIN, Grey wanted to bellow, but there was still nothing inside of him . . . his eyes seemed to have closed again . . . he couldn't see the ceiling anymore . . .

"But if he's made it this far, I think the odds are good."

"I hope so, Dr. Legrand." Now this was . . . the voice of that man, Jean-Anne d'Aumont? A friend? No, an enemy. His bitterest enemy. His bitterest enemy who continued:

"This person is of the utmost importance to the state. He must live."

He must live. He must live. He must live . . .

. . . Now Grey was on something hard . . . not the litter anymore . . . a wooden bed. No mattress. No straw. No light. No—there was light, just a hint of a shadow on the floor. A lined shadow. Faint light through bars on a window.

Ache. Aches. His head. His whole body, it felt starved of something. Starved of some vital sustenance. Like . . . like the worst hangover imaginable. Was that what he was doing here? He laughed a single grunt at the idea, and pain flashed through his gut.

He reached for its source. His hands were free. There was a heavy bandage over the left side of his abdomen. He was dressed. In his own clothes. At least, in his own trousers, and what shreds remained of his shirt.

Grey looked from himself to his surroundings. He was in a cell. Surprisingly roomy. Meant for two? Yes, he could see another wooden pallet bed on the opposite wall. It was empty. And beside it, a bucket. He hoped that was empty too. There was nothing else in the room. The window, with its bars, and a heavy oaken door were the only interruptions to the dark stone walls.

The door had a small peephole in it, for a guard to check on the cell's contents. Grey dragged himself up off the bed—he felt suddenly very light-headed, threw an arm out to the wall for balance—then dragged himself over to the door. He looked out through the hole. Craning his neck from side to side, all he could see was an empty stone corridor.

He turned and went to the window. It was about two feet tall and almost as wide as his shoulders. Quite nice for a prison—it must have been built as something else. Wasn't the Conciergerie a palace to begin with? These may once have been servants' quarters, up here in a tower, with a view of the river.

The Conciergerie was indeed where he was, on Paris's central island, the Île de la Cité, sitting in the middle of the Seine. The revolution's second most famous prison. How many men had waited in this room, waited for a fateful knock, for a blindfold, a ride in an oxcart, to the platform in the Place de la Concorde, to the guillotine. Was he awaiting the same thing? Would his head shortly be sliced off his shoulders?

As if in answer, a key turned in the lock of his door. Of course, Grey thought. In prison, they don't knock.

Grey turned. The jailor who had opened the door was giving way to a second man. Narrow face; sunken cheeks, ponderous Gallic nose.

"Captain Grey. My name is Duquette. Perhaps you would accompany me downstairs."

Grey squared his shoulders.

"Certainly, my good man. Should I dress or will this be an informal occasion?"

"Oh, what you have on now is quite adequate, Captain."

"That's just as well. I really haven't a thing to wear."

Mr. Duquette gestured for Grey to walk in front of him, behind the jailor—who was carrying a torch—and, in convoy, they proceeded down a narrow turret staircase, down a flight, two flights, three, four—into a dank basement.

"Is there anything so unpleasant as cold humidity, Mr. Duquette?" said Grey.

"I believe so, Captain Grey."

The jailor placed his torch into a sconce, among several others that lined the walls and illuminated the room. In their flickering light, Grey examined the object that stood before him: something like a wooden table, about two feet longer than a man is tall, with a horizontal windlass at either end.

"Do you know what this is, Captain?"

"I believe so . . . Of course I've never seen one before. They've been illegal in England for two hundred years."

"Yes," said Duquette, "I know. It is a popular anecdote in my profession that Guy Fawkes could not be racked, because of the English law, until a special warrant was obtained from the king James."

"Just so," said Grey.

"Normally," said Duquette, "you would begin with conversation, and then perhaps some . . . less severe methods of torture, before reaching my level. But I understand there is a certain urgency connected to your case."

Duquette took two steps back and called out into a corridor: "Gentlemen?"

Two burly, stupid-looking men walked in, their heels clicking menacingly on the stone floor.

"If you would help place Captain Grey on the rack."

The jailor had come up behind Grey, and now grabbed him around the shoulders, holding down his arms. Grey shrugged him off, wheeled around, and connected a violent right hook into the man's upper jaw. Teeth broke and flew onto the floor.

But now the two big men grabbed Grey, one at each shoulder, lifted him clean off the ground, dropped him roughly onto the torture table, wrenching Grey's arms over his head, lashing them with ropes to the windlass above him, while the jailor—bleeding from his mouth and cursing—lashed Grey's feet to the other.

"So, Captain. I will ask each of these questions just once. Do you understand?"

"No—could you repeat that?"

"One turn," said Duquette to the jailor, who was standing at the windlass by Grey's feet, who now reached for a wheel on one side, and started to turn it.

Suddenly Grey's entire body went taut. His shoulders were pulled to an unnatural angle, trying to rotate out of their sockets.

"Now you are uncomfortable, Captain. And I assure you that what you feel now is the definition of trivial compared with what will come next."

Duquette was leaned over Grey, so that Grey could see his face.

"Have you spoken to my doctor about this?" asked Grey. "I believe there was some talk of my dying from blood loss."

"Yes, I spoke to him just an hour ago," said Duquette. "He told me that, provided I didn't open any wounds, you would be no more likely to die than any other subject. But that you would be unusually slow to recuperate. You may keep that in mind, if you wish. It might save us some time. One turn."

The jailor reached again for the wheel by Grey's feet. A new course of tension ran through Grey's body. He couldn't recall his spine ever having felt so straight, or his organs so tight.

"But please do not interrupt again, just answer my questions exactly as I put them to you." Duquette stood up and walked a few feet away before turning back to face his charge.

"Captain Grey: You are an intelligence agent. True or false?"

"False."

"One turn." Now a line of agony shot through Grey's body. His elbows locked full outward. "That was a lie, Captain. Please do not lie to me again. Your luggage has been searched, and your hidden lock picks discovered. You have operated at the level of a trained clandestine soldier. You have turned over considerable, detailed information to the Maison Militaire, all of which, without a single, flawed exception, is either out of date or unverifiable. These are not the actions of a man who sells his soul for money and then suffers pangs of regret. These are the actions of a professional."

Once again, Duquette leaned over Grey:

"Do you agree or disagree?"

Grey found speaking had become difficult:

"Disagree."

"Two turns."

Agony shot through Grey's body. Something in his hips seemed to tear.

"You may scream if you like," said Duquette.

Grey opened his mouth to curse the man—but a scream was all that came out.

"Did you know, Captain," said Duquette, "that muscle which has been stretched too far for too long loses its ability to contract again? It would be a shame for you to spend the rest of your life as a jelly."

Grey drew just enough air into his lungs to hurl a single obscenity at his torturer. Duquette clucked his tongue twice and shook his head.

"We'll leave you like this for a little while. For your sake, I hope your spirits break before your spine."

In fact, the first thing to give way was Grey's consciousness. After he passed out, Duquette checked Grey's pulse, made a few notes, and then called again for his two large assistants. They dragged Grey back up to his cell, led by the jailor's torch, four flights up the turret stair, and dropped him on the cell floor.

GREY WAS BACK in Malta. He looked to his right. There was Paulette, curled in her favorite window seat, reading a duodecimo, letting the salt breeze wash through her hair.

Grey looked at his hands—covered in grease, holding a fine brush as he cleaned powder out of the lock of a pistol.

"Come here, love," said Paulette, smiling at him with some deep inner glow.

"I'll get you filthy, my dear—look at me." He held up his palms.

"Oh, never mind that," said Paulette. "Come read with me."

"What is it?" asked Grey, nodding to the book, wiping his hands on a rag.

"*Twelfth Night*," said Paulette. "Come, sit beside me. Read the duke's part. He's telling Viola, who loves him, who is disguised as a man, to convey his, the duke's, love to the Countess Olivia."

Grey shook his head and chuckled. "Very well, love. Where?"

She pointed to the page.

"Once more, Cesario—get thee to yond same sovereign cruelty . . ."

"But if she cannot love you, sir?" asked Paulette.

"I cannot so be answered."

"Sooth, but you must! Say that some lady, as perhaps there is, hath for your love as great a pang of heart as you have for Olivia: you cannot love her, you tell her so. Must she not then be answered?"

"Make no compare between that love a woman can bear me and that I owe Paulette—there is no woman's sides can bide the beating of so strong a passion as love doth give my heart; no woman's heart so big, to hold so much; they lack retention—alas—their love may be called *appetite*, but mine is all as hungry as the sea and can digest as much."

"Ay," said Paulette, "but I know—"

"What dost thou know?"

"*Too well* what love women to men may owe: In faith they are as true of heart as we—my father had a daughter loved a man . . ."

"And what's her history?"

"A blank, my lord. She never told her love, but let conceal-ment, like a worm in the bud, feed on her damask cheek: she pined in thought, and with a green and yellow melancholy, she sat like patience on a monument . . . smiling at grief. Was not this love, indeed?" asked Paulette. "We men may say more, swear more, but indeed our shows are more than will. For still we prove much in our vows, but little in our love."

THE CLOCK UPBRAIDS ME *with the waste of time . . .* When Grey came to, there was a thought already fixed in his mind: he had to escape before he broke. He couldn't trust himself to endure too many more interrogations like today's. If he were to admit to being an English intelligence agent, the questions would turn to His Majesty's secret sources of information all over the Continent. He'd used his time in Malta to expand his remit too far. He knew too much. He had set up too many networks that spread from the Adriatic back to Paris. He was a damned fool for having allowed himself into this position.

He had to escape, or he had to die. There was no third option.

The first thing Grey did—even as every muscle in his body screamed for him to lie still—was tear a bit of bloody cloth off his tattered shirt and stuff it into the cell door's peephole. It would be noticed, of course, by the first guard who happened past, and no doubt some sort of retaliatory beating would follow, but its discovery and removal would give him a few extra ticks of time to hide his more sophisticated machinations.

Next. Metal screws had been ubiquitous in England since before he'd been born. Had they reached the Continent? Continentals tended to be backward in matters of industry, and Grey had never had any particular reason to investigate how they were fastening their wood before . . .

He picked up the latrine bucket and squinted at its joins. Not screws: nails. Savages. Less than ideal. But workable.

He tried to get a purchase on one with his fingernail. No good. Smashing would get the nails out, and probably bring the cavalry running down the hall. He couldn't risk it. But the bucket's bottom . . . it was soft, slightly rotted. Rotted by whatever had been left to sit in it.

Grey overturned the bucket so it was top up, and—gingerly—stood on it. It bowed slightly in the middle, but didn't break. He stepped off.

The corner of his bed was a right angle of hard wood. He held the bucket's bottom against it and gradually moved his feet backward, pushing his whole weight on the bucket, and through the bucket, onto that single point of wood. He pushed, hard as he could, looking like a man trying to start his carriage out of a ditch.

He felt the bucket's bottom start to go . . . He pushed with every fiber of himself . . . and *crack*, the bottom splintered and shattered.

God. Had it been as loud as he imagined? Like the report of a signal cannon? He waited. No footsteps outside.

Now it was a small matter for Grey to wrench out the rest of the bucket's broken bottom, and then to force out the nails that had been holding it in place along the bucket's bottom edge: eight three-inch nails, set forty-five degrees apart. He held them in his hand like so many pearls, replaced the bucket as it had been, made everything look quite normal. He carried his pearls to the window.

The bars—there were two of them—had been added to the windows long after the building's construction. Troughs had been drilled into the stone sill and the bars cemented in place with some kind of concrete. He would have preferred the threads of screws for filing it away. With nails, the concrete would have to be gouged out. But there was no sense complaining.

Two hours and four blunted iron nails later, Grey's knuckles were raw and bloody, but he was quite pleased with his progress. Soon the left bar's cementing would be diminished enough for him to wrench it inward. And if he could get it out of its bottom seating, the top would fall free. Then he could use the first bar to pry out the second.

Then—suddenly—there was some commotion behind him, out in the hall. He heard Duquette's voice ordering the jailor to remove the obstruction to the peephole. Did Grey dare grab the bar, try to pull it out in one jerk? Stuff himself through the narrow gap and try to scale the wall outside? If he failed, there would be no second chance.

But could he hold out through another session on the rack?

He would have to. Better torture than failure . . . assuming he could keep from breaking. He had just time enough to blow away the cement dust and throw the nails under his bed before the door opened.

This time there was no invitation to follow; Mr. Duquette simply waved his two trolls into the room. They grabbed Grey without a word and dragged him down to the cellar, to the torture chamber.

They threw him roughly onto the rack and tied him down, and quickly Duquette resumed his questions.

"Are you a spy, sir, yes or no?"

"No."

"Five turns."

Grey bit his tongue as long as he could, and then started to scream.

DEPOSITED BACK in his cell in a heap, Grey was completely unable to move for several minutes. He had the not-at-all-comical feeling of being a lump of dough someone had thrown down on a baker's table, slowly regaining its form. As his muscles began to reawaken—ascending from numbness to agony—Grey began to pull himself towards his wooden bed, under which he'd tossed his precious tools. His precious escape tools, his only salvation—damn it, where were they?—the nails for chiseling away the cement. He groped, near hopelessly, in the pitch-darkness, ineffectually sliding his arms back and forth. He was confused. Had he been asleep? When had daylight passed him by? Was this an eternal night? Was this hell? He'd lost all sense of time besides the tick-tick-tick in his mind, telling him the deadline for liberty or death was fast approaching.

A guard came in behind him—Grey hadn't heard the door open; he only heard the man's laughter at what must have looked like the convulsions of an insane man. The guard left, and with difficulty Grey looked over his shoulder. A bowl of gruel and another of water had been left for him. He dragged himself towards them, gulped down the water, forced down some of the food, and fell into a semi-sleep, from which he was only able to shake himself at the sound of another screaming man, somewhere below him—the screams wafting up the stairs, seeping under the door to Grey's cell like poison vapor.

Grey's right fist was clenched. It took a moment to remember why. Yes: the nails were in there. He opened the fist. Some of the nails, anyway. Six of them. Two blunt. He shook his head, trying to clear out some cobwebs, tossed the two blunts away, and began, with the agility of a newborn baby, to get to his feet.

Chip-chip-chip. Here he was back at the grindstone, back gouging out infinitesimal pieces of concrete. But God in heaven he was close. At the front of his hole, he could see where the bar ended. He put the nails into his mouth, the way a seamstress holds needles, then grabbed the bar firmly with both hands, placed one foot on the wall, and yanked the damned thing with all his might.

The bar didn't move. He pulled again. Again it didn't move.

He adjusted his grip, put two feet on the wall, and tried once more—straining every wounded sinew of his abused body.

CRASH. He and the bar flew across the room. His thrill at success was dampened by the certainty that he had been heard. The clock in his head started to tick faster.

He ran back to the window and, using the right vertical of the window frame as a fulcrum, began to pry the second bar out.

Come on, damn you! He felt sure some vein in his head was going to explode . . . COME ON, DAMN YOU! GIVE IT EVERYTHING YOU'VE GOT! HEAVE! HEAVE!

CRASH! Out came the second bar; onto the floor tumbled Grey—and open flew the door to his cell.

"DROP THAT!" shouted the voice of the jailor, and the foot of one of Duquette's big men came down on Grey's left hand, the hand that was holding his window pry bar.

"Get up," said Duquette. The cell was crowded now with the four Frenchmen and Grey.

Grey coughed—coughed the nails he held in his mouth into his right hand.

As he pretended to struggle to his feet, Grey moved the nails

around in his fist, arranging them so that three were pointing outward from between his fingers.

"Get him up," said Duquette, to one of his trolls.

As the man pulled Grey to his feet, Grey punched him in the side
of the neck—pushed the nails into his throat and jugular vein, then
pulled them out again.

The man started to scream; the second of Duquette's big men
swung at Grey's head; Grey ducked, and punched the nails into his
thigh. The second big man screamed, and Grey punched again, an
uppercut, jamming the nails into the bottom of the big man's jaw,
and a third time, into the side of his head.

That was where the nails stuck—protruding from the man's skull.

The jailor grabbed Grey and threw him to the floor. Grey came
up again with one of the iron bars, which he crashed into the side of
the jailor's neck, loudly snapping it.

Three men lay dead or dying at Grey's and Duquette's feet . . .
Duquette, who had stood, pale as a sheet, watching the whirlwind
fight unfold.

"Not much use in a tussle, are we, Mr. Duquette?"

Duquette, eyes wide in terror, said nothing.

"Come along," said Grey—grabbing Duquette by the shoulders,
with the energy of sudden action still coursing through his body.

Having had its bars pried away, the window was now beautifully
open, and Grey was dangling Duquette out into the crisp, airy night.

"Now," said Grey, "I will ask each of these questions just once. Do
you understand?"

"Yes!" screamed Duquette.

"Good. You work for the security committee of the Maison Militaire, is that correct?"

"Yes! I am under orders—I only follow orders! You must
believe me!"

"Shut up. Where does the committee meet?"

"I don't know!"

"You'd better think; those paving stones down there look very hard."

"I don't know, I swear it! I'm a low-level servant, just a functionary! I have never met with them!"

"All right," said Grey, "I believe you."

Duquette dropped like a sack of meal. He must have fainted when he felt Grey's grip loosen, because he fell silently.

Grey cursed—he hadn't meant to drop the man. He'd wanted Duquette's clothes . . . everything else would be dripping with blood. But he was so damned tired, so tired. And with much still to do before any prospect of rest.

Grey appropriated the dead jailor's shirt; it was the least bloody of the four, including his—which, in any case, was all in tatters. The jailor's jacket, meanwhile, proved tight, but not impossibly so. The rest of the man's clothes, and the clothes of the two trolls, were stripped off; Grey made a rope of them, which he tied to one of the bars. The bar was only slightly longer than the window was wide. Grey hoped it wouldn't slip out of place as he descended.

With one last, wistful look at the hard wooden bed—which was calling to Grey like a siren on a rocky shore; calling him to sleep— Grey pulled himself, legs first, through the window; pulled the bar into place behind him; and began gingerly to descend, through the darkness, to the street below.

Hand under hand, foot under foot, walking down the wall, bearing in mind that he had dropped Duquette and could just as easily drop himself.

And then the bottom, where he let go of the rope and fell the last few feet, onto his torturer's corpse. Lucky no one had found it yet. Lucky it looked like one of so many drunks asleep in the gutters of Paris.

Grey resisted the impulse to wish Duquette better luck next time, tightened the jailor's jacket around his shoulders, and walked off into the misty Paris night.

20

WHEN GREY HAD attended that coming-out party with Branson, the debutante ball—God, it seemed such a long time ago—Branson had provided the footman at the door with his invitation, and in the process, had provided Grey with Branson's Paris address.

It was a bit of a walk, up the hill towards Saint-Georges. Not the finest neighborhood, or, under the circumstances, the most aptly named. Evidently the French government was not too concerned with making its Celtic guests feel welcome.

An interesting change to Paris since Grey had been there last—part of Bonaparte's reforms, no doubt: the houses were all numbered, and quite prominently. What a shame to lose the chaos of these lesser arrondissements, the glorious laissez-faire of sub-royal Paris. But no time to regret the march of progress. At least it made finding Branson's apartment simple.

The sound of two men walking past him, speaking Irish, told Grey he was going in the right direction.

Branson's address belonged to the second floor of a two-story wooden building with an exterior stair; Grey climbed it silently and put his ear to Branson's door, checking to make sure the man wasn't hosting a late-night Irish rebels' Tennis Court Oath.

Satisfied that if Branson was there at all, he was asleep, Grey knocked on the door. A casual knock. No need to frighten him in the middle of the night. It wasn't certain that the news of Grey's perfidy had filtered down this far: Branson might still see him as a friend. Or, anyway, as a mercenary ally.

Grey had to keep up the knocking for nearly a minute before, finally, he was rewarded by the sounds of a sleepy man shuffling about to find a candle and matches.

Then the sound of a match striking; gentle light under the door, and then the door opened.

Branson's face showed unguarded surprise.

"Captain Grey? What on earth . . ."

"May we step inside, Mr. Branson? I'm afraid there's quite a draft out here."

Did those eyes narrow slightly? Was there a hint of anger in them?

"Yes, certainly. Come in."

Grey stepped across the threshold and looked around. Like Branson, the room was rather too point-device in its accoutrements; slightly dandyish. It crossed Grey's mind that Branson might be a homosexual. The threat of blackmail might preempt something more violent, if Branson had been informed of Grey's duplicitous purpose. But the thought was quickly shelved as a girl in her later teenage years emerged from what Grey presumed was Branson's bedroom. Just as well: it might have been useful, but Grey found coercion of that sort to be, somehow, far more objectionable than violence. To kill a man is one thing—to intrude in his private life is something altogether different.

The girl said something to Branson in Irish; he shook his head at her, and said in French, "Go back to bed, my dear." Then he turned to Grey:

"Take a seat, Captain—what can I do for you? I confess to being confused by your presence here; Captain d'Aumont didn't inform me of your plans to return to the city. Even if he had, I'm not sure why you would come here. Or even how you know where I live—I believe I would recall having told you."

Grey took a seat on a chaise lounge; Branson sat opposite him in an Orkney chair.

"D'Aumont sent me. You see, a British agent has infiltrated the French security apparatus. He feared I might be a target of assassination, so he sent me here. To lie low, so to speak, until the road ahead is clear."

"I see," said Branson. "Well, what can I do for you? Would you like a glass of something?"

"Actually," said Grey, "I've just had a most important revelation— a thought as to how French single-deckers might be able to run the English blockades, something to do with their patterns of tacking and wearing on patrol. It hadn't occurred to me till now, and it might be significant. I'm most anxious to inform the security committee."

"I see," said Branson.

"But I have no way of reaching them, or d'Aumont, in fact. What with your being my liaison, I thought you might bring my news to them."

Branson nodded. "Yes, of course. Of course, though, they won't be in session at this time of night."

"No, of course not," said Grey. "But perhaps tomorrow. Do you know where they meet? I should have asked d'Aumont, had this thought occurred to me sooner."

"I doubt he would have told you; you know how the French are about this all, since the Thermidor Reaction"—when much of the old, Robespierrist security apparatus had been murdered in a coup d'état, of sorts.

"Quite," said Grey. "Quite. But *you* know?"

Grey and Branson locked eyes. Yes, Branson knew all right. He knew that Grey was not what he claimed to be. There were those eyes narrowing again.

"Yes. Here, let me get you a drink," said Branson, standing, turning towards a drinks cabinet.

"That isn't necessary, thank you," said Grey. (In fact, in his condition, a single drink would probably have put him under the table.)

"No, I insist," said Branson, opening the rosewood cabinet, reaching inside, twisting rapidly around, and pointing a pistol at Grey's head. Or where Grey's head had been.

Grey was already on the move, dropping low, tackling forward, meeting Branson's gut with his shoulder. Branson brought the pistol butt down on Grey's back; Grey was throwing him to the floor, grabbing his right hand—Branson's shooting hand—hammering it on the ground. Once, twice, three times—the Irishman's grip loosened; the pistol clattered out of his hand and onto the floor. Grey slid it away, back towards the chaise. Branson connected with the same hand, his right, into Grey's throat, and then his jaw. Grey recoiled, and Branson pushed him up and off; rolling away, reaching for the gun.

Grey was back on his feet—he kicked the gun further away; at the same time, Branson grabbed Grey's other foot, pulled him off balance, got to his feet as Grey fell down; kicked Grey in the stomach. He attempted a second kick; Grey caught Branson's foot and threw him backward, onto a coffee table—it shattered to splinters under him. Now Grey was swiveling his head about, looking for the pistol—which he found, in the hands of the girl from Branson's bedroom. She had it pointed at Grey's head. This time, where Grey's head still was.

He froze. So did Branson, amidst the remnants of his furniture, looking dazed. For a moment everything stopped. The girl pulled the trigger—

Nothing. It didn't fire. Grey took two steps towards the girl and swiped the gun from her hands.

"Forgive me," he said, and punched her lightly in the jaw, knocking her unconscious. He caught her as she fell, and draped her slip of a body into the Orkney chair, which had somehow managed to stay standing throughout the fracas.

Grey turned to Branson, who was still on his haunches.

"She didn't cock it," said Grey, pulling back the pistol's flintlock and taking a bead on Branson's face. "Now. Where were we? I believe you were going to tell me where the security committee meets."

Branson started to push himself back to his feet.

"Don't get up," said Grey.

"What the hell good will knowing where the committee meets do you?" asked Branson. "What do you plan, to attend a meeting? Or will you just assassinate its members? Who all have several-man bodyguards."

"A plan has been drawn up for the invasion of England. D'Aumont has received a copy; I assume the other staff members have received copies as well. And you will agree, I'm sure, that there is certain to be a copy on file in the committee's office. This has been a night of ultimata; nevertheless, I will make you this offer: If you will help me obtain the invasion plan, I will guarantee you a ministerial pardon for your role, whatever it may have been, in the rising of '98, and a free passage back to Ireland."

Branson sneered. "Better death," he said, "than to live in a captive Ireland."

"Yes," said Grey. "I expected you to say that."

Branson cleared his throat.

"If you're going to kill me now, let me stand first."

"I'm not going to kill you. If you will give me the committee's address, and your word not to interfere, I will accept your parole."

In this rather bloody and uncivilized war, at least one shred of chivalry had survived: the practice of a surrendering gentleman giving his word to refrain from further belligerence, and that word being accepted at face value. He was then free to return to his home and carry on with his life—honorably abstaining from any participation, direct or indirect, in the fight—until such time as an on-paper prisoner exchange freed him to return to service.

"In this case," Grey continued, "being, as it were, a captive of circumstance—I will deem myself to be your opposite number. Once I'm out of the picture, you might consider yourself free from your obligation."

Branson took a few moments to consider. Grey's appeal to his sense of honor had caught him off guard.

"Very well," said Branson. "I accept, and give you my parole. The committee meets in a building on the Rue de l'Université, on the

Rive Gauche, where it becomes the Rue Jacob. The name on the building is 'l'École Nationale d'Histoire Militaire.' Much good may it do you. You'll never make it inside alive."

"Thank you, Mr. Branson." Grey uncocked the pistol. "I'm afraid I'm going to take this," he added, slipping the gun into his jacket pocket.

"How I wish I'd never laid eyes on you, Captain Grey," said Branson.

"If you had never laid eyes on me, Mr. Branson, I would now be sleeping in the sun on a New England beach. But no man's the master of fate. Good morning, Mr. Branson."

"Good morning, Captain Grey."

"Morning" was a generous description; the sky outside was still perfectly black; however, it was close enough to dawn that to get across the Seine to the Rive Gauche . . . no, there wasn't enough time. At least, Grey hoped there wasn't: the alternative was that he was lying to himself, as an excuse to sleep. But either way, to sleep was where he was going.

Fortunately, Saint-Georges is quite filled with disorderly houses, which are quite happy to accept customers at any time of the night, without feeling the need to pry into anyone's business. Grey went into the first brothel he came to. He found the morning mistress—a woman of perhaps fifty—leaning over a desk at the center of a bare wooden room, playing patience.

She looked up at him as he came in, raised an eyebrow at his tousled clothes and hair, then looked back down at her cards.

"You want a girl?" she asked.

"No," he said. She raised another eyebrow.

"Just a bed, thank you. Though I'm happy to pay for both."

"How long do you want it for?" asked the mistress.

"Have you the time?" asked Grey.

The mistress sighed just loudly enough to make it clear that she was not in the mood for this sort of trivial negotiating. She removed a chain from around her neck, found the key dangling from it, and unlocked a drawer in her desk. Inside was a silver pocket watch, which she removed and squinted at.

"Half past four," she said.

"Then," said Grey, "let us say sixteen hours."

"Sixteen hours? What are you, a man, or a bear in winter?"

"I assume," said Grey, pulling the dead jailor's purse out of his relinquished jacket, "that you'd like to be paid in advance?"

"I would. It will be a sou an hour."

"Very good," said Grey, handing the woman a gold franc. "There's for twenty hours. Have a nap on my account."

She didn't smile. "Take number twelve, last on the left"—nodding over her shoulder—"it isn't locked."

Grey politely bowed his thanks and started down the corridor. "Have a girl wake me up at eight this evening, won't you?"

"As you wish. Blonde or brunette?" said the mistress, dryly.

Grey looked back at her. Now she was smiling. He chuckled.

"Surprise me. Or come yourself." He winked. She shook her head and went back to her cards, saying just loudly enough for him to hear:

"It takes all types, doesn't it?"

Inside of three minutes, Grey—confident of his anonymity and feeling reasonably safe—was sound asleep, and deeply dreaming.

21

Paulette Grey wiped her brow and reached down among her gelding's saddlebags for a waterskin. It had been three days' ride through the dry, brown, rock- and brush-covered Moroccan desert from Mogador, and she felt she had inhaled enough sand and dust to cough out a beach. But finally, this morning—not half an hour after the tents had been taken down and rolled up—the peaks of the High Atlas Mountains had peaked over the horizon. Now, ahead of her, high up on the slopes, there was a stripe of green: a thick and shockingly incongruous forest enveloping the mountaintops. For three days they had seen no animals but snakes and scurrying lizards. Now there were circling birds—bearded vultures, she thought—and they meant good things to come. Not in the sense of augury, God forbid. Where there were vultures, there were carcasses; where there were dead animals, there were live ones. Bears, boars, deer, monkeys of types she'd never before seen—some likely unknown to science. And how she longed to see a leopard, or a Barbary lion!

Along with two able seamen and a marine—from the crew of *Constance*, the sloop that had brought her and her husband from Malta—Paulette was being led towards the mountains by a Berber desert guide, with a second Berber along to interpret. The marine had, in very game fashion, caught or shot one of every lizard they'd come across, for Paulette to skin, dissect, and examine each evening. Now he carried some of those skins and dozens of little skeletons in his own saddlebags. He'd insisted at the outset that he would keep them close at hand, rather than relegating them to the tent-bearing pack mules—skeletons being quite fragile. Paulette had thanked him for the notion, but warned him that they would start to stink most horribly. He had insisted also that, as a solider, he was unfrightened of smells. Now, on the morning of the fourth day of their journey, his face betrayed his discomfort. The rising sun began to beat down in earnest, and her collection had resumed putrefying. His was the last horse in their convoy; Paulette slowed slightly and waved the two seamen past so she could ride beside him.

"Lieutenant Gillum," she said to the marine, who was now attempting an expression of pure stoicism, "lasting this long with my samples hanging about your shins would be counted among Hercules's most trying trials. But you've done enough. Let me hang those bags among the tent poles; they'll be fine."

"Nonsense, Mrs. Grey," he said, with the slightly hoarse voice of a man who has been breathing too shallowly. "I could ride them all the way across the continent. To the Gulf of Aden."

"Gallant of you, Lieutenant, but I'm sure that won't be necessary. I hate to pull rank on you, but I'm afraid I must insist: hand them over."

Paulette extended a graceful hand, and the marine grinned at her cocked smile.

"If you insist, Mrs. Grey, I will relieve myself of them. But allow me to attend to it."

She acceded with a nod. "Just as you say." He slowed to match pace with the mules, and she spurred her gelding to a slightly faster trot, heading back to the head of the column. "Don't think your efforts have gone unappreciated!" she said, over her shoulder.

Gillum touched a knuckle to his brow in the traditional seaman's salute. "My duty, madam."

Back at the front of the line, the guide Aziz said something to the interpreter Hamza, who translated: "Aziz say, missus, that by midday we be upon the foothills, and before nightfall, at Oasis Aderdour."

"Thank you, Hamza," she said, inclining her head to each of the two men in turn. "Please ask him to keep an especial lookout for mammal tracks as we get near."

"Yes, missus; Aziz say that leopards home at Aderdour. They property of pasha, not hunted by Muslim or Sahwari men, only by pasha's people like missus, and lion too. Many there. Many many."

Paulette felt the excitement rise up into her throat. "Thank him for me, Hamza, would you?"

"I thank him already, missus. If I embarrass him, we slow down." He laughed; so did Paulette.

The Oasis Aderdour began as a rivulet running out of a crack in a gravelly stone escarpment, flowing down to a very small spring-pond—no more than twenty feet at its widest point, and vaguely triangular in shape. However, as they were still half a dozen miles below the mountain's rain line, this first glimpse of moisture at the edge of the desert was enough to make the surrounding hillside lush and green, like an emerald set in sandstone.

Above the gravel slope was another wide band of desert, and beyond that, the legendary cedar forest of the High Atlas Mountains. A mist of romance seemed to roll out of the trees, down the slope, towards the camp. Which was, as she looked about, rising up around her.

The two seamen were setting up Paulette's tent—an elaborate, embroidered four-pole affair; a gift from the pasha whom her husband Tom was now waiting upon—while Lieutenant Gillum and the two Barbary men set up their own, less impressive shelters.

"Ho!" cried Aziz, pointing at something, gesturing to Hamza, who went over to him. They spoke together briefly, debating some point, then Hamza called to Paulette:

"Missus, there are tracks here, a she-leopard and a cub! Aziz says two cubs. He is wrong."

Paulette walked quickly to the spot where Aziz and Hamza were now locked in aggressive debate about the nature of the set (or sets) of smaller, cub's prints.

As soon as she could get a word in, Paulette asked—

"How fresh are they?"

Hamza translated the question, and the debate's subject changed.

"Aziz say less than half a day. He is wrong. They are very fresh, less than an hour."

"Could we catch up with them?"

Hamza asked Aziz; Aziz answered and Hamza snorted at him.

"Leopards hunt in night and sleep during day—they only awake now because we come. Aziz say maybe we could catch them, but they will be hiding again. Very hard to find in day. Hard to see, they look like wood and rocks. They have spots. Also Aziz is afraid. He does not say it but I see in his eyes."

"Yes," said Paulette. "I understand."

"I can help you, ma'am, if you like," said Lieutenant Gillum, who had arrived at the edge of the conversation. "I've hunted tiger on the Indian station and lions at the Cape, I don't think I'll have any trouble following these"—he gestured with his foot to the tracks. "Big cat spoor is old hat to me. And it is my duty to supervise, and keep you from harm."

"That's most kind of you, Lieutenant—but I fear trespassing too far on your sense of duty. You needn't feel compelled to tackle a leopard."

"Fear not, Mrs. Grey—I assure you, the pleasure will be mine. I'm no naturalist, but I do enjoy a good fight with a beast who knows how to fight back. Even numbers, you know, are even rarer in a hunt than in a sea fight."

"If you're certain, then, let us set off at once; tide and time wait on no man, Thomas—Mr. Grey—always says. Waste not a moment."

"Only let me load the guns, ma'am, and I am with you. We'll go on foot."

. . .

The spoor was good and the trail was clear, but it was long: after keeping to the edge of the oasis and running orthogonally to the slope, the leopards' tracks turned upward, crossing the last miles of arid desert beneath the tree line, and slipping into the distinctly alpine forest.

Here at the forest's edge, Paulette and the lieutenant stopped to catch their breaths, and for a conclave on their pursuit. The shadows were getting long and the sun would soon dip behind one of the southern peaks. Paulette asked Gillum if, were they to follow the trail further, he would be able to retrace their path in the dark.

Gillum smiled a smile of supreme confidence and assured her he would.

"Then lead on," she said, hoping the man wasn't letting his hubris run away with him—but willing to take that chance, in order to see her *Panthera pardus.*

Stepping into the woods was like stepping into a fairy-tale menagerie; all at once, the two Englishmen were surrounded by a swirl of tropical-seeming birds of every color. The trees were not overthick—this was no jungle—and yet the intensity of their green, and the green of the tall grass encompassing them, seemed more appropriate to the River Plate (or to a fresco, thought Paulette) than to a place surrounded by valleys of dry bones.

Mrs. Grey was less an ornithologist than she might have been; her study ran more towards the beasts of the field; yet this was an undeniable wonderland. Larks of a dozen plumages, swallows and thrushes, warblers, flycatchers, finches, egrets—egrets? Yes— waterbirds, everywhere. Bitterns, herons, egrets, ibises shooting overhead in great, unconcerned crowds. Where were they coming from? The answer came after a few more thickets had been pushed through: a watering hole, a very large one—a lake, really—with its surface half covered by flamingos. A shock of pink.

Paulette edged along the water, brushing past reeds growing on the shore, climbing over some low boulders, feeling glad she had chosen to change into her duck trousers while Gillum had loaded his rifles.

And then suddenly: there they were. The leopard cubs. Two of them, playing in a small tributary pool, splashing and wrestling. O brave new world, that has water-loving cats in it! Then behind her:

The sound of sawing? A low grumble . . . building to a roar. Paulette spun around, just in time to see the mother leopardess charge at her through the tall grass. Paulette wore a knife on her belt—not a large one—it was for taking floral specimens—better than nothing—but her mind of reflex told her there was no time to unsheathe it—

The leopardess was still charging—roared again; leapt into the air—

Then the BANG of a gunshot, and the animal was thrown backward, tumbling, scrambling back to its feet, issuing a loud whine and disappearing into the brush with its children beside it.

And there was Lieutenant Gillum, acrid smoke wafting out the barrel of his gun, saying something to her, lips moving—no sound—ringing in her ears.

"Are you all right?" he repeated.

"Yes, God, thank you, I'm fine. Damned stupid of me, should have known the second I saw the kittens."

Her heart was pounding; after a long climb with little water and no food, she felt suddenly very faint. She wobbled on her feet; the lieutenant caught her and guided her softly to the sandy ground, kneeling beside her and adopting an expression of concern as he searched her face.

"Are you certain you're all right?"

She smiled at him gratefully. "I am," she said. "Thanks to you."

He smiled back at her, leaned slightly forward, kissed her on the mouth.

She recoiled, twisted her head away. "I am *married*, Lieutenant. As you well know."

He leaned forward again, this time kissing her neck, now running his hand up her leg, up her thigh—

"Stop! *Stop it!*" she screamed at him. He pushed her to the ground, began to yank at her trousers.

She screamed again—no words this time, just a guttural scream of hatred and anger. For a split second she fantasized the leopard might return—she fought away the hand at her waist, at her thighs—she reached down—the knife was in her hand, slipping out of its scabbard—

She thrust it into his neck. Now he was screaming—rolling off her—struggling to his feet—falling to his knees at the water's edge—falling face-forward, with a splash—a narrow stream of blood, now thickening, mixing into the fresh water.

And she was panting, panting, trying to catch her breath.

It was long after dark when Paulette stumbled back into the oasis camp. Of the other four men in her party, just one was there— one of the seamen, instructed to stay in case Paulette and Gillum reappeared. The other sailor and the two Berbers were searching for them. The seaman fired a shot in the air; the signal that they'd been found. Or, anyway, that Mrs. Grey had.

When the others returned and Paulette had composed herself, she told them that Lieutenant Gillum had been killed by a mother leopard defending her cubs.

But after their return to Mogador, Paulette told her husband the whole story, omitting no detail. From the cold, steely hatred in his eyes, she could feel keenly Tom's regret at not being able to kill Gillum personally. She could see too that he was directing much of his hatred at himself, for his choice of an escort for her, for his having allowed her to come at all.

When, less than a week after that, she was dead, the image of the French captain of the French ship that killed her—the image supplied by Grey's imagination—wore the face of Lieutenant Gillum.

The image persisted until he clapped eyes on Jean-Anne d'Aumont; the thing itself. Yet in his dream, their features were confused, mixed up, like a portrait whose subject had been changed halfway through the painting.

22

A SHARP KNOCKING ON the door pulled Grey out of his long dream; a voice from outside the door called, "It's eight o'clock, sir," and Grey tried to return himself to the land of the living, after sixteen hours of sleeping like the dead. He could still see Paulette's face, pained, red with such utterly undeserved shame, telling him about the animal Gillum. As Grey swung his legs over the side of the bed and felt around for his boots, he tried to put it out of his mind. Though if nothing else, the long rest had refreshed his desire for revenge. Killing Gillum—not Gillum; d'Aumont— killing d'Aumont was a consummation devoutly to be wished. He wouldn't have to wait much longer.

But first, to have a look at the work of the Committee for State Security. Duty first. He sighed—yawned—pulled on his shirt, and stood, ignoring the defeatist groans of his musculature. Duty first. There was something about duty that Paulette had said to him once, needling him when he was off to Illyria on some mission or other. He couldn't quite remember. Every subject's duty is the king's, but every subject's soul is his own, something like that. But she always had been three-quarters heretic.

He went out to the corridor, where he found a healthy flow of customers and girls coming and going. He bid adieu to the mistress at the desk—not the same woman who'd been there the previous morning—and stepped out into another Paris night.

It was an hour's walk to the Rue de l'Université, and another ten minutes to arrive at its change to the Rue Jacob. Here was a slightly busy cluster of buildings, half a dozen on each side of the street, bearing various academic names. What studious students to be leaving their libraries only at nine at night; weren't the children of the revolution supposed to be greedy and lazy? A man had set up a vending stall at the corner, and was selling tobacco and paper to the departing scholars. Grey bought a pouch and a few strips, and took his time rolling a cigarette as he stood across the way from the École Nationale d'Histoire Militaire, glancing casually up at it.

It was an unremarkable, though quite attractive, neoclassical building, built in the Royal Academy style, and quite close to its neighbor buildings on either side. Though it was, Grey saw, the only building on the street that was separated at all from its neighbors—every other edifice on the block touched the building beside it, while the security building was set off by narrow alleys, of about five feet across. It was also the only building to be set back from the street, with a small courtyard separating the front door from an iron fence and a locked gate. The front door was recessed as well, in a curious rococo alcove with mirrors on either side. Half silvered, no doubt, so anyone seeking admittance could be given a thorough looking-over before the door was opened.

Clearly this was a building that had been designed with security in mind. And yet—secrecy-wise—Grey was forced to admit that it was most effective in appearance. Had he not known what he was looking for, it was unlikely that any of these details would have announced themselves to him.

Either way, the front door, as obviously well guarded as it was, could not be Grey's way in.

The next building down the street was the École Nationale de Musique, with a rather more inviting façade. At its doorway, two young men were discussing the tuning of a fiddle that one was plucking at intervals. Grey approached them and asked if one might have a light for his cigarette. When neither did, Grey shrugged and walked casually past them, into the music school.

The entrance hall was a grand baroque room with a central, hemi-circular staircase, up which Grey walked—past another couple of departing students—with the total authority of one who belonged. At its top, a short hallway led past several lecture rooms to a second, rather less graceful staircase, in its own stairwell, leading to the floors above. Grey followed it to the top, where it terminated at the base of a ladder, which led to a trapdoor and the roof.

After a quick check to make sure that there was no one around and no one following him, Grey ascended, careful to keep the lively rooftop breeze from loudly snapping the trap shut again.

The music school and the security building were the same height, which gave Grey a good look at his goal: invisible from the street, the edge of the security building was "ornamented" with faux-decorative, vaguely Venetian spikes, there to prevent anyone from doing what Grey had planned to do: jump the gap. Grey returned to the trapdoor and climbed back down to the music school's top floor.

The corridor that led away from the stairwell was lined with offices. Grey walked along the row of doors whose windows would be facing the security committee's building, trying their knobs, finding them all locked. The last door belonged to the office furthest back from the street, and furthest from the stairwell—which, Grey hoped, would reduce the chance of his being heard: he stepped back a few paces, charged the door, and threw his shoulder into it.

The lock snapped, the door flew open, and Grey followed it into the office. He was in a small, dark room, lit only by a window, which was, fortunately, quite large. It clasped in the middle; Grey opened it, and looked across to the *école d'histoire militaire*. The window at which Grey stood faced a window belonging to the security building, almost but not quite directly across. There was about five or six feet worth of empty space between them, four stories up.

Grey turned to the desk in the center of the office, which was stacked with staff paper and notes. Grey selected a good, solid paperweight—polished stone, about the size of a cricket ball—took aim, and let fly.

Crash went the glass of the target window. About two-thirds of it, anyway. Grey grabbed a second paperweight, and with a second throw, cleared out the remainder.

He put his foot up on the sill of the music school window . . . he would have to measure his steps carefully. Now he backed up, till he was standing at the office door, took a deep breath, and ran forward—planting his foot on the sill and pushing off, hurling himself out into air.

Time seemed to slow down.

He flew through the smashed-open window and landed in a heap, amidst shards of broken glass.

Grey got to his feet and dusted himself off. He let out a long, relieved breath and examined his surroundings:

He was standing in a large room, much longer than it was wide. It ran the entire length of the building, front to back. It might have been unpleasantly dark, thanks to a maroon motif that extended to the painted ceiling, but the dim light coming in from the three walls of windows was reflected; concentrated; amplified by the fourth wall, which was covered in mirrors—each the same size as the wall's large central door, in individual bossed bays. The mirror-wall bounced the light back and forth with smaller mirrors tucked into the gaps between the other walls' windows. This was a room, thought Grey, that had been decorated by a man who missed Versailles. Or possibly by one who had spent too much time in expensive bordellos.

In the room's center was a long, narrow, oval table, surrounded by high-backed chairs. So this was where the Committee for State Security met. Lucky—the door was surrounded with a leather gasket; apparently the room was soundproofed. Just as well. Grey had half expected a guard to burst through the door as he arrived through the window, alerted by the sound of glass breaking. Grey still had Branson's pistol, which meant one bullet of security. One bullet only. He was glad still to have it in reserve.

Grey's quick survey of the room suggested no strongbox, no safe, no locker. Here was a formal meeting room, not an office. Where did the committee keep its working documents? Surely there would be a file room nearby. Grey rounded the table, opened the door, and stepped through it into a small anteroom. Perhaps this was another (perhaps unintentional) sound dampener; when Grey opened the anteroom's door out to a hallway, he came face-to-back with a French guard—a soldier, in uniform. Caught unawares.

The soldier spun his head round, looking to his rear, over his shoulder, startled out of his wits. Grey grabbed him, dragged him backward, threw him to the ground, and—softly as he could—shut the door again.

Before the soldier could comprehend what was happening, Grey had Branson's pistol out and pointed at the man's forehead.

"Where is the document room?" asked Grey, in French.

"In the basement," said the soldier, almost in shock.

"How do I get there?"

"Down the stairs, to the bottom."

"Where is the stairway?"

"Down the hall on the left."

"Is there more than one?"

"No."

"How many guards?"

"A dozen, perhaps more."

"Doing what?"

"Guarding!"

"They make no rounds?"

"Only on the ground floor."

"How well do the guards know each other?"

"Not well, they change them regularly, for security. Who are you?"

"Is the document room guarded?"

"Yes."

"Is it locked?"

"Yes."

"Do you have the key?"

"No."

"Oh well."

Grey cracked the soldier across the face with Branson's pistol; the soldier slumped back, unconscious. Grey began to take off the man's clothes. The uniform would fit him. But damn it all, it smelled most unpleasant.

His new uniform was composed of white trousers and knee boots; a white shirt beneath a white-and-blue jacket, and a tall, cylindrical shako hat that Grey carried under his arm, with Branson's pistol hidden inside. He also had the soldier's musket, with a bayonet fixed, slung over his shoulder. For the first time in a long time, Grey felt adequately equipped.

Brass buttons blazing in the light of several wall torches—and the guard's candlestick, which Grey now carried—Grey walked along the corridor, into the stairwell, and downward. One floor; two; no sign yet of another guard. On the ground floor, Grey could hear soldiers' boots clicking on marble tiles as the rounds were marched, but he saw no one. Down one more flight, and Grey was on the underground level, where a single long hallway extended to a large metal door, with a guard standing before it.

Grey walked straight up to the guard, without a beat of hesitation: "I need to retrieve a document for Captain d'Aumont."

For a moment the guard said nothing; just looked at him. Grey didn't flinch, awaiting a response with his long-practiced, cool impatience.

"Well?" said the guard finally. "You have a pass?"

"Oh yes," said Grey, rolling his eyes, shaking his head. "How stupid of me."

Grey reached into his hat, searched around a moment, and once again pulled out Branson's pistol, which—in a single smooth motion—he whipped over the guard's face. The guard fell, his broken nose bleeding profusely.

Grey ran his hands along the unconscious man's belt, found a key on a stout cord, and unlocked the door. It swung outward, forcing Grey to push the unconscious man out of the way, before dragging him into the file room and safely out of sight.

Inside, Grey closed the door behind him. Before him: three rows of shelves, each about eight feet high and a dozen long, each filled with individual wooden cases, each of these carefully labeled with their contents: expense reports, background investigations, the movements of politically suspect individuals, detailings of assets— all of it domestic, unfortunately; after all, the Committee for State Security was a secret police organization. It was only through their handling of imported spies—Grey, and whatever worms Branson's circle had sifted up—that they were concerned with the foreign side of Napoleon's empire. Fortunately for Grey, the more dictatorial the tyranny, the more complete its bureaucracy—and there was a narrow file case marked "From the Maison Militaire: Plans for Future Channel Operations and Operations in England and Ireland."

Grey opened the case and leafed through its contents . . .

Here were maps and lists, just as d'Aumont's letters had suggested, of the yards building the ships, the ships carrying the troops, the troops being assigned, the units, the commanders, the supply lines, the rations, the pay requirements, everything the Little Corsican had in mind for his first foray into Britain. Plans too for an uprising in Ireland, to be backed by French troops. Damned meddlers. But this, this was priceless. In his hands, Grey was holding information that could save the lives of tens of thousands of Englishmen, and Irishmen (not to mention Frenchmen; not that Grey permitted himself to dwell on such sentimental thoughts), not to mention saving the United Kingdom and democracy in Europe. Grey carefully folded the papers—one copy of each; for some reason these people insisted on everything in triplicate—and slid them gingerly into his undershirt.

. . . Then he turned to the personnel files. Under "A," *d'Aumont,*

Capitaine Jean-Anne, adjoint de so-and-so, and the address of his Paris apartment on the Rue des Gravilliers, third arrondissement, back on the Rive Droite.

With that safely locked in his memory, there was only one thing left to do—of course, he would have loved to stay and read and pick out every detail he could, take every file that might be useful, which might very well be all of them—but he knew he might have only seconds till the absence of the guard at the door was noticed, and an alarm raised. He couldn't risk the papers he'd taken already. No, the only thing left to do was quickly to empty out a dozen or so cartridges from the powder bag of the unconscious guard, as fuel, and set the room on fire.

Once the powder was scattered carefully and extensively—once Grey was sure everything would burn—he tore a strip of paper from a random file, held it to his candle, and tossed it on the powder. As the room went up with a great *whoooooosh*, Grey hauled the unconscious guard up, over his shoulder, and ran—trundled, more like—up the hall, screaming:

"FIRE! FIRE! FIRE IN THE BASEMENT! FIRE IN THE FILE ROOM! FIRE! HELP! HELP!"

He coughed, and hacked, as chaos broke out; men in uniforms running down the stairs, fetching buckets of sand, helping him up the stairs, tending to the unconscious man.

In the confusion—and still playing the part of the smoke-injured, coughing man—Grey slipped outside for fresh air. As an alarm bell started to clang, Grey melted into the crowd of onlookers, and into the night.

23

As Thomas Grey walked away from the panicked guards and the chattering onlookers and the clatter of the arriving fire brigade, he became aware that the principal emotion he felt was not satisfaction at a job well done, or the hatred that had sustained him over the last few, trying days—but hunger. All-consuming hunger. Lord in heaven but he was hungry. Why hadn't he noticed before? His stomach had had its mind elsewhere, he supposed. Now, it could no longer be distracted. For a moment Grey had even to steady himself against a lamppost, to keep himself upright as his body dizzily evaluated itself.

Using the authority of his uniform, he flagged down a passing cabriolet—the foot traffic had all rushed up to the fire—and shouted to its driver:

"My good man, where is the nearest place to eat?"

The cabdriver looked at Grey with the special expression metropolitan natives save for out-of-towners, and jerked his thumb backward over his shoulder.

"The Palais-Royal, friend," he said. "In the cellars under the colonnade. Only place open for hot food this time of night. And it's open all the night long, with whatever other services a man like yourself might be looking for."

Quite a cheek to this man, thought Grey.

"Thank you, friend," said Grey, pushing onward, annoyed that there was nowhere to eat this side of the Seine. What was it with these Parisians and their goddamned Palais-Royal?

"You're welcome, friend," said the cabriolet driver, annoyed he hadn't been tossed a centime for his services.

It was a walk of just ten minutes—but ten excruciating minutes— to the palais, and two minutes more to find his way down into the cellars, where the choice of cafés and restaurants was, indeed, sur- prisingly extensive. And surprisingly democratic. Peasants and laborers were thoroughly mixed with craftsmen and officers. Even the upper classes were well represented, those who had come to the colonnade after the Comédie-Française let out, and, when the more discriminating, upper-level establishments had closed their doors for the evening, had not been prepared to call it a night.

Grey was in no mood to be discerning. He stepped into the first café that had an empty table, and waved over a waiter.

"Welcome, sir," said that waiter, "to the Café des Aveugles. The performance will begin in three minutes and a half; and please allow me to introduce our dishes for the evening."

"Please do," said Grey, and, before the waiter started, "What performance?"

"Why, sir, the blind orchestra. Our marvelous orchestra of the blind maestros." He seemed confused that Grey should not have known.

"Very well. The food?"

"Yes, sir," said the waiter, handing over an embossed card to Grey, then pointing to each item as he spoke: "To start, you have the choice of nine different soups, which are followed by seven sorts of pies; those who do not like pies may have oysters, by the dozen. Succeeding these are thirty-one *entrées* of wild and tame fowls, and twenty-eight of veal, mutton, and beef. We proceed then to the fish, of which there are fourteen kinds, and to join these, *entremêts* in forty- eight forms; eggs and pancakes, jellies and creams, macaronies and truffles in champagne, champignons and craws, cherries and apricots and a wide variety of fresh vegetables. And finally, should you still have a little room left, thirty-one articles of dessert will afford you an opportunity of filling it. If you are not fond of sweets—preserves, confectionary, fresh or dried fruit—perhaps you will not refuse a slice of *fromage de Rochefort, de brie, de Neufchâtel*, or even *de Cheshire*."

Cheshire! thought Grey. What industrious smugglers these gourmets employ. The waiter continued:

"And of course, to moisten these solids: twenty-two sorts of red and seventeen of white wine; seven kinds of liqueur wines, and sixteen sorts of liqueurs."

The waiter bowed from the waist.

"Is that all?" asked Grey. The waiter smiled proudly. "I'm afraid so, sir, though our chef can make something special if you like."

"Bring me a rump steak, some brie, and a pot of coffee, would you?"

The waiter frowned and—Grey thought, in the dim light—blushed slightly.

"No coffee, sir. With the blockade it is already heavily rationed."

"Never fear. Have you champagne?" The waiter brightened again.

"Yes, sir, of course, an extensive collection—" Before he could begin naming the houses, Grey cut him off.

"Château d'Aumont?"

"Yes, sir, I believe so."

"Bring me a vintage bottle, then, and I suppose you'd better make that steak a bird. The *galantine*? And bring a pot of tea."

"It will be my pleasure, sir," said the waiter, bowing again. "Straightaway."

The waiter backed away from the table, and (his exit timed perfectly) a curtain rose on the opposite wall, revealing a small stage where a string quartet began to play Vivaldi; something from *The Four Seasons*; very upbeat and evidently a crowd favorite, as a dozen or so patrons began to clap time and hum along.

As Grey sat and listened—unexpectedly rapt; the violinists were very good—a bottle of d'Aumont's champagne arrived and a voice came from the next table:

"Why, Captain Grey—I see you've accepted a commission."

Grey froze. Of course, by now, word of his escape from the Conciergerie would have spread around. Nothing he could do about it. Fortunately, he hadn't met enough people for his face to be a risk . . . So he'd thought, anyway. Grey looked to his left—

And looking back at him was Sébastien Berger, the surgeon who'd stitched his arm after the duel.

"Why, Dr. Berger—an unexpected pleasure." Grey rose from his seat slightly and bowed; the doctor did the same.

"Unexpected it should not be," said Dr. Berger. "My practice is directly above us; I often eat here after the last splash of blood has been washed away." Berger's dinner companion rolled his eyes. "Forgive me my vulgar humor, Captain Grey, allow me to introduce Mr. August von Kotzebue."

Grey nodded politely; Kotzebue nodded back: "A pleasure, Captain."

"An equal one, sir," answered Grey.

"How is your arm, Captain?" asked Berger.

"Beautifully healed, thank you." This may or may not have been true; after the racking, Grey had only a dim idea of which parts of his body were and were not working properly.

"I'm glad to hear it. Are you dining alone this evening?"

"I am, for my sins. I value a little solitude."

"Well, don't let me disturb you," said the surgeon, who had evidently had a good deal to drink, and was manifesting it in chattiness. "Though I must say I find solitude to be a most deleterious actor, professionally speaking. Our friend Jean-Anne, for instance. He makes a good show when he's called on to socialize officially, but aside from that he's become quite withdrawn since the death of his wife. I tell him he's still young, he must meet someone else. But will he listen to me? A veteran of more years than he, an old comrade-in-arms? No."

"Captain d'Aumont is a widower? I didn't know."

"Yes, I'm afraid—very common; all too common. His wife died in childbirth—and the child too—several years gone now—in the year one, I think. I tell him it's a fact of life—that maternal mortality is one-in-five; that until we defeat puerperal fever, it will remain so. I tell him death is a fact of life, a fact of birth. Will he listen? Oh well. He'll come out of it—all such do, in time. At least he hasn't any motherless children to worry about."

If Berger had anything else to say, it was cut off by a sudden increase in speed and volume from the musicians. The surgeon and his dinner companion turned back to the music; Grey looked down at his wine flute, emptied it, refilled it, and waited for his food to arrive.

IT WAS A twenty-minute walk to the building where d'Aumont lived, and a short climb up the stairs to his third-floor apartment. On the way, Grey dissected what the surgeon had told him. D'Aumont was a widower too? Well, what difference did that make. D'Aumont had lost his wife to an act of God. Grey had lost his to an act of d'Aumont's. No doubt d'Aumont would have liked to exact his vengeance on God. It was hardly Grey's fault that he wouldn't have that opportunity. At least—if Grey had his way—d'Aumont would have the chance of becoming acquainted with God very shortly.

Grey knocked on d'Aumont's door. There was no answer.

Grey knocked again.

"One moment, I'm coming," came the voice of Captain Jean-Anne d'Aumont.

A moment passed, and the door opened—as it did, d'Aumont was saying, rather curtly: "What is it? Do you know what time of night—?"

When d'Aumont saw who it was, he stopped talking. The blood rushed to his cheeks. When Grey pushed a pistol into d'Aumont's chest, it rushed out again.

"Back into your room and make not a sound," said Grey.

"When word reached me of your escape," said d'Aumont, doing as he'd been told, "I assumed—everyone did—that you'd be making for a frontier . . . traffic on the roads out of Paris is being interdicted and searched as we speak . . . What on earth could have possessed you to come here? Do you have a death wish?"

"Yes," said Grey. "But not for my own death. Sit." Using the barrel of his pistol, Grey motioned to a chair at a small, round dining table.

"And what's your obsession with me? Is this revenge for the small knife to your belly? Or does it go back further than that? Perhaps you were disappointed with our '86 vintage. We all were."

"You killed my wife," said Grey, sitting down opposite his hostage.

Silence hung heavily on the room. The two men stared at each other.

"I think not," said d'Aumont.

"My wife Paulette," said Grey, "was, with me, a passenger on a British-flagged sloop bound for Malta. The *Constance*. About a year ago. Perhaps you remember."

D'Aumont said nothing.

"Our sloop was hit by a single shot fired by the French frigate *Fidèle*. Your command, I believe."

After a moment d'Aumont said simply, "Yes, it was."

"The shot splintered one of the ship's knees as it raked her. You're a seaman, I know you've seen men die of splinter wounds."

Grey had been in his traditional place among the sloop's rigging—with a telescope and a rifle—when the shot was fired. He had left Paulette safely in the hold, and had no notion of anything being amiss until one of the ship's boys began to run up the ratlines calling for him.

In a panic, Grey had slid down a backstay, dashed through the nearest open hatch, torn past the gun crews to the cockpit, where he found Paulette still conscious—but almost unrecognizable amidst the daggers of wood protruding from her face—limbs—chest—stomach—as might be a person who had fallen onto a bed of glass.

The sloop's surgeon had done his best to close the lacerations over the arteries. There just wasn't enough time; Paulette didn't have enough time left for his attempts to make any difference. Grey had held her in his arms, told her it would be all right, as the life drained out of her, onto the sodden deck. She'd died with her eyes open, staring horrified up at him, her mouth contorted for a shout of pain she didn't have the breath to utter.

The funeral had been at sea. Grey had wanted to see Paulette buried properly, with a priest, in Sliema, but her body couldn't stand up to the heat, and his hand was forced. The sloop's captain delivered the prayer, with Paulette hidden by a Union Jack, in recognition of her service to the Crown at Grey's side.

> *. . . There is no searching of his understanding. He giveth power to the faint, and to them that have no might he increaseth strength. Even the young shall faint and be weary; the young men shall utterly fall, but they that wait upon the Lord shall renew their strength; they shall mount up with wings as eagles; they shall run and not be weary; they shall walk and not faint.*
>
> *Thou knowest, Lord, the secrets of our hearts; shut not thy merciful ears to our prayer, but spare us, Lord most holy—suffer us not, at our last hour, for any pains of death to fall from thee. Yet forasmuch as it hath pleased Almighty God in his wise providence to take out of the world the soul of this woman, we therefore commit this body to the deep, to be turned into corruption, looking for the resurrection of the body, when the sea shall give up her dead.*

Grey was looking down at the pistol in his hand. D'Aumont was looking down at it too.

"You know," said d'Aumont, in a tone hoping both to show sympathy and to solicit it, "there are always unintended casualties in war. I didn't intend to kill your wife. I didn't choose to find her aboard a vessel of war flying the flag of an enemy power. I am sorry to have played a role in her death. But surely you see that to view it as a personal act calling for personal revenge is absurd. It is illogical."

"Yes," said Grey. "I do see that." Grey sounded wistful . . . almost mournful . . . as if he were back at Paulette's funeral. After a short pause, Grey continued: "It is not, however, illogical to kill a senior staff officer in an enemy's navy."

His pistol was pointed at d'Aumont's heart, and he wanted very much to pull the trigger. After all, to find and kill this man had been the whole point of the exercise; his whole reason for coming to France. Why else had he risked life and limb, but to avenge his beloved Paulette?

Yet: like a hunter who has eagerly ridden himself ragged to bay a fox, and then cannot bring himself to break it, Grey was beginning to grasp his inability to kill d'Aumont. Grey had prized nothing in life even remotely as he had prized his wife. And yet, of the things he had still, he prized nothing so much as his own particular rectitude. What d'Aumont said was true, and to kill him would be murder. It would be, perhaps, a murder Grey would shed no tears at, hearing of it committed by another man. Grey was vengeful. He was a killer.

But he was no murderer. Here, with d'Aumont at bay, and with no more excuses to delay ending the man's life . . . perhaps it was time to stop deceiving himself. He was, simply, not going to kill the man in cold blood. Perhaps it was time to stop indulging a fantasy of finding a way to substitute anger for grief. Or of putting right things that could never be put right.

Grey set his jaw and began to lower the pistol. "I would like very much to kill you," he said to the French captain. "However, if you will give me your pa—"

Before he could get the word "parole" out of his mouth—as soon as the gun was pointed away from d'Aumont—the Frenchman shoved the table at which the two men sat, shoved it hard into Grey's gut, knocked the wind out of him. Before Grey could recover, d'Aumont had thrown the table aside and tackled him, knocked him out of his chair and onto the floor. The gun fell out of Grey's reach, and d'Aumont began to strangle him. Grey stretched his arm out, feeling for the gun . . . he couldn't turn his head to look for it; d'Aumont had his throat in a vise grip. Now Grey groped at d'Aumont's sides, trying to get hold of something he could use to pull d'Aumont off.

Instead his hand found the square shape of d'Aumont's cigar case.

Grey didn't have much time left as he slipped two fingers into the pocket that held the case. His vision was closing in to the size of a pinprick; d'Aumont now looked very far away as he straddled Grey, choking him to death.

Grey was almost unconscious as he slid out the paring knife, wrapped it in a weak fist, and stabbed it into d'Aumont's hip.

The Frenchman screamed and let go Grey's throat. Grey gasped for air, which flooded back into his lungs and brain. He took aim now at d'Aumont's throat, bringing the knife up and slicing from ear to ear.

D'Aumont's hands flew to the gash, his face instantly white. He gazed down at Grey in horror, then crumpled sideways onto the floor.

"God damn it, man," said Grey, wiping d'Aumont's blood out of his eyes, speaking to d'Aumont's corpse. "I was going to let you live."

24

AFTER WASHING OFF as much of the blood as he could, and covering d'Aumont's body with a sheet, Grey began a careful search of the apartment.

D'Aumont had no servants in his Paris home; apparently he had chosen for the metropolis a more austere, professional-soldier-esque life. Or at least, a more austere, professional-soldier-esque appearance.

The desk was locked, but it yielded to a member of a key ring Grey found in the dead man's pocket. Inside the desk were various reports of naval affairs from the Maison Militaire, which Grey placed with his other captured documents. In d'Aumont's bedroom was a wardrobe; inside it, another safe—happily, one of the regular variety, no number dials to deal with. The lock opened with a second key from d'Aumont's ring.

The safe held nothing of significance; a smattering of jewelry, and some more money. Grey helped himself to some of the latter— only, though, what he thought he would need to get himself home; he left the rest for d'Aumont's family. He was no thief. Just a simple soldier doing his job . . . Though of course he had stolen quite a lot this particular night, he reminded himself, still standing in another man's dress-uniform pants. In fact: he opened the side of d'Aumont's wardrobe opposite the safe, the side that actually had clothes in it, and pulled out a captain's uniform. It would give him more freedom of movement than his infantry duds. On the other hand . . . he tore off the epaulettes; turning it into a lieutenant's uniform. A happy medium; he wouldn't want to draw attention in the other direction either, by appearing too grand.

An even more valuable prize, though, was hiding—or at least, standing—in d'Aumont's wardrobe behind the clothes: the Girandoni air rifle.

Grey held it in his hand like the Sovereign's Sceptre. And given a choice of the two, he would much rather have the rifle. What a weapon! He shook his head in admiration. By God, it was almost a work of art. He dropped the musket he'd picked up at the security building, and slung the Girandoni in its place, along with the air rifle's tool kit and bullet bag.

He made a quick search of the rest of the wardrobe—holding briefly to some hope that he might find his St. Vincent sword there too. He didn't. A shame. But after all, it was just metal and wood . . . not some friend who'd been with him for years . . . through thick and thin. Grey sighed.

Satisfied, anyway, that he would leave behind nothing of importance, Grey returned to d'Aumont's desk, sat for a moment, took a sheet of paper, dipped a pen, and began a letter to Julia:

My dear Miss d'Aumont,
    I feel it is my duty to explain my behavior towards you

Grey tore this up and began again:

My dear Miss d'Aumont,
    I wish to reiterate my sincerest apologies for

No, that wasn't right either.

My dear Miss d'Aumont,

We will certainly never see one another again. I came to your home to settle a private matter between your brother and myself. Please accept my regrets at the necessity of things turning out the way they did.

With all the earnestness at my command,
Thomas Grey.

Grey read the letter over, then held it to a candle on d'Aumont's desk and dropped it into an ashtray. The ashes of the torn-up drafts followed. No explanation would be suitable, and none would give Julia any comfort. Grey was glad d'Aumont had forced his hand, in the end, but there would be no sense making that point to a member of his family.

In any case, he had more immediate things to worry about.

With his forearm, Grey swept everything on d'Aumont's desk-top onto the floor, and used the uncovered surface to check and reload his pistol—the pistol he'd taken from Branson, which had been knocked about during the fight with d'Aumont. He checked that the Girandoni's magazine was fully loaded, and topped off the air canister with its hand pump. (No easy job, as it turned out.) Then he got up, walked to the door, walked through it, walked down the stairs and back out to the street, ready and eager to shake the dust of France from his feet.

25

WELL. HERE HE WAS. A heavily armed fugitive spy in the center of the enemy's capital, carrying documents whose successful return to England might change the outcome of the war. How was he going to get them there?

He had an inkling of a plan. After paying his bill at the Café des Aveugles, and before leaving, he had handed over the balance of the Conciergerie jailor's purse to the waiter, sworn him to secrecy, and asked the details of the route by which English cheese was arriving on French restaurant tables. Grey made himself out to be a connoisseur, and the waiter was happy to oblige with the smugglers' path, as he understood it. It was a path Grey now intended to follow in reverse.

For a pair of countries that had been at war for nearly all of the last eleven years, France and Britain had continued a lively trade, entirely through smuggling. French clothes, wine, and spirits crossed the English Channel going north, while coffee, sugar, spices, and, apparently, cheese flowed back in the other direction.

Unfortunately, the des Aveugles waiter, though expert in his trade, had only an approximate knowledge of this smugglers' trail. But at least he was able to point Grey in the right direction: a tavern on the Boulevard de Rochechouart, just inside the wall of the Ferme Générale.

How much trouble that wall had caused France, Europe, and the world! The Ferme Générale was the organization of French tax collectors; the construction of their wall around Paris—to collect duties on everything coming into the city—was one of the final straws on the broken back of the French poor. There was an irritated wordplay regarding the wall, composed during the 1780s and known, by the time of the revolution, all over Europe: *Le mur murant Paris rend Paris murmurant*: "The wall walling Paris is making Paris murmur." The wall was almost finished when the Bastille was stormed, and the *octroi* tax it charged was among the first things abolished by the revolutionary government.

. . . Of course the revolutionary government ended up walking the same path, economically speaking, as the royal one before it, introducing price controls and production mandates, and by '98, the brave revolutionaries had brought the *octroi* back, realizing that it was, of course, the patriotic duty of every Frenchman to empty his pockets for the new patriotic government.

Napoleon had moderated things, keeping some of the price controls while abolishing some of the wall duties, but wine remained heavily taxed. This had three principal unintended consequences: first, tavern villages started to spring up just outside the Mur de la Ferme Générale, where the lower classes could drink for half what they'd pay in the metropolis; second, bars in Paris now had a much tonier average clientele; and third, the earth beneath the wall was so perforated by smuggling tunnels that a special police squad had had to be dedicated to tunnel duty. This according to the waiter, anyway, who said that so far this year no fewer than seventeen tunnels had been seized and filled in. One, the waiter swore, had been nearly a quarter mile long and had had sixty barrels of *vin rouge* in it when the gendarmes arrived. "Sixty barrels," the waiter had proudly whispered, never breaking the rhythm of his confidential smuggling lecture, "is equal to eighteen *thousand* bottles."

In any case—the Ferme Générale wall had its famous sixty-two tollgates, one at every legal entry point to the city. Grey was forced to assume that there would be a man or men at each waiting for him to make his escape. A smuggling tunnel, therefore, was the logical way forward.

There was one such tunnel that the waiter knew of, for wine, et cetera, located at the Yellow Fish tavern on the Boulevard de Rochechouart, fifty yards inside the wall. Its exit was a grain warehouse fifty yards outside the wall, on the hill of Montmartre. A tunnel admission could be had for ten francs—if you knew whom to ask. According to the waiter, the man to ask was a friend of a friend of a friend of the café's cheese man: a tall Breton with bright orange hair. That was all Grey knew. He hoped it would be enough.

AN HOUR LATER, Grey stepped through the open door of Le Poisson Jaune into a rambunctious and smoky atmosphere. The tavern's main room was two stories tall with a balcony ringing the second, opened onto by private rooms (for let, by the night or the hour). On the ground floor, a band was playing angry fiddles and patrons were dancing something that, Grey guessed, had started life as a naval jig.

Grey negotiated his way through the crowd, to the bar, and ordered a brandy. When the barman brought it, Grey offered a large tip and asked where he might find a large, redheaded gentleman of Brittany. For a beat the barkeep stared Grey down, then nodded upward, and said "Number two. Follow the smell of wormwood."

Grey swallowed his brandy and climbed the stairs. The door he took for "number two" had two white lines painted on it; Grey knocked, and when there was no answer, banged, fearing perhaps he couldn't be heard over the fiddling.

"WHO THE F— IS BANGING ON MY DOOR," roared a voice from inside. The door flew open, revealing a very tall, very muscular red-haired man, who grabbed Grey by the jacket and lifted him clean off his feet.

"WHO THE F— ARE YOU, SEAMAN MARTIN?" the giant Breton demanded. Grey chopped his fist into the giant's Adam's apple; the man made a choking sound and dropped Grey back onto his feet. Grey leaned forward, grabbed hold of the man's head, and spoke directly into his ear—*"I'm here about a trip to the warehouse."*

For a moment the big, redheaded man's face was blank . . . then he understood, and started to roar with laughter; now coughing, now slapping Grey on the back as if they were old friends.

"For the holy's sake, why didn't you say so?" He wiped a tear from the corner of his eye, inhaled deeply, and said, "Follow me."

The Breton led the way down to the main floor, around the bar, through a door, to a stair, down into a cellar.

"I think," said the big man, "that this absinthe—have you heard of it? It comes from Switzerland. It's green! Made of herbs. Anise. And alcohol. And wormwood. Comes from Switzerland! They say it's a medicine. I think perhaps it's made me better. But who can say! I'm certain I can't. Here we are."

There was another man in the cellar, reading a newspaper by candlelight. Saying nothing, he stood, and with the help of the Breton, began to move a pyramid of six wine barrels away from the wall, uncovering an unremarkable section of the room's wood paneling. The big Breton pushed the wall, and a yard-square secret door swung inward on a hinge, exposing a pitch-black passage behind it.

"Have you your ten francs?"

Grey reached into his pocket and pulled out two large silver coins, which he deposited in the redheaded man's outstretched hand. The man put them in his right front pocket, and from the left, removed a small candle.

"The candle," he said, striking a match and lighting it, "is included in the price. Are you a murderer? Most of the people going this way are murderers, or pederasts. Who did you kill? But no, don't tell me. I do recommend this absinthe, though, you know. It comes from Switzerland." He laughed from his belly, then shushed Grey, and waved him towards the opening.

"Safe passage," he said as he pulled the panel closed. "Most of the rats are friendly, if you are."

"How do I get out at the other end?"

"Knock. But not too loud. The other him"—the tall man pointed to the silent man who had returned to his newspaper—"will open it for you."

Through the wall, Grey could hear the barrels rolling back into place.

"Christ Almighty," said Grey aloud, permitting himself a rare oath, "what a peculiar man."

THE CANDLE WAS smoky and not especially bright; the noxious tallow smell it gave off was intensified by the close quarters. Though, in fact, for a tunnel, it was quite roomy: wide enough to roll a barrel, with a high enough ceiling for Grey to stand upright (if only just). An impressive construction.

And so Grey forged ahead, hemmed in by dirt walls and wooden beams, up a gentle slope, which made him wonder if smugglers were ever crushed by runaway wine casks.

He counted his paces. As the crow flew, the tunnel's two exits were about a hundred yards apart. In reality, the tunnel curved here and there along gentle S's, to accommodate, Grey supposed, underground boulders or building foundations. At a hundred and twenty-one paces, he began to feel a light breeze, and the flame on his candle grew brighter.

At a hundred and forty-eight paces, Grey reached a dead end. He looked to his left and found a ladder in a small nook; he climbed upward about ten feet to a bedrock landing and knocked softly on the wooden wall before him.

He waited. After a few long moments, the silence gave way to the sound of wood scraping on stone, and the wall swung open.

"Come through," said a man on the other side. Grey stepped past him into what appeared to be the inside of a large barn, stacked high with bales of hay.

"Where can I get a horse?" said Grey.

"How should I know?" said the man, before pointing to the far end of the barn. "Out that door and turn right, follow the road for most of a mile. There's an inn. Ask there. Coaches pass there too, if you like, for the ports."

Could he chance it? Well, why not. Who would recognize him? If someone stopped the coach, he was prepared. And to sit . . . to sit down for a while . . . his sixth sense might be against it, but the whole rest of him was numb.

Twenty minutes later, Grey was talking to the innkeeper, buying a cup of wine, secreting himself in a dark corner to wait for the morning coach to pass by. For a half sou, the innkeeper flagged the coach down, checked if there was room, and summoned Grey to take the sprung carriage's sixth and last seat, between two strangers, facing backward. Grey paid his money and told the driver to let him off at Ardres, on the road to Calais.

Thirty seconds later, the coach began to rock gently back and forth, and Grey decided to permit himself some optimism. As the hills of northern France rolled slowly by, he told himself that there was little for him realistically to fear, for the moment. This tunnel had light at the end of it.

He looked around at the faces of the two women and one man sitting opposite him. All three were staring blankly out the carriage windows. To Grey's left, an elderly gentleman began to snore.

26

GREY WAS A lieutenant again, in the bright red jacket of his best uniform, standing at the altar of Sherborne Abbey. Paulette, also in bright red—in a silk gown—stood before him. There was only a small crowd; Paulette's family and her closest friends, Grey's family and a few fellow officers. The organist had been playing elder Bach—"Wachet auf"; Paulette's favorite. The priest had spoken, and now it was Grey's turn.

"I, Thomas, take thee, Paulette, to be my wedded wife, to have and to hold, from this day forward, for better, for worse, for richer, for poorer, in sickness and in health, to love and to cherish, till death us do part—and thereto I plight thee my troth."

"I, Paulette, take thee, Thomas . . ." God, she was beautiful. Beautiful, perfect, a nonpareil of womanhood. What had he done to deserve her? What could anyone do to deserve her? " . . . till death us do part, and thereto I plight thee my troth."

The priest placed a ring on the open pages of his prayer book. Grey picked it up and, taking Paulette's right hand with his left, placed it onto her fourth finger. With every ounce of earnestness at his command, he looked in her eyes and said, "With this ring I thee wed, with my body I thee worship, and with all my worldly goods I thee endow—in the name of the Father, and of the Son, and of the Holy Ghost. Amen."

"Those whom God hath joined," said the priest, "let no man put asunder. Forasmuch as Thomas and Paulette have consented together in holy wedlock, I pronounce that they be man and wife.

"God the Father, God the Son, God the Holy Ghost, bless, preserve, and keep you; the Lord mercifully with his favor look upon you, and so fill you with all spiritual benediction and grace, that ye may so live together in this life, that in the world to come ye may have life everlasting.

"*Amen.*"

Life everlasting . . .

"LIEUTENANT. *LIEUTENANT.*"

When Grey was shaken awake, after some seven hours had passed, it was to the disapproving faces of his fellow passengers. They were tired, hot, and sweaty, envious of Grey's evident, somnolent mastery of coach travel, and displeased at an unscheduled stop.

The coachman was reaching in through the carriage door, jostling Grey's knee, telling him they were at Ardres. In his stupor, Grey could not at first understand why the man kept calling him "Lieutenant" . . . was he back at Sherborne shaking hands, walking under the crossed swords . . . No, imbecile. Your clothes.

Grey climbed down from the carriage, tipped the driver, and after watching his coach roll away, took his bearings from the setting sun. From Ardres east-northeast to the coast would be about fifteen miles. So the Café des Aveugles waiter had told him, anyway. Grey bought an apple from a man with a horse, and set off across a field.

It was late evening when Grey caught the first sounds of breaking waves wafting towards him on the wind. Here was where the waiter's information ended. Now Grey could only hope that

France's smugglers hadn't changed their habits since the early days of the revolution, when Grey was still on active duty in the Channel squadrons.

The prevailing winds blow north-northeast from Calais, so smugglers liked to touch off from the western edge of the Pas—still near the closest point in France to England, but from the proximal place they could expect the best chance of being ignored by English blockade ships: an English two-decker on patrol would be unlikely to break formation in order to chase a minor prize when the chase would mean having to tack back into the wind to resume her station.

As he walked down to the beach, the salt breeze seemed to pour life back into Grey's body, and even though the night air was brisk, he indulged himself by taking off his boots and letting his sore feet luxuriate in the soft, spongy sand. He was so close to home now, he could taste it.

He turned west and walked along the coast, keeping his eyes peeled for any twinkle of light that would tip off the location of a "death-or-money" boat, one of the little smuggling racers: unarmed, unarmored, designed only for speed—rowing shells, most of them, with crews of seven or nine men who never had to worry about tide or draft, and only about the wind so far as it made the sea rough. The "death" part of the name was not hyperbole. The prospect of drowning dissuaded as many would-be smugglers as the prospect of prison, or of being blown out of the water by a gunboat or a revenue cutter or even a ship of the line. Each poor outcome was as common as the next.

Perhaps that explained Grey's disappointed search. It couldn't be that the local smugglers had gone out of business, could it? But for mile after mile—long after sunset, approaching moonset, there was no sign of any soul besides Grey. If he failed, he would have to find a cave or a breakwater to hide in for the next day . . . and then what? On to Boulogne-sur-Mer and pirate a fishing boat?

CRACK

The sound of the waves was suddenly shattered by a gunshot, and a lead ball whizzing past Grey's ear.

As Grey dove to the ground, he couldn't help but smile: here was his ferry home!

"Hello, friend," called Grey. "I mean you no harm. I have custom to offer you!"

"Well then, friend, stand and deliver your proposition. With your hands above your head, please."

Grey got to his feet, carefully keeping his hands in plain sight . . . as plain as could be, anyway, with the moon almost to the horizon.

"Well, well, well, what have we here?" came a voice from the darkness. "An officer in naval service to the Republic . . . and a well-armed one. Let us see."

From the gloom stepped a man with a rough, weather-beaten face; he reached for the pistol in Grey's belt. As he did, Grey's hands snapped onto the smuggler's own pistol, twisted it out of the man's grip, turned it back at the smuggler's face. The man froze.

"Don't touch that, please, it might go off," said Grey. "Now, I wonder if you might be able to offer me passage to Dover, or thereabout."

The man nodded. "Certainly, friend, for a price."

Keeping the man's pistol trained on his face, Grey reached into his own pocket, pulling out the balance of his French currency and counting it.

"I'll need one of these gold chaps to get me from the seaside to London . . . But I've no objection to your taking the rest, provided you behave yourself. That's about eighty francs."

"Well, well," said the smuggler, smiling widely, "that would be most satisfactory. Will you shake?"

The man stuck out his hand; Grey shook it, and then offered the man back his pistol.

"Forgive me," said Grey as the smuggler replaced the weapon in his pocket. "Force of habit, you know."

"Never fear," said the smuggler. "It isn't loaded. She's the same instrument that sent you to the ground."

Grey chuckled and followed the man up the beach, to where the death-or-money shell was hidden among the reeds.

There were six men more there, lashing down some crates—"the spring fashions," one said, after Grey's escort explained the passen-ger he'd collected. They drew lots for who would give up his seat for Grey, and after the man with the short straw waved goodbye, with ten unlooked-for francs jangling in his pocket, Grey and his new friends began to slide the boat down to the water.

Good God, but it's cold! Grey thought as they launched the death-or-money into the surf, scrambling aboard, each pulling with every sinew to get her swiftly over the breakers. And then, quick as you like, they were onto the smooth rollers, and with the steady rhythm of a Norman rowing song, pulling towards England.

And so it went, for three or four songs, and more verses than Grey could count, until they were almost out of sight of land. Until suddenly the coxswain—Grey's friend, the man steering, and the only one facing forward—stopped singing and focused his eyes on something off the boat's starboard beam.

"Shhhh!" he said, squinting hard.

The rowers—Grey included—followed the coxswain's gaze out into the clear black night. They saw nothing . . .

But after a moment heard the gentle toll of a distant bell.

The changing of the watch, on a ship. They were not yet far enough into the Channel for this to be a British blockader.

"Gunboat," said the coxswain. "Up oars."

Grey didn't dare interrupt the proceedings to ask questions or argue; clearly in the smugglers' experience, the best thing to do was to be still and silent and hope the starshine of a clear night wasn't enough to betray their position to the French coast guards.

For ten minutes, they floated along with a following tide, taking them further out into the Channel, away from France. A black silhou-ette on the horizon had turned into a full-dimensioned object in the sea: a French gunboat, coming back towards land, likely to cut over the death-or-money boat's bow. Every man in the shell had his eyes trained on the enemy, the rowers twisting their heads back over their shoulders, some silently moving their lips, praying not to be seen.

The first sign that their prayers would not be answered was a flash of light. The sound didn't reach them for another full second. Then, a second after that, an iron cannonball flew over their heads, throwing up a great white splash twenty yards away.

This was a warning shot. The next would be shoot-to-kill.

A wave of grim resignation passed over the smuggling boat. Instead of a rich payday on the shores of England, each was now facing prison. Not an easy medicine to swallow.

And Grey? England; home; safety for his country; all within a few more hours' rowing—how bitter a thing it is to have defeat snatched from the jaws of victory.

The terrible black hulk of the gunboat was now only a few hundred yards away, and shortening sail. This was defeat itself. And for Grey, not just a prison cell, but the rack, and in time, the blade of a guillotine.

If that's where he was heading, though . . . well, he wouldn't be taken without a fight. He pulled off his jacket and his boots (slipping the captured papers into the latter as discreetly as he could), then pulled Branson's pistol out of his belt.

"Here," said Grey, handing it to the coxswain, who was seated directly before him. "Don't shoot until you hear the commotion start. And if I'm killed, throw my things into the sea."

"Very well—" said the man, confused. "But what are you doing? Friend, what about your powder?" The coxswain nodded to Grey's rifle, the Girandoni, still slung on his back: a gun with wet powder is as useful as a sword with a meringue blade.

Grey was already lowering himself over the side, into the freezing, inky water. "This gun doesn't use powder," said Grey, and then his head disappeared under the waves.

Lord in heaven! The chill of the water spread instantly through his skin and into his flesh, and he had to fight a powerful, unthinking impulse to turn instantly around and climb back into the boat. But he kicked forward, downward, putting as much distance as he could between himself and the smuggling boat, underwater.

A minute. Stroking forward, being jostled by the tide, consumed by the cold. Forward, forward. Ninety seconds. His lungs screamed at him. His whole body was yelling. How much more did he dare put it through? Forward, forward, forward, another few kicks, another few feet, every inch counts.

He exhaled, finally, and pushed himself to the surface. He'd covered about fifty yards, he estimated—and now, starkly visible with its newly lit side lamps, the French gunboat was between him and the smugglers; about thirty yards from the smugglers, and something less than twenty from him.

It was a sloop of about seventy feet; likely with a crew of a dozen or so aboard; one twenty-four-pounder cannon fore and another aft. Looking at the gunboat's larboard side, he saw no one aboard. All hands must be on the starboard rail; all eyes on the death-or-money boat. Every eye probably with a pot of gold in it, thinking of the prize money the capture of a smuggling shell would net them.

Now a voice called from the gunboat's bows:

"Under the authority of the French Republic, you are hereby placed under arrest! Make no attempt to resist or you will be killed! Our swivel guns are trained on you now; we will send you to hell or the bottom!"

Grey's breaststroke soon had him at the gunboat's larboard-side chain; the small platform under the mast shrouds. He was pulling himself up, his bare feet fighting for purchase on the slimy wood. The voice had begun demanding each man in the smuggling boat identify himself.

Now Grey was on the chain, tipping the water out of the barrel of the Girandoni, slinging it back over his shoulder, pulling his head up over the gunwale, getting his first look at the gunboat's crew—the backs of five men, one of them standing on the starboard rail. This was the man shouting instructions to the smugglers. Four more men were standing, two apiece, at the two swivel guns, one on the forecastle and one at the stern. And two men more were hanging about in the rigging.

None of them had the slightest notion of Grey's presence, and with the speed of the Girandoni repeater, massacring them would be child's play.

. . . But they were simply men doing their job, and to shoot them in the back—to give them no chance to surrender? No, it just wouldn't do.

"HANDS IN THE AIR!" bellowed Grey. "YIELD OR DIE."

And chaos broke out on the deck. The man who had been standing on the gunwale drew his sword, twisting around towards the sound of Grey's voice; two of the other men on the rail were now staring at Grey dumbly, while two more, seeing the gun in Grey's hands, were diving for the fore-hatch that led belowdecks—and presumably, to a small-arms chest.

Grey's focus, however, was on the swivel gun crews: The aft were the quicker to respond, swiveling the small cannon on its shaft, towards Grey.

Pffft

Pffft

went the Girandoni, and the two men lost their heads in backward sprays of blood and skull.

The other swivel gun had now been brought to bear, and with a great

BOOM

a ball tore through the shrouds. Grey sprang forward over the gunwale, vacating the ball's target a split second before it hit; now he was diving behind a heavy coil of rigging, popping up from behind it, putting the bead of the gun's front sight on the two men in turn.

Pffft

Pffft

CLANG

The man with the sword had now crossed the deck—had taken a swing at Grey's head—Grey ducking out of the way, the blade connected with an iron cleat. Grey—still ducked—grabbed the man's left knee, yanked it forward, sent the man tumbling backward onto the deck, and then—

Pffft

Grey put one of the Girandoni's .46-caliber lead balls in the man's chest, shattering the deck beneath him.

The two other sailors who'd been standing dumbly beside the dead swordsman were now charging, as if they'd been on a slow-burn fuse. One was waving a boat hook and the other a small dagger.

Pffft

Pffft

And they fell—Grey had to bound over the crumpling body of the man with the boat hook as his momentum carried him forward even after his rib cage and lungs had been shattered.

Grey now swung the barrel of the Girandoni up towards the rigging, where the two mast jacks had been trapped, unarmed and confused by the assault. Grey took a bead on the first:

The man was waving his hands and shouting—

"I yield! I surrender myself!"

Grey moved his sights to the second man, who had to swallow twice before being able to speak loudly enough for Grey to hear him:

"Me as well!"

Grey nodded his acceptance to the men, and turned towards the fore hatch, which would lead to the hold. At least two men, possibly more, were down there, waiting, and likely armed.

With the Girandoni pulled tightly into his shoulder, Grey crouched above the hatch's steep companion ladder. Dim light flickered up from a lantern. He saw no one; no movement, no shadows.

Grey backed away, slung the Girandoni back over his shoulder, and grabbed one of the dead fore-swivel gunners. Dragging the corpse by the collar, he hauled it over to the hatch, then to its feet . . . then dropped it down the ladder, like a man jumping from the deck to the hold.

Two shots rang out; two lead balls hit the dead man's trunk. Now Grey dropped himself down the ladder, before the two French sailors had time to reload.

Pffft

The first man fell, his musket in one hand, a ramrod in the other.

Grey turned to the second man, in the same state of unpreparedness—he was reloading a pistol—but before Grey could fire, someone—a third man—seized Grey from behind, pinned his arms to his sides, brought a knife to his throat—

Grey dropped the Girandoni, grabbed at the arms grabbing him, and flung himself backward. He landed on the new attacker, who let out a shocked shout as the air was driven from his lungs; at the same time, Grey grabbed the hand with the knife, twisted his own body along its long axis—so he and his attacker were now facing each other—and drove the knife into this new man's chest, scraping his ribs as the blade slid home. The man gasped and died.

Now Grey spun back around, knowing full well what he would see there: the other shooter, with his pistol reloaded and pointed at Grey's head. The man's finger was on the trigger; an unspoken prayer passed through Grey's mind, a final request that his sins be forgiven.

BANG

The sound of the pistol shot tore through the small sloop's hold.

Grey looked up. Smoke trailed out the end of Branson's pistol, in the smuggler-coxswain's hand.

"Your timing, friend," said Grey, "is impeccable."

Grey leaned back on the companion ladder and slowly released the breath he'd thought would be his last.

"Is there anyone else?" asked the coxswain.

"Not down here," said Grey. "There are two men in the rigging who surrendered."

"Yes," said the coxswain, "we have them on deck. They will have to be killed—if any word of this reaches shore, our heads will be forfeit."

He emphasized this with a slicing gesture across his throat.

Grey was still panting lightly from the exertion. "Or," said Grey, inhaling deeply, exhaling deeply, "what if there were a way to keep them from returning to shore without killing them—and getting you head money in the process."

As Grey spoke, the coxswain climbed down to the body of the man he'd killed. He knelt, took a ring off one of the dead man's fingers, and began to rifle through his pockets. He looked up at Grey with a pondering look on his face.

"That would be most satisfactory . . . Please explain."

"I will," said Grey. "First give me my boots back."

27

IT WAS DAWN before the smuggling shell had been hoisted aboard the sloop. After its loot crates had been hauled aboard, the death-or-money boat itself had been rigged to some half-inch line and pulled slowly from the water with the gunboat's capstan.

The two captured members of the gunboat crew—the mast jacks—had been sent back into the rigging. They'd gone eagerly once Grey had explained that, though he had negotiated for their lives, their best chance of survival lay in passing speedily out of the hands of the smugglers. They'd gone right back to work as if nothing on deck had changed, and begun helping the sloop make sail with as little delay as possible. The smuggler coxswain had taken the helm, and with the other smugglers all reasonably experienced seamen (enough to hand, reef, and steer, anyway), the gunboat—*Clémence* was her name—was underway before the first hour of daylight had passed.

A course was laid east-northeast. After an hour's sailing, their destination was in sight: a line of sails, hull up on the horizon.

The English fleet.

A half hour later, the fleet caught sight of *Clémence*, and a frigate was dispatched with the customary order to either take her a prize or sink her. Grey couldn't help but smile at the confusion he was about to create on the frigate's quarterdeck as he shouted instructions for the men in the rigging to pull down the *Tricolore* and run up a lily-white square of virgin sailcloth in its place. He didn't like to disappoint the hardworking men of the Calais blockade—but *Clémence* was a prize that had already been taken.

When Grey had informed the smuggling crew that he was an Englishman, they had expressed surprise, confusion, some hints of anger—after all, he spoke French like a native and was still wearing the uniform of a French lieutenant. It was lucky that every member of the smuggling crew was a cutthroat whose loyalties lay only with himself, or else there might have been violence. And once Grey had explained that, as an Englishman with a captured French gunboat, he had prize money coming to him—and that, as his crew, they were all legally entitled to share in it—and even more, that Grey intended to remit to them his share as well—the mood lightened substantially.

Grey told his prize crew, truthfully, that an undamaged French gunboat sloop bought into the service would profit them something in the neighborhood of seven thousand pounds sterling. Instantly, each man began to spend his one and one-sixth thousand pounds in his head, wondering which tropical colony he would retire to, and what sort of beach house he would build there. Only one of the six men had a wife, and he said he felt she would, in any case, be better off without him—after all, he didn't dare go back to France, did he? Better for them both if he started a new life in Tahiti. It was common knowledge, the coxswain told Grey, that a senior civil servant in Napoleon's government earned eight thousand francs a year, and that—as a franc-to-sterling smuggler—he could vouch for an exchange rate of about twenty-five-to-one. This meant that a single night's work had netted him a rich man's salary for the next three years and more. He clapped Grey on the back and, grinning from ear to ear, said that this was a very good night's work indeed.

Grins abounded still when the English frigate—HMS *Phoebe*, thirty-six—arrived at hailing distance and reefed her sails. Standing on the larboard, leeward side of his quarterdeck, *Phoebe*'s captain called out—his voice carrying well over the calm sea:

"FRENCH SLOOP *CLÉMENCE*, THIS IS CAPTAIN SIMMS OF HIS MAJESTY'S FRIGATE *PHOEBE*. IS IT YOUR INTENTION TO SURRENDER?"

Grey stepped to the larboard, windward side of the *Clémence*'s taffrail and shouted back:

"SHE'S ALREADY SURRENDERED, CAPTAIN, AND I'VE TAKEN CUSTODY OF HER—THIS IS CAPTAIN THOMAS GREY, LATE OF HIS MAJESTY'S ROYAL MARINES. I WONDER IF YOU'D SEND A CUTTER OVER TO TAKE ME OFF AND PUT A SKELETON CREW ON, AND I'LL MAKE THE SITUATION UNDERSTOOD TO YOU."

(How good it felt to speak English again!)

Grey could see the curious faces on the *Phoebe*'s quarterdeck, but a moment and some brief discussion later, Captain Simms called back, "VERY WELL, CAPTAIN GREY—THE BOAT WILL BE OVER SHORTLY."

And so it was. *Phoebe*'s cutter delivered a dozen British seamen to take over the sloop's sailing, and—after Grey swore on his sacred honor that he would not forget his commitments to his French crew—it took him back to the *Phoebe*. There Grey eschewed the bosun's chair and pulled himself ably up the companion ladder, the physical trials of the last few days temporarily forgotten.

Once again, his feet were on English territory—even if it was just a collection of oak boards floating in the sea, to him it felt as homely and solid as St. James's Park. In fact, it somehow felt more like home than the last time he'd been on English soil, just a month ago. It was a curious feeling, and he chose not to delve too deeply into it.

Grey saluted the quarterdeck and the assembled officers, then the assembled marines—a handful of whom he was pleased to see were familiar faces—and then accepted the outstretched hand of Captain Simms.

"Captain Grey," said Simms, "you'll forgive me pointing it out, but that isn't the uniform I'm accustomed to seeing His Majesty's Royal Marines dressed in. Even ones who have resigned their commissions."

"No," said Grey, "I would imagine not. I assure you, though, that you'll find my explanation for it satisfactory. Though I'm afraid— duty compels me—it is not for the general ear."

Simms raised an eyebrow but made no objection. "Certainly, Captain," he said, waving over his steward, "let us speak in my cabin. Hansen—bring us tea, would you? Or would you prefer coffee, Captain Grey?"

"If you have coffee, Captain Simms, I should like it of all things."

Grey followed Simms down the quarterdeck companionway and followed him into the great cabin, with its characteristically beautiful spread of stern windows.

Simms sat down at his desk and motioned for Grey to take the seat opposite. Grey sat down and began to struggle with his left boot, which—since being reinstalled in the aftermath of the taking of *Clémence*—seemed to have grafted itself to Grey's skin.

Simms stared at him with only a hint of disapproval, and after a moment ventured to ask, "Captain Grey, is your foot troubling you?"

With a sucking noise, the leather finally released Grey's leg. "In this boot," said Grey, holding it up, "I have papers of the utmost importance secured from Paris. Before I explain further, may I ask: Do you know, is there any representative of Sir Edward Banks's in the fleet?"

CAPTAIN SIMMS gamely accepted that Grey had not the authority to let Simms read the papers he had produced, but a few key phrases he spoke—"Nothing so strange as a whitecap on a perfectly smooth day"; "I can't recall the last time I saw Ushant in the daylight"; "Was that the year they laid down the *Prince George*?"—worked into otherwise pointless small talk, demonstrated to Simms Grey's authenticity as one of Edward Banks's spies. Grey hadn't had to use them in a while; he was glad they hadn't been changed.

With this certification out of the way, Simms dispatched *Phoebe*'s cutter—carrying his first lieutenant, who carried a letter from Grey—to the blockade squadron's flagship . . . HMS *Royal Sovereign*, one hundred. Simms's first lieutenant had instructions personally to deliver Grey's letter into the hands of the fleet admiral's intelligence man. Less than an hour later, the cutter returned with new orders, under the admiral's seal, for *Phoebe* to break formation and make at once, with all dispatch, to the Nore, thereupon to provide Grey with the cutter and anything else he might need to proceed up the Thames to Admiralty House. With equal dispatch.

Back in his cabin, with Grey, Simms read the orders with an emotionless face. He called for the officer of the deck and rattled off a quick series of instructions: beat the men to quarters, make all plain sail, set a course north-northeast, order the skeleton crew on *Clémence* to take her into Portsmouth, and ask the port admiral to commend her to the prize court. To this he added instructions for the officer of the deck to ask the first and second lieutenants and the captain of the marines if they would care to join him at six bells in the afternoon watch for dinner, where he hoped Grey could be induced to tell the story of the *Ruby*'s heroic beating off of the *Diligente*—a most valorous sea fight that had already been gazetted, in the form of a letter from a passenger aboard her, a botanist, one Mr. Kefauver.

Simms directed this final request to Grey himself, who—having spent the intervening period between the dispatching of his letter to the flagship and the arrival of new orders from the admiral on the sun-soaked quarterdeck—was finally dry, but still dressed as a French lieutenant.

"It would be my great pleasure to join you for dinner, Captain," said Grey, "but I wonder if I could have a few minutes first with your sailmaker, to see if he can't turn this outfit into something less Gallic."

Simms—who had a very deep voice—chuckled briefly. "Captain Grey, I assure you that your dress will be of no account, under the circumstances. However, Mr. Bradley will be at your disposal"; and to the officer of the deck, a youngish midshipman who was becoming nervous he wouldn't be able to remember everything: "Mr. Llewellyn, pass the word for Mr. Bradley, would you?"

"And now," said Simms, standing, "I must get on deck; there's much to be done. My cabin is at your disposal, Captain Grey."

WHEN, ALMOST EXACTLY one day later, Grey climbed out of *Phoebe*'s cutter at Westminster Bridge, it was in a smart blue jacket—now with its gold lace and naval accoutrements gone, and with a less feminine waist. "These French and their nonsense patterns," Bradley had said when Grey presented him with the jacket. "Have they got men over there, or is their navy run exclusively by Sapphites?"

Grey climbed the steps away from the river, looking once over his shoulder to see the cutter already casting off, heading back to rejoin the *Phoebe* at sea—its small crew frowning wistfully at London, cursing the fine weather that had murdered their hopes of a brief liberty ashore. It was only a two minutes' walk to the Admiralty building, and two minutes after that, Grey was standing at a window in Sir Edward Banks's outer office.

After a wait of perhaps twenty minutes, "Well, well, well," said someone behind Grey. "I had been under the impression that you didn't work here anymore."

Grey turned around, to the widely smiling face of Aaron Willys, Sir Edward's chief of staff—the not-yet-forty but prematurely gray man whose job it was to manage the everyday business of the Admiralty's secret intelligence service.

Grey grasped Willys's hand and shook it vigorously. They hadn't seen one another for more than three years—but they'd come up together, years ago now, in the Royal Marines—their paths parting only when Willys had been forced to tender his resignation from the service, unable, because of certain personal convictions, to take an officer's oath.

"There had been some considerable debate," said Willys, "as to whether or not you had actually gone to America. You see word had reached us of some rather unremarkable ship-to-ship fighting—nothing too warm, mind—which included some raggedy ex-marine, who then decamped in Portugal and disappeared. Have any idea who he could have been?"

"Aaron, how have you kept yourself, you old dog? You'll forgive me, I hope, for not dropping in to see you when I was last about."

"You needn't explain, Tom; I'm glad to see you yourself and in decent spirits. The old man will be with you presently. He's just returned from the House. The papers you brought are on his desk."

As if on cue, the sound of a small, tinny bell came from Willys's office—the bell connected, by a series of strings and pulleys, to a cord on the wall behind Sir Edward's desk.

"Go in," said Willys. "We'll speak after."

A sudden, unaccustomed twitch of nerves passed through Grey as he reached for the tarnished brass knob. He pushed the heavy ebony door open and stepped into Sir Edward Banks's inner sanctum—feeling for a moment as if he were again a junior agent, desperate to make a good impression.

"Come in, Grey," said Sir Edward. He was leaned back slightly in his chair, holding a page out of Grey's captured Paris dossier, reading it over. He looked at Grey for only a brief moment, returning to the paper as he waved Grey forward. Banks made no indication that Grey was to take the chair opposite his own, so Grey remained standing, silently. Sir Edward continued with the paper for nearly a minute before setting it facedown on a stack of like pages and looking up.

"This is a copy," said Sir Edward, placing his palm over the document with which he'd just finished, "of your original. A dozen more are being made next door"—he gestured to the larger, corner office he used sometimes for meetings, and more often, for his staff of secretaries to do their clerical work in a place that provided sunlight and a little fresh air.

"Those copies will be distributed to the relevant ministers and officers by special courier, each with its own armed guard. An emergency meeting of the cabinet will be scheduled for this evening. You will attend, and when I've finished with you now, you'll sit down with Willys to give, for transcription, a complete account of the events surrounding your discovery of these data, and anything else relevant to them that you can think of."

It was strange, thought Grey, to picture now the avuncular figure of Sir Edward that had briefly appeared at Grey's home only a month earlier.

"That makes an issue of this letter, which I received here"—Sir Edward retrieved another paper from atop a different stack, among the many that scattered across his desk—"dated May the sixteenth of this year: 'To the Honorable so-and-so, regarding our meeting of Tuesday last, I hereby tender, and hope you will accept, my resignation forthwith from His Majesty's Secret Service.'"

Sir Edward set the letter down again and fixed his eyes on Grey's. For a moment he looked coldly into them, before continuing:

"Under the circumstances, I cannot accept it, and would ask you to withdraw it, until—at least—the matters you've brought to our attention are dispensed with."

He paused and allowed his face to soften very slightly.

"Will you?"

Grey hesitated before answering. In his mind's eye, he saw Boston slowly disappearing over the horizon, taking his fresh start to life with it.

"I will, Sir Edward."

"Thank you, Thomas," said Banks. "Very well. That's all; I'll speak to you this evening." And without another glance in Grey's direction, Sir Edward Banks returned to his work.

Back in the outer office, Grey was received again by Willys, who said:

"Before he let you in, he sent me a memo round the corner to have your office reconstituted—'reconstituted,' it said—as it had been prior to your assignment in Malta. No foreign postings at the moment, I'm afraid, Tom, so we'll have to have you around the office for a while. Presuming you agreed to withdraw your resignation."

"I did," said Grey. "Though he certainly didn't bend his masts inducing me to."

Willys chuckled. "Come on, then," he said. "We have work to do. I hope you're in good voice. I gather you have quite a story to tell me."

AFTER INNUMERABLE tellings and retellings of the events of his past two weeks, Grey was relieved when the organs of government had, at last, moved from establishing the facts to establishing a plan of action. This meant, of course, that Grey's role in the proceedings were at an end. He was given the customary thanks, along with the customary implication that it was now for greater minds than his and greater men than he to take over. Grey's final involvement in the matter was to deliver a final mention of the Admiralty's obligation to the French smugglers, and to put in a good word for the Irish rebel Donald Branson, who Grey felt had ultimately behaved in an honorable manner. (Grey felt sure that some remonstration with the United Irishmen would be in the offing.) After that, Grey was dismissed and—late on a Friday—made his way home to Kent, to Marsh Downs, where the first to greet him was Fred.

"And where's the rest of the detachment?" asked Grey, after a few minutes' vigorous scratching of the dog's cheeks, ears, and belly. "Have Canfield and Mrs. Hubble taken new posts already?" Grey had attempted to learn the disposition of his house and household from his man of business Pater, but an associate at Pater's office had been able to say only that Mr. Pater would be away "for some days," and that a date for the auction of Marsh Downs had not yet been set. Grey told the associate to scratch it off the agenda, and to have Pater look Grey up if he ever resurfaced from Buttle's. The associate said he would.

"Why, Mr. Grey!" said Mrs. Hubble, answering Grey's question of Fred. "Why, I knew you wouldn't go through with it. My bones told me so."

"Mrs. Hubble," said Grey, standing up, to the mild consternation of the dog, who felt he had not yet been adequately scratched, "how good to see you. I was afraid you had gone."

"Oh no, sir," said Mrs. Hubble. "Sir Edward told us weeks ago that if the house came to auction—which he very much doubted—he intended to buy it and keep us on."

"Did he?" said Grey. "Did he indeed." Why, that old so-and-so. "So Canfield's still here as well."

"He is, sir, he certainly is. Shall I fetch him?"

"No, that won't be necessary, Mrs. Hubble, I can find him. Though if you could make me something to eat, I would be forever in your debt."

"Why, certainly, sir—is there anything particular you'd like?"

"No, Mrs. Hubble, anything will be quite fine—anything warm would do me beautifully."

"Very good, sir."

"And if you could give me Canfield's heading?"

"I believe Mr. Canfield's at the shore garden, sir—he said there were some unruly vines about that needed to be taught a lesson."

"Thank you, Mrs. Hubble."

Grey stepped into the mudroom, where he was finally able to switch Jean-Anne d'Aumont's boots for a pair of his own. He walked out into the garden, with Fred at his heels. It was a warm, almost hot, midsummer's evening, and the gardens were in fine fettle: blooms everywhere, and a pleasingly high volume of leaves on the various rhododendron bushes.

Fred ran ahead, and Grey couldn't help but wonder if, with his comings and goings, the dog wasn't still expecting Paulette to return as well. How could he think otherwise? As a puppy, whelped less than two months before Grey's assignment to Malta—and Grey was still surprised the dog knew his face—it had been Paulette with whom the little Irish setter had spent most of his time, and she who had become tearful when they'd decided that Fred was too small to make the trek to the Mediterranean. Now Fred was bounding excitedly around the garden that Paulette had planted with Fred's mother at her side. That was Canfield's dog Lydia. Lydia had died during the Greys' time in Malta; a letter from Mrs. Hubble to Paulette had informed them of her passing, and Paulette had been tearful at that too. Grey wondered if these intertwining tragedies meant anything to the rambunctious dog, who was now woofing at some unseen squirrel. As a puppy, barely able to open his eyes, Fred and his four sisters (who had all made good matches and were living on various nearby estates) had triggered a doleful discussion of the future.

Grey had carried a basket of five puppies out to the garden to be with Paulette and their mother, who were jointly at work turning soil and planting bulbs. Grey had, the day prior, received his assignment to Malta, and had been irritable ever since. It was a promotion, certainly, but one he wished he could refuse. Here he was with a new house he wouldn't be living in and a new wife he might not be living with— he feeling that it would be dangerous to bring her along, she insisting that Malta proper was peripheral to the war, and that, anyway, she wouldn't be parted from him. And here: new puppies to boot.

Grey had set the basket down at her elbow, taken a seat on a bench, and watched her. Paulette was whistling as she worked, with a trowel in one hand and her bulbs in the other. Of course she had to come along to Malta. Perhaps it would be dangerous. But how could he be parted from her? She was right, of course: it was ludicrous even to contemplate. After all, they were in this together. For better or for worse.

He, on the other hand . . . ascending to a spot as head of station in the center of the Mediterranean . . . he knew what sort of work was waiting for him in Italy and Dalmatia and the Adriatic. Possibly Egypt and Tunisia as well. He felt a twinge of excitement—yes, surely, it would be the most exciting time of his life. But the twinge was mixed with concern for his blissfully whistling wife. He had a sudden premonition that she would end up a war widow. He was coming up to a period of much greater sustained danger than he'd ever faced before; not just danger on isolated assignments, but as a prime target from the day he stepped off the boat at Valetta.

"What will you do if I'm killed?" he asked suddenly—quickly wishing he'd kept his thought unexpressed.

"I would go entirely to pieces," she said dryly, gently tamping down soil over a bulb.

"Well, of course," said Grey, now committed to the conversation. "But what would you do after that, with the rest of your life?"

"I don't want to talk about it," said Paulette.

"I think we should," said Grey, rising from the bench and sitting down on the lawn beside his kneeling wife. "We have to at some point. Perhaps we should have long ago."

"What are you asking me, Tom? Would I remarry?"

"Would you?"

"What an asinine question," she said, leaning away from him, troweling up a new hole.

"Well, I won't say I would want you to . . . but I do need to say that I'd want you to be happy. Cast thy nighted color off, and so forth; not let the clouds hang on you forever."

"I don't want to talk about this," said Paulette with more conviction. "Nothing is going to happen to you; what nonsense. So long as you're careful—and I would remind you, you've promised to be careful."

She put a dirty finger on his forehead and made a little cross. "You know what happens to vow-breakers."

"But you must promise too," said Grey, "to be happy. How miserably earnest you've turned me! But promise, and then we don't ever have to discuss this again."

"Very well, dear heart, I promise. Now leave me alone." She kissed him on the cheek. "And leave the puppies."

Three short years ago, thought Grey, looking at Fred . . . who now had a dead squirrel in his mouth.

"Good boy," said Grey. "Good dog. What an admirable fellow you are, Freddy."

Together they walked down towards the marshes, where Grey could see Canfield attending to some creepers.

"Mr. Grey!" said Canfield, catching sight of the pair. "I knew you'd be back. Mrs. Hubble kept saying so. Said she felt it in her bones. And I've never known her bones to be wrong."

"It's good to be back, Canfield, very good indeed," said Grey. "I wanted to show you this."

Grey swung the Girandoni off his back and held it out at arm's length for Canfield to examine.

Canfield looked it curiously up and down.

"I've never seen anything like it, Mr. Grey . . . What's the container at the end for?"

"Air!" said Grey.

"Air, sir?"

"Yes—compressed air—it's an air rifle, a 'Girandoni,' from Austria. It's a repeater!"

"No! Is it really? I've never *seen* a repeater," said Canfield, now looking covetously at the Girandoni.

"This rifle can fire twenty-two shots in twenty-two seconds, Canfield. This tube along the barrel is a magazine; twenty-two .46-caliber balls. You load them into the breach with this lever here."

"Remarkable, sir! What's its range?"

"Accurate to a hundred and fifty yards. Would you like a go?"

"I most decidedly would, sir. May I?" Grey handed the rifle to Canfield, who—in his excitement; not knowing what to do with them—handed his pruning shears to Grey. Grey chuckled and clicked the shears open and shut a few times, as one invariably does with such things.

"Mr. Grey!" called Mrs. Hubble, back up towards the house. "Your supper is ready!"

"Thank you, Mrs. Hubble, I'm on my way!" answered Grey, hanging the shears from a mulberry sprig. "In any case, Canfield, get a feel for it, and then, after I've eaten, you can give me a hand recharging the air chamber."

"Absolutely, Mr. Grey—thank you!"

Grey patted him on the shoulder and started back towards the house. Passing through the mudroom, he caught the smell of freshly cooked eggs and toasted cheese wafting through the air, and the sound of footsteps on the gravel path leading to the front of the house. A moment later there was a loud, firm knock on the front door.

"I'll get it, Mrs. Hubble," said Grey, passing by the kitchen.

The door opened to an unexpected sight: a young deputy from Sir Edward Banks's coterie.

"I'm sorry to trouble you at this time of the evening, Mr. Grey," said the deputy, "but Sir Edward wonders if he might have a word, at the Admiralty."

Grey felt a chill of excitement run over the surface of his skin. So. He was back on the job.

"Let me find a pail to toss my dinner in, and I am your man."

The End

Historical Note

I've STOLEN FROM the great Bernard Cornwell—author of the Sharpe books, about a rifleman in the Napoleonic Wars—the idea of ending with a historical note. I always get a kick out of discovering how neatly woven into fact Richard Sharpe's adventures have been—and though, like Sharpe, Thomas Grey is fictional, much of the story that surrounds him is real.

When the Peace of Amiens ended on May 18, 1803, Napoleon really was planning to invade Britain, claiming that he required "only a favorable wind to plant the Imperial Eagle on the Tower of London." He really did begin construction of an invasion fleet on France's northern coast, and—in July of 1803, shortly after *Hold Fast*'s story ends—Britain began to fortify her southern coast to defend against it. Fifty new battalions, totaling about fifty thousand men, were created as a home-front "Army of Reserve," and by autumn 1803, King George had drawn up plans to guarantee that, should an invasion occur, he would need no more than a half hour's notice to go personally to battle.

The Society of United Irishmen was a real organization; its members worked with and were assisted by the French, and in 1803 they were planning another uprising against English rule in Ireland. In July 1803, an explosion at one of their secret munitions depots forced them to begin the rebellion before preparations for it were complete; consequently, it was defeated almost before it began.

As far as possible, the more minor details of *Hold Fast* are real as well. The Girandoni air rifle existed exactly as described, and was every bit as remarkable as Grey and d'Aumont found it. It was never to play a major part in Europe's wars—but it did play an interesting role in American history: Meriwether Lewis took one on the Lewis and Clark expedition. In his journals, he writes frequently about using it to "astonish" people.

The laws and bans regarding the card game Basset are all real; Louis XIV really was forced, by the astonishing sums of money his noblemen were losing, not only to ban Basset, but to offer bribes to courtiers to rat out secret games.

The Café des Aveugles was real; its menu was real too, though it belonged in reality to the nearby restaurant Véry, and was taken—in all its glory, and almost word for word—from Mr. Richard Phillips's 1804 English edition of Mr. August von Kotzebue's *Travels from Berlin, Through Switzerland, to Paris, in the Year 1804*. It was too beautifully written to alter.

On a less cheerful note, the savage Republican marriages were real, as were the revolutionary prohibitions on church-bell ringing and Catholic vestments. On a more cheerful note, the story about Jacques-Louis David and Maximilien Robespierre is real too. So is the history of the French in Malta, and the toll wall around Paris, and the profusion of smuggling tunnels under it. The process of "riddling" champagne really was invented by Veuve Clicquot in the early nineteenth century, and since the technique was soon adopted by every other champagne house, I can only assume that espionage was involved.

Sir Edward Banks is fictional, but has several real-life counterparts, and espionage really did play a major role in the Napoleonic Wars, with both the British and French having sources and agents spread out over Europe. However, the book's biggest liberties are taken in placing the job of spying in the hands of British naval intelligence and the secret service, neither of which had quite come into existence in 1803—though their progenitors had.

I hope that doesn't spoil it for you. But after all, it is fiction.

Acknowledgments

THERE WERE A LOT of people involved in the writing and production of this book, without whom it would still be an untitled text file on my desktop. First was my brother Dan, who, from the time I began writing *Hold Fast*, was an indispensable reader and advice-giver. Also indispensable in reading and advice-giving has been my agent, Warren Frasier, to whom I will be eternally grateful for picking my manuscript off the pile and taking a flier on it.

Star Lawrence, my editor, is a literary giant, who has edited a large slice of the generation's most important books, fiction and non-fiction. Along with *The Perfect Storm*, *Moneyball*, *The Blind Side*, *The Big Short*, etc., he edited Patrick O'Brian's Aubrey-Maturins, which were the inspiration for *Hold Fast*, and are, simply, my favorite novels. Getting Star's notes on a novel of mine was like getting pointers on red Italian sports car design from Enzo Ferrari.

I am deeply indebted to W. W. Norton for publishing me, and to everyone who works there, and to everyone who worked on this book, including the invaluable Nneoma Amadi-obi, who coordinated everything, the splendid team of project editor Rebecca Homiski and copy editor Amy Robbins, and a legion of typesetters, designers, producers, and marketers, without whom *Hold Fast* would still be a typo-filled Word doc in an inbox somewhere.

I am deeply indebted too to Patrick O'Brian, my particular literary hero. No accounting of the twentieth century's best writers can be complete without him in it; the best lists have him near the top. And I want to acknowledge my debt to Ian Fleming: beloved inventor of James Bond, underappreciated writer qua writer, and a big influence on me. In some ways, *Hold Fast* is as much an homage to him as it is to O'Brian.

Much thanks is owed to the many great writing teachers I've had over the years. (If I were to single one out, it would have to be Charlie Rubin, a professor of mine, and subsequently a great friend.) Ultimately, though, I was taught to write by my father, who was relentless in making sure I learned the elements of style, the wittiness of brevity, and the dangers of adverbs. More than that, he, in tandem with my mother, worked tirelessly to teach me history, art, and science, without which no writer ever gets past page one. They have been the best teachers (and parents) one could wish for. That's why I dedicated the book to them. But I figured they deserved a curtain call too.

Finally, I need to thank a few tremendous friends who are always willing to read and proofread, without whom this book would not have been finished. Specifically: Allison Holcomb, Steve Socha, Beth Christenberry, Monica Mierzejewski, Nimisha Jain, and Anthony "Tony Nickels" Nicholaysen, MD. They're a good sample of the best friends a guy could have.

Even more finally: because I'm writing this approximately one year before it's going be published, I would like to take this preemptive opportunity to thank the New Jersey Devils, New York Mets, and Kyle Busch, for all delivering championships in 2020–21. Way to go, boys.